I0612027

NUMEROLOGY

A Book Of Insights

By

Anne Burton

Anne Burton

Numerology, A Book of Insights

Copyright © 2007 Anne Burton

All rights reserved.
Printed in the United States of America. No part of this book may be used or reproduced in any manner whatsoever without written permission except in the case of brief quotations embodied in critical articles and reviews.
All people and facts in this book are fictions. Any resemblance to real people or facts is coincidental.

Fifth Estate Publishers,

Post Office Box 116, Blountsville, AL 35031.

First Printing 2007

Cover art by An Quigley

Printed on acid-free paper

Library of Congress Control No: 2001012345

ISBN: 1933580453   ISBN13: 9781933580456

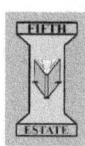

Fifth Estate

2007

Anne Burton

Table of Contents

Anne Burton

INTRODUCTION

The eternal "why" has been with us since the dawn of mankind. The oldest books in the world deal with the "why." Why do bad things happen to good people? Why do the good suffer and the evil go free? Why me? Why now? Or why not?

All major religions seek to answer the questions of "why." From Job to Lao Tsu, from Buddha to Jesus, the same human condition and the same questions have stared us in the face. There are a myriad of ways to look at the mystery of life, a plethora of ways to deal with it, but the question remains the same. Why?

Numerology seeks to answer the age old question by use of patterns and mathematical principles applied to time and the human Soul. These patterns do not care for rich or poor, good or evil; they simply exert their influence as a wave washing and pushing this way or that. What is done with these tides of time becomes a matter of personal choice. It is about these influences and personal choices that this work was written.

THE QUEST

Life is a journey, although seldom smooth and never tidy. Any journey must have at least a general direction and a path. If one does not have these things, one simply wanders. The human problem is how to chart and travel the course.

The journey, or rite of passage in life, is that of the Soul's sojourn from its pristine, unaware state to the full, healthy, self-aware Expression. Anything that would force the Soul off this path or slow its journey is the enemy of the Soul.

The journey itself is one of overcoming the obstacles that stand in the way of reaching the precious goal. Anything that would prevent wholeness must be dealt with.

When one looks closely, it may be discovered that the obstacles may not be what force us from our course. It is our reaction to the obstacles that waylay us. Thus, we may be able to "intuit" or feel what is coming, but if our reaction to the situation or event is not wise and appropriate, it will not matter if we were expecting the situation or not. We will be detoured. The enemy is ourselves. Our reactions, and how we handle the events thrown at us determine our growth. We are the enemy or the hero of our journey.

Human weaknesses and strengths are discussed in the system of Numerology used in this book. Numbers will assist us in finding our way home. The numbers in our name tell the story of our personality. They represent our starting point and our goal. We will start with these.

The Soul number, derived from vowels, represents our heart's desire. It is the untainted state of the real being. It is the driving force and who we are beyond all outer trappings.

The Quiescent Self number, derived from consonants, is how we appear to others. It represents what we wish to be, what we project, the initial impression we leave on others.

The Expression number, derived from the total name, is how we conduct ourselves, how we act and perform in the world. It is the combination of our true self and how others see us.

It is the journey from the Soul number to the fullness of the Expression number that represents the evolution of the person. What we will encounter along the way, and what life has in store for us during our mission is represented by the Life Path, which is derived from the birth date. This number is the road we will travel in our quest to reach our full Expression. Only by reaching the fullness of this potential can we achieve our correct destiny.

Thus, when all is laid bare, we have the circle of our humanity before us. We have our Soul number. It is our primal energy, motivation, and heart's desire. It is at once the raw building material and our motive. The raw material is built into our destiny only by traveling the Life Path to reach our fullest Expression. After all, potential is nothing unless it can be expressed through mind and body.

Is it mind or body that moves us toward our destinies? Is it not time itself that moves us on? The numbers kindly perform for both those amassed and bereft of understanding. The oracle is moved by time itself. That thing, like the ocean tide, that ties all things, living and not, together into the dance and rhythm of synchronicity.

The tide is discerned by the swaying rushes, the wind by a bending bough, and the tides of time by the pattern of numbers. Understanding these things allows us to ride the tides, just as any master sailor, to anywhere in the world.

What will the tide of time wash upon the shores of your life? Where will they take you? Read and see.

HISTORY

The Greek philosopher, Pythagoras, is credited as being the father of numerology. Born on the island Samos, approximately 174 miles from Athens, Pythagoras lived from 582 to 500 B.C.

Pythagoras is most noted for mathematics rather than for philosophy. Students of geometry recall the Pythagorean theorem about right-angled triangles: $a^2+b^2=c^2$.

However, the Pythagorean theorem was not actually discovered by Pythagoras. The earliest known formulation of the theorem was written down by the Indian mathematician, Baudhāyana, in 800 B.C. The principle was also known to the earlier Egyptian and the Babylonian builders. This "personalization" of previously discovered knowledge may also apply to his invention of numerology, since systems of like kind were also in use earlier in the Middle East, with the Chaldean and Egyptian system being the earliest.

Pythagoras is acclaimed as one of the brightest figures of early Greek society. The Pythagorean theorem is often cited as the beginning of mathematics in Western culture, and ever since the deductive reasoning behind mathematics has held a profound influence on Western philosophy and science. Pythagoras' influence has also been felt in music, philosophy, math and science.

Pythagoras founded a society of disciples which was very influential for some time. Men and women in the society were treated equally - an unusual thing at the time- and all property was held in common. Members of the society practiced the master's teachings, a religion the tenets of which included the transmigration of Souls and the sinfulness of eating beans!

Metempsychosis, or the transmigration of the Soul into the same or different animal species was a cornerstone of Pythagorean philosophy. This gave way to the thought that eating meat was an abomination, since the Souls of all animals enter different animals after death.

Pythagoras' contact with the idea of reincarnation was derived from his exposure to Egyptian beliefs. He introduced this concept to the Greek society, which soon absorbed and popularized it.

The belief in the existence of eternal cycles led the group to assert that there was a higher or universal structure and a divine order. Pythagoras believed the Soul was influenced by these constant cycle, and cycles within cycles.

His attempt to understand these cycles is reason for Pythagoras' study of mathematics. He was convinced that the principles and actions of the universe could be understood and expressed in numbers. He applied his studies of math to music and philosophy, part of which was numerology.

This eventually led to the famous saying that "all things are numbers." Pythagoras himself spoke of square numbers and cubic numbers, and we still use these terms, but he also spoke of oblong, triangular, and spherical numbers. He associated numbers with form, relating arithmetic to geometry. His greatest contribution, the proposition about right-angled triangles, sprang from this line of thought.

Just as there is convincing evidence that Egyptians knew of the 3,4,5 relationship of the legs and hypotenuse of the right triangle, there is also evidence that numerology was in use thousands of years ago in Egypt, centuries before the birth of Pythagoras.

We also know that Pythagoras journeyed into the Middle East, where it is likely he also encountered these ideas. It was after he returned from his journey that he set about to put his own spin on these sciences. At that time he developed his ideas on numerology and the human psyche.

It should be well noted that in the Middle East at that time, there was a body of knowledge containing the basic personality descriptions of nine types of individuals. This knowledge eventually found its way into the mystical

13

teachings of the Sufis. The body of knowledge is now known as the Enneagram.

The earliest appearance of the Enneagram that has been historically documented is in the teachings of G. I. Gurdjieff (ca. 1870-1949), which are recorded in the books of his student P.D. Ouspensky. The first documented correlation of the nine points on the Enneagram to nine personality types occurs in the teachings of Oscar Ichazo (b.1931). While Gurdjieff considered the Enneagram to contain the key to knowledge of all that is in the cosmos, it was Ichazo in the 1960's who first developed a theory of nine personality types corresponding to the nine points of the Enneagram. Most Enneagram teachers believe that it is more ancient than Gurdjieff or Ichazo, though they do not agree on its precise origins and offer no solid historical evidence for their various theories. Gurdjieff asserted that knowledge of the Enneagram has been passed down in secret circles devoted to esoteric wisdom, perhaps for thousands of years, though he evidently never divulged from which group he supposedly learned it.

Many Enneagram teachers believe that he learned the Enneagram from Sufi mystics, though in saying this they do not necessarily mean to deny that the Enneagram could be older, since the Sufis themselves are reputed to pass down forms of wisdom that are older than their own school. Others assert that the Enneagram has its origins in the numerological speculations of the Pythagoreans or the ancient wisdom of the Chaldeans.

If this connection is true it points to an ancient and central pool of knowledge that spawned both numerology and the Enneagram.

Whether Numerology gave way to the Enneagram. or the body of knowledge that became the Enneagram was used by Pythagoras, the central pool of wisdom does exist.

By comparing and contrasting these two disciplines one can expand and integrate our knowledge of numerology. We can recreate the lost reservoir of wisdom accessed by Pythagoras some twenty-six hundred years ago in his search to qualify and quantify the human soul.

In the end, the secret of this art is the realization that all numbers reside within all of us. Understand the numbers and understand yourself.
EXPAND YOURSELF TO INCLUDE ALL NUMBERS.

FORMULAE OF NUMEROLOGY

Alphabetic to numeric conversion chart:

A J S = 1	B K T = 2	C L U = 3
D M V = 4	E N W = 5	F O X = 6
G P Y = 7	H Q Z = 8	I R = 9

To determine soul and quiescent self numbers, convert the entire alphabetic name to a numeric name of one digit:

Vowels include A, E, I, O, U.

In certain circumstances Y and W are considered vowels. When the "Y" makes an "E" or "I" sound it is considered a vowel. When the "Y" makes the vowel before it long it is a vowel. Examples of these two rules are the names "Lynn" or "Gray."

In names where the "Y" makes its own sound, such as in the name Yolanda, is it a consonant.

"W" is considered a vowel only when it makes the vowel before it sound like a long "O" such as in the words such as "low" or "show."

Example of how to break down a name:

Billy Bob Smith:

Vowels   9 +7 +6 +9 = 31

Consonants   2 + 3 + 3 + 2 + 2 + 1 + 4 + 2 + 8 = 28

Soul = sum of all vowels reduced to a single digit, in the example, it is 3 + 1, or 4.

Quiescent Self = sum of all consonants reduced to a single digit, in the example, it is 2 + 8, or 10. 1+ 0 reduces to 1.

Expression = sum of Soul and Quiescent Self numbers reduced to a single digit, in the example, 4 + 1 = 5.

To determine the Life Path number, convert the entire birthday to a single number:

Example:

September 9, 1970 = 09/09/1970 = 9 + 9 + 1 + 9 + 7 = 35 = 8

Life Path = sum of numeric birthdate reduced to a single digit, in the example 3 + 5 = 8.

DEFINITIONS AND EXPLANATIONS IN NUMEROLOGY.

To use numerology one must first convert the full name into numbers. Only when converted to numbers can the formulae be used and the main personality be revealed.

The following is the chart that must be used for converting the name to numbers in order to use numerology. Each letter of the entire name as it appears at birth is assigned a number in the following manner.

A J S = 1	B K T = 2	C L U = 3
D M V = 4	E N W = 5	F O X = 6
G P Y = 7	H Q Z = 8	I R = 9

Example:

Billy Bob Smith:

Vowels   9 +7 +6 +9 = 31

Consonants   2 + 3 + 3 + 2 + 2 + 1 + 4 + 2 + 8 = 28

All numbers are reduced to a single digit. Reducing is done by adding the digits of the number together until the result is a single digit. If the number before reduction is eleven or twenty-two this should be noted. They are considered to be "master numbers" and have special meaning. This will be discussed later.

The vowels represent the Soul Number. It is the drive, inner personality, and heart's desire. The number is 31. 3 + 1 = 4 So, the Soul is 4.

The consonants represent the Quiescent Self. It is the first impression and the ideals of an individual. It represents the kind of person we wish we were and thus what we strive to be. The number is 28. 2 + 8 = 10 But this is not a single digit, so we have to add the resulting digits again. 1 + 0 = 1. The Quiescent Self is a 1.

The sum of the Soul (4) and Quiescent Self (1) is called the Expression. 1 + 4= 5

This represents how the person will act. It is their destiny, what they will become, and how they will grow. It is the combination of the heart's desire and what they wish they were. The following pages give a more in depth definition of these forces.

INFORMATION ON THE SOUL VIBRATION

The Soul is one of the most important numbers for discerning the personality type. It is the inner wants, needs, and drives of the person. It is what they are below the games and masks. It is the true motivating force and heart's desire, as well as feelings and talents. It is derived from the total of the vowels in the name.

INFORMATION ON THE QUIESCENT SELF

The Quiescent Self is that part of our psyche that contains our ideals. These values were instilled by our parents, family, society, and those who had profound influences in our lives. The Quiescent Self is our inner guide and internalized parent. It gives us a clue as to what ways of conduct and thinking a person might find acceptable, and a standard to be sought. It is interesting that between many good and stable couples one person's Soul or Expression number will show up in the partner's Quiescent Self. Usually it only works one way; that is, spouse "A" will have the Quiescent self number of spouse "B" Soul or Expression, but not the other way around. This attraction only makes sense.

If the Quiescent Self represents the qualities that we admire and seek for ourselves, we should also find them desirable in the person with whom we wish to spend our life. The Quiescent Self is an indication of the first impression that we leave on others. It is how others first judge us. This is slowly altered according to our Expression number but it never goes away, since it is what we are striving for. It is your first impression personality, but not the true you. The Quiescent Self is the reduced value of the consonants in the full name.

INFORMATION ON THE EXPRESSION

The Expression is the total of the name. It is both vowels and consonants, which are added and reduced to a single digit. The Expression represents the way that the Soul is vented or expressed to the outside world. It is the combined influences of what we are at our deepest (the Soul), and what we think we should be (the Quiescent Self). It is how we will act out our part in life. It should be kept in mind that no one is what they appear to be. We are each a combination of many layers of influences. What we truly want to do and be is held in check by the restraints of society, family, and self-image.

The Expression is the result of this process. If the person is not in touch with their feelings, they may think that they are the Expression. It is, however, a face that we present to the outside world.

The Expression needs to be compatible and harmonious with the Soul in order for the person to express themselves in a productive way. The incompatibilities between the Soul and the Expression represent possible personality dysfunctions.

We should also remember that, as people, we are susceptible to any ongoing influence and therefore by

21

attempting to present a false face or a façade, we distort who we are and are able to vent less and less of our true selves. This will lead to repressed emotions.

For more information on the Soul and Expression please refer to chapter entitled, "Enmass." (This word was chosen because it refers to a grouping, gathering, or collection of things. It is where much of the synergy of the two systems – the Enneagram and Numerology - can be seen) For a 6 Soul refer to Enmass 6, for a 1 Soul refer to Enmass 1, etc.

ENMASS INFORMATION

Although this entire book is based on a combination of the Enneagran and Numerology, this section will bring them both together.

The Enmass information is based on the combined knowledge of Numerology and the Enneagram. The application is straight forward. After calculating the name numbers of a person, the most powerful of which are the Soul and Expression numbers, you then read the Enmass information for those numbers. You will find that one of the numbers is in force more than the other. The dominant number will give insight into the formation and evolution of the person. The other number will give you an idea as to what was happening in the background as a group of secondary issues.

The dominant number is the one that the person relates to and recognizes. If you have chosen not to use the formulas of numerology but instead choose to use the empirical approach of the Enneagram you must question, observe, and match the main attributes of the Soul and Expression to the person. Once this is done, turn to the Enmass section and read those numbers for a complete understanding of the person and how their personality was formed.

The dominant number will also give insight into the formation and evolution of the person. The other number will give you an idea as to what was happening in the background, as a group of secondary issues. Each number is broken down into three classifications, healthy, average, and unhealthy. This is a gauge of the integration of the personality.

There are also two other classifications within each type. The superior and inferior functions. An easy way to view this classification is that the superior function is the one that you are aware of and you use. You control it The inferior function is the subconscious soft spot. It controls you.

The Enneagram is simply a personality typing system which is related to Numerology. Numbers start with 9 then go from 1 to 8. It is broken into three triangles representing three "planes or centers."

The feeling triad is made up of 2, 3, and 4. They all have problems with this area. 2 is overdeveloped, expressing only the positive and repressing their negative feelings. 3 is out of touch with their feelings. They project only a facade. 4 can only reveal itself through its work, art, form or music. In other words, its feelings are reflected.

The doing triad is made up of 5, 6, and 7. 7 tends to think, plan and dream instead of doing. 6 can't act on its own, but tends to fall back on its authority figure or rules, to tell it what to do. 5 can become manic, hyperactive, out of control.

The relating triad is 8, 9, and 1. 8 sees itself bigger than life and wants to take over. 9 is out of touch and relates to an illusion, idealized person. 1 deals less with people than with its ideals and whether they are attained or not. 3, 6, and 9 are the most blocked and out of touch. They have the most trouble in their triads. The other types are more mixed in their effects.

There is no one who is all of one type. We are combinations of all types. We will see that, as always, a number or type is a two-sided coin containing within itself both the very positive and the very negative parts of the same personality functions.

The 2, 3, and 4 have a problem with hostility. 2s deny and conceal it.

Each number is classified as either an introvert or an extrovert. These terms relate to how the person processes information and therefore how they relate to their environment. Numbers are further divided into "Planes of Expression," which are Mental, Emotional, Physical, and Intuitive. These planes represent how the person functions and learns. Information on the Planes of Expression as well as other centers and divisions can be found on pages 144 – 160.

Definitions and explanations for terms such as "ego, id, and super-ego, " as well as "parent, child, adult, and inner-voice" can be found in the section beginning on page 323.

As the personality disintegrates, it passes through stages. It starts at its base number and goes from there, descending following a path of 1-4-2-8-5-7-1-9-6-3-9.

If the personality is on the upswing and is integrating itself, it will grow through a process, ascending in the following manner: 1-7-5-8-2-4-1-9-3-6-9.

If the personality is striving to integrate and improve they are said to "work out." However, if the person is descending or not integrated he or she is said to "act out."

ONE EXPRESSION

1's have ambition, drive, strength of will, self-concern and are not easily swayed by the opinions of others. Their temper shows when they are disagreed with. Domineering, they dislike being directed or bossed around. 1's are individualistic and nonconformist. They are loners, self-reliant, argumentative and must be heard. They are quick-witted and can become sarcastic if angered.

This Vibration is best for salesmen or persons who must put ideas across. They may proclaim their love too quickly. 1's may have an interest in teaching, law, writing, preaching, selling, collections, or owning a business of their own, needing to direct, and spearhead. A 1 adds drive to the Soul number bringing out a more individualistic and willful nature in the given Soul. They believe in and stick by their own judgments and ideas. If they are healthy, the 1 is capable of persisting and enduring to the point of success. This is a blessing. If they become convinced of the moral rightness of their stance, they will not relent. 1's have musical talent, executive ability (director, department head, group leader, etc).

1's may be self-centered. They must take care not to be arrogant, selfish, or stubborn. They must learn to consider others first. They usually don't think about others since they assume others function as they do and will take care of themselves. 1's need to remember that they could be wrong. They may need to learn to control their temper. They may choose their mate based on status, outward appearance or what he/she could provide them. 1's may come across as strong and certain, yet most times they are insecure and more uncertain than they appear. It is their nature to be capable of delivering a convincing, strong, or persuasive point, not even knowing if they are correct. Often they begin to believe their self-image. This will bring them to a place of egocentric stubbornness.

ONE SOUL

1's do not like to be told what to do. They have ego, drive, and are impatient with slow minds. They may seek praise or try to prove self. They may think of people as an extension of their own will. They are decisive, creative (usually in writing). They may be critical, but unable to take criticism because they may get their feelings hurt. They are opinionated. They are individualistic. 1's are resilient in love and will not be dominated. (This can be changed by a 2 Expression.) They have a need to direct. They are usually the head of the house. They have a gift for art, writing, and usually music. Many can play by ear. They are good at conveying an individualistic opinion. Many do favors with the idea of what they can get back in mind.

They are happiest when they're in control. The 1 seeks praise or leadership position. They may want to own their own business. Beware of lack of consideration of others, or lack of compassion because of selfishness. If not, they are harmonious, stubborn, procrastinating. They won't admit mistakes or change their mind. Because of their self-centered viewpoint they may take money, status or outward show into account when they marry. Seem to be swayed by the year Vibration more than most.

ENMASS 1

1 is the type of the leader/reformer. They want to be right, to strive to improve others, to justify their position, and to be beyond criticism so as not ever to face condemnation. The ego looks strong, but has been damaged in childhood. They aim for the ideal, not content to be as they are. They keenly feel the struggle between good and evil, head and heart, irrationality and their own rational minds. They are sure of themselves, (less because they are perfect and more because they are sure of their ideals). They see themselves as less than the ideals for which they strive. They subordinate themselves to an abstract ideal such as truth or justice. They embrace a work-oriented theology and ethic, thinking that one must work and strive toward an ideal. They may seem confused

and disbelieving when they see that effort and hard work sometimes don't pay off. Whether it is because of fate or personal failure, 1's don't consider it fair when a return for effort isn't forthcoming. They feel uplifted and set apart from the norm by this striving.

So as not to be condemned, they act as if they are perfect and right. They constantly measure the distance between themselves and the ideal, and also how far they have come. They are caught between having these ideals, and implementing them in the world. They repress many emotions and impulses, riding herd over them to keep them in check and live up to their idealistic aims. Despite their apparent strength of will and character, this repression and striving (which may be to seek the father image's approval), can cause obsessive/compulsive behavior.

They desire to be liked and accepted. They get very lonely at times inside of their self-sufficient facade. 1's are the extroverted thinking type. They elevate objective reality and formula to the ruling principle for themselves and their environment. By this criteria all abstracts are measured (good, evil; beauty, ugliness).

Everything that agrees with the formula is right, and the rest is wrong. People must also conform to it. All who don't are immoral, wrong, and are going against the universal laws. As we can see, if this law is broad enough it may serve a sociological purpose; however, it seldom is,

29

and provides nothing more than a whipping post by which he forces himself and others into his mold. They will get angry at others when they are really angry at themselves for not being perfect

The superior function of 1 is mental or thinking, the inferior function is emotional or feeling. In childhood the 1 identified negatively with the father image. The father may have been critical. In some way the child got the message that they were not acceptable as they were. They tried to become blameless by shifting blame, avoiding blame, and trying to be perfect. The message of "you must be better" drove them to repress many emotions and impulses.

They probably had help from a parent who punished them if they let an impulse slip or told them that they were bad, wrong, or unacceptable. He had few kind words for them. The father could have been stern, abusive, missing, critical, cold, or alcoholic. The child was forced to be an adult and not to do or say anything wrong for fear of being punished. The child was not able to be a child, especially in the sense of the needed emotional freedoms. They may have been called on to help raise younger siblings or keep the household running in some way. This can truncate a childhood and stop growth. At first they did not rebel; instead they felt guilty for not performing up to some expected level and they felt frustrated.

The feeling of failure for not being good enough and the pressure of the critical environment begat anger, both at the parent and themselves. They tried to internalize the anger. The anger increases when they see that others do not have to conform to the same perfection that was laid upon them. The super-ego of the 1 now is imprinted with the values and critical inner voice of the parent. The voice that we all have that talks to us, critiques us, encourages us, and gives us that running commentary comes partly from the super-ego. It is our internal parent. They push themselves toward perfection, just as they felt in their childhood. At its worst, they repress their wants and desires in exchange doing only what is right and correct in order to silence the inner voice.

Isn't it odd that from the time we are old enough to identify with those in authority over us to the time that we die, we strive to please them, or rebel against them. This is the choice that the 1 type will make. They will either be hard, egocentric, willful, and defiant; or they will be perfectionists, driving themselves to the point of exhaustion, probably remembering words from their past such as, "you are lazy", or "you are stupid."

They don't understand that others are not driven as they are. They usually don't really understand what drives them until they are stopped by some situation that forces them to take time enough to look inside. They can come to

31

resent those who can do as they wish without the interference of an inner voice. As the 1 goes to the limits they may forsake trying to quiet the voice, and rebel against all social rules. They may even form a kind of split in which they perform as adults when around those that they know, and as a child at other times.

The child within them is forced into a defensive attitude due to the discomfort of being wrong "all of the time", (even though by now the majority of the insufficiency that they feel is from themselves), so they have a hard time admitting that they are wrong. They become opinionated and loud so as not to be challenged. They become critical of others as a defense against being criticized. At this point, they usually show signs of stress and nervousness, having repressed much anger and fear from their past. The aim is to silence the critic within, so they may turn to excesses of drink, drugs, or sex. They may have crying spells or spells of rage that temporarily reduce the pressures.

The 1 has to realize that their way is familiar to them, but it is not the only way. Others have different stresses driving them. There is more than one right way. They also need to see that when they were young, love was a reward for being good, but that is not the way that it should be. True love asks nothing but its own expression. They must break with the old ways and old voices within and come to accept ourelves and others without a fear of rejection.

We are all imperfect, yet we all should be loved. We have to forgive all of the cuts, criticisms, and demands placed on us in the past, and to allow themselves to be less than perfect. We should see ourselves as the people that we are, better than some, worse than some, just a person who is trying, and if we could be satisfied with that, we could feel a release from our self-imposed prison.

1's deepest need is to feel that they are loved even though they are imperfect. The sad thing is, they can't love themselves due to the inner voice of their parents judging them all of the time. This view of the 1 allows us to see a vulnerable, needy side of the 1 type. The child within has braced his small frame against the next cut, and waits with defiant tears for the one who will accept him as he is. The defiance is what shows, not the child. They are very concerned with how others view them, although they may not admit it. They judge situations against a view of potential perfection (how perfect it could be versus how far it falls short). Those are old ways that did not serve them well. They must seek a release from them now.

Healthy 1's are wise, discerning, and tolerant. Realistic and balanced in judgment. Rational, moderate, principled, objective, ethical. High integrity, a teacher, leader. They try not to let their feelings get in the way of good judgment. They allow their emotions to surface, and they discover that they are not as chaotic as they had been led to believe. They lay aside the rules to try simply to become complete people. They have a moral vision and are sought for guidance. They can understand and tolerate different points of view without having to agree or enforce them. They are passionate about righteousness and justice. They live their convictions, even if it means going against civil law. Their goodness is a deep satisfaction to them. Original, creative, progressive, determined, optimistic, willpower, leader, individualistic, direct, to the point, self-starters, courageous, pioneering.

Average 1's are high-minded idealists, striving for excellence. Reformer, crusader, advocate. Orderly, efficient, impersonal. They are too emotionally controlled; they can also be critical, judgmental, opinionated, perfectionists, and moralizing. Indignant, angry, abrasive. They can exhort themselves and others to improve. They find it hard to allow others their views. They have an elitist, noble, lofty sense of self. They take on the challenge of righting moral and social wrongs, educating and guiding others. This is because they do not trust anyone else to do it correctly. They have classified almost everything as right or wrong, and expect others to do as they are told. They have the zeal of a missionary. They are articulate and love to debate points of view. They want the rational mind to rule everything. Meticulous, precise, sticklers. Life is serious business. They cannot delegate work.

The unhealthy 1 can be very self-righteous, intolerant, dogmatic, and inflexible. They cannot stand to be wrong. They tend to preach one thing and do as they please. They can be cruel and punitive with others.

Obsessive/compulsive behavior or sudden nervous breakdown and depression is possible. They think in error that they have attained the unattainable ideal for which they strove. They think that they alone can do the job or have the truth. They are argumentative. They view people as malleable to their will. Nothing is ever good enough. "I'm not having fun, so neither will you." They are dogmatic. They are so aware of their thoughts and impulses that they can become obsessed because of impulsive thoughts of sex, heresy, violence, that they may even think that it is demonic. (This is also a way of shifting blame). They have no mercy, love, or sympathy. When others don't act according to the 1's moral code they can have them burned at the stake. In their fear of being condemned they will quickly and mercilessly condemn others. Selfish, egocentric, aggressive, arrogant, bullish, bossy, proud, unable to admit mistakes.

1's will act out by setting very high standards and obsessing about not living up to them, and by rationalizing their way out of admitting their shortcomings. They have feelings of bitterness and disappointment at having fallen short of some mark. These feelings are often blamed on others, or the world in general. They become angry, impatient and rude. They judge others and feel "put upon." They become rebellious and tyrannical, leaving no room for any opinion but their own. They won't listen to reason. They think that everything is imperfect, and it's their job to tell others the best way to set things right.

All of their angst of what they are feeling about themselves is projected into others. They feel imperfect, yet driven to be perfect. Anger and despair can be the only result. The 1 needs to let go of unreasonable standards, the fear of losing control, being blind to their own inconsistent thoughts and ways, disappointment with themselves and the world, driving themselves and others too hard, and being easily annoyed. The 1 should focus on his ability to be independent, self-motivated, creative, pioneering, capable, and a leader.

1's will work out their problems by reminding themselves that it is all right not to be perfect...that others count just as much as they do. 1's must learn to differentiate between the rights and lives of others and themselves. Relax and trust others to do things their own way in their own lives. It will take much pressure off. Slow down and be softer, more compassionate, more concerned for others. Enjoy life more. Understand that the feelings that you have about your self-image are not fact. It is the echo of long past voices of those who had their own ego problems.

We must all learn that feelings are not facts. They only become facts when they line up with reality. If you stop right now and make a checklist of what most people consider normal and correct, you will find that you fall well within the limits of being an exacting person. This being fact, now you must work on adjusting your feelings accordingly. In a nut shell, be less critical of all, and that includes yourself.

TWO EXPRESSION

2s are kind, tactful, patient, cooperative, diplomatic, and sensitive. They are slow to anger and able to see both sides of any given situation. They may often be placed in the middle of a fight to make peace. This may aggravate the over-sensitive 2s. They may seem to have the "middle child complex" lacking proper emotional attention in their childhood, especially if they are too shy or quiet. They may feel overlooked at times. They overcome this by being able to sense the feelings and emotions of others, then to mold themselves to the needs at hand. This, however, could allow them to lose their identity in others.

2s often get caught up in details. Not only can they lose the "big picture," but it could lead to pettiness. They may seem naive and insecure in relationships. 2 is the receptive type. They are often dependent on others. A sense of harmony and rhythm is part of the 2. Talent with music, or color is indicated. Their interests are in religion, art, photography and science, decorating or music. They are able to retain detail and have an above average memory. Detail retention is best with art, music, numbers, dance, banking, statistics and logistics. These people often make good teachers. With a 7 Soul they may be blunt or outspoken. A paradox exists if emotions are submerged for too long; the Expression may become repressed.

The temper is often soft-spoken and passive-aggressive. They have an easy-going nature. They are patient and considerate. If affected or under stress 2s could lose tact, and become blunt or resentful. If stress is long-term, 2s may vacillate from quiet and patient to rude and short-tempered. This is due to the nervousness which is a part of the 2s makeup. 2s are faithful and forgiving in love, possibly to the point of blindness. The harmony experienced or sought after by the 2 may be best expressed through eastern philosophy, metaphysics, or religion. This goes along with their search for inward peace.

They need to experience balance, harmony, and unity with others. Proper expression may not be possible with a docile nature. Emotions, especially anger, must be properly vented or the anger may be later directed toward themselves. This may occur when the 2 fails to speak their mind, or they become too caught up in trying to please and mold themselves to the one that they have chosen to serve. They repress their own needs and feelings. This also gives way to passive/aggressive acts as they find ways to covertly express the emotions that they are afraid to openly express due to a fear of rejection. 2s tend to be neat people. They are drawn to neat, clean environments. They are able to pay close attention to detail to the rhythm, balance, harmony and other's needs.

TWO SOUL

Sensitive, diplomatic, peacemaker, buffer. They crave affection. 2s are gentle, patient, considerate, passive, and can be nervous. They are sympathetic. They want someone to be the center of their world. They are tactful, slow to anger, possessing a sense of rhythm and harmony. Some 2s have musical talent. 2s are tolerant, diplomatic, and able to see both sides. They can be overly dependent or unable to make decisions for themselves if they were too dominated in childhood. Their world is made up of family and a small group of friends. (Note a possible inner conflict of a 7 Expression and dissatisfaction or need to have companionship.)

2s can make good teachers. They have the ability to sense the needs and feelings of others. They are drawn toward serving others. If they go too far, or if they get involved with a person who is too strong or demanding, the 2 may start to lose their identity. They will repress their needs in order to continue to mold to the one whom they wish to serve. This can build up resentment, anger, or other unexpressed negative emotions to the point that they lash out, or become manipulative and petty. 2s have a fear of rejection that keeps them trying harder. They also tend to take blame too easily, but this is because they think that if they are at fault then they still have a chance to fix the situation and make peace.

If affected by lack of expression or understanding, 2s can become rude and insensitive, with bursts of temper, and sullenness. There are times that the 2 will show most of what the reverse of 2 is; for example, when they are alone and do not want to be, or are unhappy with themselves. This also stems from lack of self-certainty and confidence. 2s could have the sensitivity to deal with fine details in colors, textures, or sounds.

2 Souls need a peaceful, placid existence. Their family is a group of friends and loved ones. The 2 seeks companionship, love, marriage. Some 2s are apt to deal with logistics because they are precise. Usually, 2s are faithful and forgiving in love. They seek harmony, balance, unity and love. They are drawn to dominant mates. Art, music, painting are usually loves of theirs.

Some 2s like collecting as a hobby. They may think of the past too much. May do intricate or detailed work with hands.

ENMASS 2

2s want to be loved, to express their feelings for others, to be needed and appreciated. They will coerce and manipulate others using guilt or passive-aggressive acts to get their emotions out and keep others where they want them. They also need others to need and want their love; they need to think that they are emotionally correct and will hide their true motivations from others and themselves. Healthy 2s make wonderful mates. They are capable of sensing and serving the needs of their mates, at times, even before they verbalize them. They are individuals yet are able to be very empathetic.

If the 2 is not healthy they will have strong feelings that tend to be over-expressed. The positive will be stressed and the negative side will be ignored. This leads to obsessions and self-deception. They may be blind to their own aggressive feelings making them manipulative, passive/aggressive, and selfish in the name of love.

The negative 2 is the most insidious of personality types. Their love is not free but many times has strings attached. This is because the parent communicated his love in a conditional way, the parent withheld approval and affection if the child disappointed them, or they did not approve of the child's actions or decisions. The child grew up expecting this and thinking that it was correct. Yet they feel hurt and anger, and are ill-equipped to reason out why. They grow up on the emotional edge of love and anger.

They are an extroverted feeling type. Often only a small change in situations is needed to cause a large emotional shift. This is because of an unacknowledged anger present just below the surface. There was an ambivalence to the father or father image. This sets the stage for ambivalence toward those who can give them love. This problem of relating to the father makes their love conditional. They seem to think that they have to be absolutely good to deserve love, even to love themselves. This may explain why they must ignore the bad in themselves and others. It can get bad enough that they will defend their manipulation in the name of love, even against the facts. Religion plays an important part in the life of 2s'. It gives them a value system that they can relate to, with which to verbalize their emotions.

The opposite is that they are busybodies, and meddlers, not knowing the difference between what is good and what is God. They wear themselves out being good, and can be heard to say, "I believe God told me to do this." We must be very careful not to use phrases like that lightly. It leaves others in a position of not being able to help them for fear of having it said that they are fighting against someone who is following a higher leading. 2s must also be aware that since the super-ego is the internalized parent, and God is the ultimate parental image, we can easily

43

confuse the echoes of what our internal parent is saying and the leading of our higher power.

It is easier to see the 2 in catch phrases such as "I'm just trying to make things easier for you," or "I'm doing this for you." They usually have ulterior motives. Most of the time we all have an aim for doing our good deed and we should acknowledge it, at least to ourselves. Honesty to ourselves is the most important thing. If we were totally honest about our actions and goals we would find that the early church fathers were correct when they said that every action and thought of man stems from some form of selfishness. The 2s won't acknowledge this in themselves but will remind you of your problems and prick at your heart's wounds while saying that they'll be there for you because you need them. They are ever trying to create the need so that they can fill it.

2s need to be needed. 2s often feel a pull between heart and head. If it gets too bad there are obsessions, and hypochondria, headaches, migraines, or stomach problems. As a last word we should "love and do what you will," and not let the word love be a license to do what you want.

The superior function of a 2 is emotional or feeling, the inferior function is mental or thinking. 2s need to feel liked and important in the lives of others. As children they felt as though they had to earn the affection of the parent by service, compliance, and by being careful not to go contrary to the emotions of the parent. They may flatter and serve in order to "buy" a person's love. They need approval. This may be a transference from the fact that they worked so hard for a parent's approval. They then tend to transfer that action over to others that they love.

2s will try to become what others need. They will say what others want to hear. This suppresses their real personality, as well as spawning an insecurity about being "found out" not to be real. This may drive them deeper to the point of losing their identity to their partner's will. They trade this for security and protection that is associated with the partner, who has usually been chosen for their strong will and personality. They believe that they know the innermost feelings of others, and they strive to serve and anticipate the needs based on that feeling

The 2 is the most subservient of numbers. Those in the subservient role have to develop a sensitive empathy, or a feeling of being almost telepathic at times in order to better fulfill the role of helper. The mature 2 is a model of the caring, sensitive person who is still an individual. It isn't until the 2 is mature that they realize that what they want out of the relationship is what they are putting into it. They will swing in their personality traits from extreme to extreme. Saint to whore, happy to angry, as they try to find a balance in themselves. It reveals situations where love was used as a tool, a reward system. Love, respect, and approval were used as a carrot in front of the child's nose to motivate them.

When unresolved anger is the driving force, there is always going to be pain inflicted. It can come with a gift, such as a comment like, "Here is a gift for you. Boy, did it cost, and I'm excited at having to go through so much to get it." This give and hurt, or give and take is very common with 2s until the anger is dealt with. The catch is that since open anger is equated with doing better in school, being a good child, or performing better, they continue this in adult life by trying to anticipate their mate's wants and desires in order to be a good little boy or girl, and to get the love that they need. As they grow more insecure they will stoop to flattery, manipulation, and passive/aggressive pressure to get the mate to feel as if they owe the 2 something.

Rejection from the 2s point of view is the worst possible outcome and is to be avoided at all times. Even the feeling of this is repressed in the 2, so you may hear things such as "I'm not angry. I've forgiven the son of a bitch." 2s can serve so intently that they lose part of their identity. They put their needs on the shelf in order not to disappoint, and therefore lose connection with the loved. This yields the insecurity of being found out, and the stress of suppressing part of themselves. Thoughts and statements such as, "They wouldn't like me if they really knew me," can be common for the insecure 2. Even if they flirt outrageously, they usually just seek attention, to feel wanted or needed.

2s watch for clues to see what people want or like, so they may be the provider of it and earn a place in the life of the lover or friend. They are truly givers. In the romantic phase of a relationship the 2 is totally committed to serving and fitting themselves to the mate, but as pressure starts to build there can be emotional, hysterical, or angry outbursts which may seem unprovoked or out of proportion to the stimuli. It is. It has only been "crow-barred" into activity by the present problem, and like a snowball headed downhill, it has little relevance to the people that started it.

Here is a test for any number to see if you are talking about the base issue that is bothering you.

1. Ask yourself if talking about the issue in a non-confrontational way is helping to dissipate the emotions.

2. Do you keep going around in circles so that in the same conversation the same issues come up over and over?

3. Does the argument get side-tracked? That is, does it branch into unrelated but volatile areas?

4. Are you having the same arguments many times, thinking it is taken care of, only to have it come back up again?

If the emotions peak instead of recede, if you find yourself back at the start with nothing accomplished, if you find yourselves arguing about many things, and if you continue to have the same fights after thinking it is resolved, you are probably not fighting about what is really at the base of the issue. 2s are good at hiding in the role of the victim, even though they may have created the hostile environment by reminding their mate about their mistakes, and giving rise to their pain only to point out how good the 2 is because they have forgiven them and will help them be a better person.

Sounds good on the surface, doesn't it? When God said that he would forgive us, he said that he would throw our sins into the sea of forgetfulness and he would remember them no more. We must all strive to be more God-like. This doesn't mean that we should let someone hurt us over and over. God's prerequisite was that we were repentant, and a truly repentant person will strive not to make that mistake again. That is not a guarantee that they will be successful, only that they will try.

The 2 should follow this simple rule: if you can forgive a shortcoming, then forget it. If you can't forgive it, then tell the person openly that you can't, and that you will probably nag them about it. You could try a time of honest "in their face" anger, and vent what is really bothering you.

I would be willing to bet that it will clear the air and a healing will start. Just be sure that you know the real issue.

Healthy 2s are unselfish, altruistic, caring, empathetic, helpful. They are capable of unconditional love. They understand that love is a gift. They find joy in giving. Able to love the sinner and forgive the sin. Philanthropic, uplifting, the good parent image. Looking out for others first, healthy emotional attachments, sympathetic, patient, diplomatic, receptive, considerate, maternal, sensitive to rhythm, detail-oriented, collects and assimilates information well. In Numerology, the healthy, integrated 2 is referred to as an eleven. These are the progressive, diplomats, and reformers. They are idealists, inspiring the people around them to higher levels.

Average 2s are emotional, demonstrative, friendly, overly personal, mothering, possessive, thinking their emotional input is more important than it is. 2s are somewhat histrionic. They have the ability to declare their feelings. They like physical and emotional contact. They can meet people and immediately regard them as friends. The average 2 talks about love and caring more than they act on it.

Unhealthy 2s are manipulative, using guilt or casting themselves as martyr, victim, or using hypochondria to get their way. Feelings of anger, bitterness, resentment, especially if others don't feel the way the 2 wants them to. When they do not feel loved it hurts the 2 and it calls into question their self-worth. They can prick at the soft spots of others with one hand and soothe them with the other. This passive-aggressive action confuses others. They can love and hate them at the same time. They will remind you of your shortcomings and bring you to self-doubts while telling you that they are good and forgiving enough to stay with you.

The unhealthy 2s are self-deceived and do not believe that they are anything but good and caring, even while they kill you with their kind of kindness. Fearful, dependent, overly sensitive, shy, petty, sullen, pouting, apathetic; 2s may try so hard to please and appease that they make themselves into a slave.

2s will act out by emotional outbursts that may be triggered by a relatively small and unrelated issue, which is used as an excuse to vent their feelings regarding the real issue. They will point to the secondary issue as the cause of their rage and emotionally destructive behavior. The real problem is that they feel unappreciated, unloved, or unneeded. They are angry that they have not achieved the desired response from their efforts. They will attempt to manipulate or force the wanted feelings and reactions from the other person.

2s need to let go of feeling abused or taken advantage of, resentment, anger, hidden agendas, passive/aggressive behavior, trying to manipulate others into feeling or doing as they wish, fears of being alone or unloved, whining and complaining. 2s should focus on being a balanced, integrated part of a team effort, sensing what would help others, being a "helpmate," and their ability to be devoted, have patience, be precise, attend to detail, sensing rhythms and harmony in people.

2s will work out by understanding their true feelings and why they feel it. They must then understand that no one has a right to manipulate the feelings of another. They must realize that just because others don't react in a particular way, it doesn't mean that they don't love you. The 2 must see that they are whole, complete, and lovable even if no one is "coupled" with them at the time.

THREE EXPRESSION

3s can be perfectionists. They strive to be perfect in the area that they are dealing with at the time. They can be very picky and uptight at times. Due to this need to have things "just right," they can drive themselves much too hard, and the people around them a little crazy. This characteristic is usually from the child within them trying to win the parents' approval. This type can be repressed at times. There is a need to loosen up and care less about what others think. Artist, writer, optimist, outgoing. 3s may seem superficial. They want to be the center of attention. 3s may be influenced easily (especially by flattery).

They are cheerful, but sometimes flighty. 3s are proud and can be jealous. They tend to seek the "perfect" lover or relationship. 3s want candidness but often get their feelings hurt from it. 3s are drawn toward people and are very social. They are very concerned with the way that they appear. Because of the concern with outward show they may be somewhat stingy since money buys status. They meet people well, and enjoy socializing, dancing, music, parties etc. They are able to mingle, fit in to a number of environments, and make people feel at ease. They sell themselves by acting in the way that the social strata and circle that they want to move in would approve of. They may tend to alter their personality to suit the group.

3s are an interesting number because they are light and airy which means they can be very fun-loving and able to uplift others. Their major problem is in taking themselves too seriously. They can become vain and narcissistic to the point that they are so self-absorbed there is no room left in them for having fun. As a general rule, 3s who don't get too caught up in how they look to others, and having everything just right, socially will have a happier life. If not they will probably look back at all of the time that they wasted on useless things they wanted in the first place. 3s put on a happy face and cover their true feelings with an outward show of lightness. They use chit-chat to keep people from getting too close. Although they appear to be superficial and light it must be remembered that they are caught up in being accepted, and what you see is a cover-up. If they are in touch with their true feelings they will be hidden for fear of rejection.

THREE SOUL

Self-expression, art, music, creativity, a flair for languages, painting, drawing, writing. Charm, social graces. Proud, jealous, learns quickly. Flirtatious, popularity is important. This is the selling, public, performing number. They may bid for the spotlight. Most

3s end up at the center of attention. 3s tend to be picky at times. They seek to be perfect in whatever area they are pursuing at the time. They can drive themselves too hard because of this.

Insecurity may arise leading to a need for the attention and/or affection of others to strengthen their own image. They wonder if their mate really loves them or needs them. 3s exude lightness and optimism. They may want their mate to be candid, but they get hurt because of it. They are stylish and place a lot of importance on associating with the "right" people. They may search for perfection in love and therefore may leave relationships too quickly. The 3 wants to make people happy. They may sing well.

Scattered energy and a tendency to get sidetracked is a problem for 3s. These people can have a light, vibrant, radiant personality. Status symbols are important in the way of clothes, cars, jewelry. Some tend to be verbose (especially with a 1 Life Path). Some 3s don't know when to shut up. They may have many "faces." Seek surroundings of groups, parties. If affected, may be superficial, lack concentration, exhibit gaudy taste, false vanity.

With a 6 Expression it will supersede the 3 and become more calm. The person may hold back in conversation, remaining quiet until they are sure that they can add something worthwhile.

ENMASS 3

3 wants to be affirmed. They thrive on attention, usually this is the lime light but it all centers around a feeling of being admired and accepted. They like impressing others with looks, talent, or ability. They can be status, style, and image-oriented. They are narcissistic. They interact with others well, but it is to defend against rejection which they fear. They are able to sense and respond to the emotions of others the way that plants respond to the sun - they turn toward the attention. They bask in it. They respond to the attention of others by imitating the values and ambiance of their psyche.

When the other people see themselves reflected favorably in the 3 they feel good about themselves and the 3. This establishes the "friendship" and the interaction is sustained. In childhood 3s identified closely with their mother image. They were given much attention when young. They were praised for performance, image, looks, or social skills. Because of this they have a high and strong self-esteem. They expect others to accept and love them the same way the parent did. If they don't, this causes a feeling of rejection.

The 3 has an underdeveloped superego and an overly developed id and ego. This adds to an arrogant air. They can manipulate and use others without remorse. At times if others don't admire them as the 3 thinks they should, they will strike out in anger, pouting, or vindictiveness as a child would. 3s need assurance and their way to feel like the spoiled child that they were with their mother image. 3s are performers, knowing what buttons to push to get people to like them. They seem sincere but are often empty. When the 3 turns to examine self and gets a balanced view of their self- worth and their abilities, acknowledging their faults and the equal worth of all, they will be modest, real, genuine, adaptable, social people.

They strive to be the consummate type of the image that they have chosen. If they chose to be a yuppie , they will be the epitome of a yuppie . This is why there can appear to be a wide variety of kinds of 3s. They are activity and achievement driven. As children they could have been "Shirley Temple" types, as adults they may be socialites or workaholics, but they will perform in whatever they do. Like number 2 types, they can get lost in their own games. They can easily come to believe that they are the character that they play. If they dig deeply enough they will find that the role that they play is chosen to produce a certain kind of reaction from the "audience." They play for attention. As a child they were praised for achievements, as adults it is simply carried on.

It matters to them that a good image is presented - a perfect home, a perfect family, the storybook lover. They can even play the part of the sympathetic or suffering person, and not feel nearly as deeply as they can project. The first movement has to be to get in touch with their true feelings, with which they are very out of touch. Those they seem to have are the false stage that they often work from (a self-delusion). 3s were children who were asked how they did, not how they feel. They were rewarded for their performance. Image became more important than emotional connection. They learned to suspend their feelings in order to focus on getting attention and status.

Being chameleon-like, they will adopt the image of the group. 3s can take it one step further. They are usually upbeat and optimistic. Their true identity becomes eclipsed by the game.

They tend to keep a surface optimism. Activity is an antidepressant for them. They are capable of doing and thinking of more than one thing at a time. If handled well and focused, this can be a great asset. If left unfocused, they can be scattered and "air-heads." 3s work toward material and financial acquisition in order to feel more secure about self.

In relationships 3s can put on the face of love. They may say and do what they think a lover should say and do without having the true feelings. They can easily deceive themselves. They try to fill as much time as they can with activity in order to keep inner emotions at bay. The actress or chameleon tendency is highest in the struggle to be accepted in the teens and young adulthood. They are competitive, with a type of competitiveness that lends itself to gossip, back stabbing, and being seen with only the right people.

3s are narcissistic in the fact that they are convinced that their way is right because they are superior and competent. This, however, is pride based on the false them, not the real. Emotional intimacy is held at a distance due to the fact that they are afraid that the real self won't be loved. They, like the 2s, might say, "If they really know me they won't like me." But 3s have too much pride and an image to maintain, so they will continue until their ship sinks.

3s have a lot of energy and can think or do more than one thing at a time. In this they resemble the 5. This can keep things lively, or can be a source of scattered energy where there is much activity and little accomplishment. The saddest thing about this number is that they fool people, and they know it. They are angered at the fact that people are fooled by their false face, yet they are afraid to show the real one in order that people love them. In a crisis, such as a mid-life crisis, a 3 may wake up to the fact that they were just playing a game, or aren't expressing the real them that has been bottled up for so long, at which time one should prepare for a change because they aren't the type to take it in stride. They will act.

3s should ask themselves, beyond the games and below the masks, what is my true face? Until a 3 can look in the mirror and know in their heart who and what they are, they may easily and frequently fall victim to self-deception and the waste of time and pain it can bring for all involved. We all play games at one time or another. We all want to be something or someone else now and then, but we must keep in mind that it is only a game. Trying to make it permanent is a lie and is dangerous. 3... show your true face!!!

It will help the 3 immensely to know that most of us see through the exaggerations and games, and we have already accepted them in spite of the "crap." People would like them even more if they didn't have to wade through it. So the fear that they have about falling short in people's eyes has already been realized, so they might as well relax and enjoy the unconditional love that they already have and don't know it. The superior function is emotional feeling, the inferior function is mental thinking.

Healthy 3s are inner directed, authentic, self-assured, energetic, adaptable, ambitious. They like self-improvement. They can motivate others to be like them since they have many qualities to emulate. They are people in their potential state (in the process of making something out of themselves). They spend time on making themselves better, more desirable, more attractive, smarter, socially better. They are the all American boy or girl - expressive, social, ambitious, conversational, inspirational, charming, gracious, artistic (through words, music, dance, sculpture, painting), and romantic.

Average 3s are concerned with prestige and status. Career and success are important. Image is top on their minds. They can be calculating manipulators, arrogant, pretentious, and narcissistic. They want to establish their superiority over others usually through competition. Being acknowledged by others as better raises their self-esteem. They compare job, salary, ability, looks...as if to say "Mine is better than yours." Because of this competitiveness, they may have trouble sustaining friendships. They have an egotistical air. They feel comfortable only around those they feel superior to. They are usually very successful since they pursue being the best with all their strength. They plot advancement relentlessly. Some have a "whatever it takes" approach. They are a marketing oriented person (sell yourself). They seek to perfect their image instead of themselves. When an image is practiced long enough it takes on a false and empty life of its own.

Unhealthy 3s are exhibitionists. Sex, appearance, attraction, to influence others and get admiration. They may hold themselves away from others in a "look but don't touch" attitude. They get a kick out of frustrating others. They will do anything to "make it." Because of the child being spoiled or allowed to run wild, they have a superego shortfall, leading to a sociopathic treatment of others. They will use anyone that they need to.

A tip-off to this is the large number of relationships that they go through, none of which is long-term. They are sneaky, jealous, two-faced, and back-stabbing. Their battle cry is, "It isn't enough that I win, but others must fail." They enjoy lying, even if about nothing important. It gives them a rush. If the deterioration continues sociopath becomes psychopath and they could do anything. Since the problem stems from their mother, most acts will be against women. The unhealthy 3 is conceited, rude, a braggart, a liar, superficial, jealous, careless, a gossip, a flirt, a dilettante, shallow, and insincere.

3s act out through jealousy and revenge. They care so much about their image that they will do or say anything to establish and keep it. This includes exaggeration, verbosity, conspicuousness, and driving themselves too hard toward being the ideal of what they have chosen as an image. The image is not truly them; it is what they think others want to see. 3s need to let go of jealousy, envy, fear of rejection, fear of being humiliated or being inadequate. 3s must stop denying their feelings in order to fit in. Cease the thirst for admiration, need for constant attention, arrogance, driving too hard to be perfect, and the impulse to be fake. They need to focus on their ability to meet and interact with people; their flair for fashion, communications, or art; their persuasive personality, spontaneous creativity, and social sense.

3s will work out by trusting that the real self has more value than a fake self. If people like you when you are real they will like you for life. If they like the false you, they only like you as long as you are "playing." Realize that if you are secure in your own worth, you will not be threatened by the success of others.

FOUR EXPRESSION

4s are practical, orderly, methodical, stern, enduring. They are mechanically inclined, good with money, logic, and math. They are hard workers, practical, and down to earth. These people make good welders, engineers, carpenters, plumbers, butchers, mechanics, performing sewing, knitting, refinishing furniture, painting, music, or most any job requiring good manual dexterity. Many 4s, especially women, are repressed emotionally and do not have a good outlet for venting their feelings. 4s find it difficult to express emotions. They may read to relax, or cook, watch TV, be involved with team sports on TV or have some other non-physical outlet, but that is not enough to relieve the pressure. Because of the emotional blockage that some 4s have, women can have problems in reaching an orgasm during intercourse. This may not be the case during masturbation, however, since another person is not involved. 4s need to let go emotionally and enjoy the act itself. 4s are tolerant of the faults of others; however, they should avoid flighty and superficial persons.

They have little interest in metaphysics or abstracts. (If it cannot be touched or seen it does not exist.) Falling into ruts or routines is common among 4s. This may lead to escapism through drugs, alcohol, sex, food, or eating disorders. If this escapism is more balanced and less destructive it will turn toward reading, movies, and working with their hands in order to escape. At times their emotional needs are filled by religion, sports or partying. If they are faced with too many changes of pace they could suffer mentally or physically. Their body clocks and sense of regularity are sensitive.

They require a certain amount of routine in order to function normally. 4s need to learn to express emotions freely. Avoid becoming lazy, stubborn, or narrow-minded. Be careful not to hold back emotions too much; this leads to escapism and swings of emotion, such as being a cold, logical person one moment and effusive the next.

This is a good military number. Good memory and learning ability. It has been noted that a large number of 4 women have problems with their legs (circulation or joints).

FOUR SOUL

Control, restraint, discipline, order, form, precision, reliability. They may not like abstracts or philosophy, yet 4 has a great sense of ethics, and is conservative. They have fixed opinions and are stubborn. They are drawn to technical, mechanical or construction fields. They may like to work with their hands - cars, contracting, building.

They don't trust their intuitive or emotional responses. Due to an inability to get in touch with their feelings, the 4 can be an escapist with habits of drinking, drugs, or eating to relieve tension. All of these must be kept in balance. If the escapism is turned to the positive, they will tend to escape by reading, watching movies, working with their hands, or watching sports. They will swing between stern and tolerant. They know the limits of self and others. They may become frustrated with a fickle or flighty mate.

They are down-to-earth and can do plumbing, welding, farming, construction, carpentry, electronics, refinishing furniture. Butcher, electrician, mill worker. When immature they will be intolerant if they haven't learned their limits. They think people should carry their own weight. May have a do-it-yourself attitude. They are motivated by a sense of duty and responsibility.

4s are given to above-average memories because they have minds that can organize and categorize facts (law, drafting, medicine). If the 4 is afflicted with a low self-image due to abuse or neglect in childhood, they can have a subservient, worker ant mentality. If this is the case the 4 may be dominated because of a subordinate frame of mind and a lack of self-worth.

With a 9 Expression: music, art, interest in workable, established systems. With a 7 Expression: could vacillate between down-to-earth, and happy. A 7

Expression adds a soft, religious, sensitive aspect; less of the "good old boy", and more of the soft-spoken, sensitive type.

Women tend to be dominant or less ladylike (harsher in nature this can be swung by Life Path or Expression). If affected, lazy, resists change, lacks emotional expression, too serious. They usually cannot stick with one thing too long (marriage, money-making, schemes that aren't stuck with long enough). They are usually quiet with people they don't know. 4 females usually breadwinners or co-workers. With an 8 Expression: a combination of stubbornness and insecurity. May lack true self-appreciation.

ENMASS 4

4s want to understand themselves and to express this in some way that has beauty. They withdraw to attend to emotional needs or the pressure may overwhelm them. They are craftsmen. There are two motives for creative or artistic work; to communicate self, or to lose themselves in their work. There are two results from artistic or creative output: one is to transcend self, the other is to become self-aware.

If they choose to run from themselves the result will be delayed growth, lessened self-evaluation, lack of dependability, and escapism. It is only the healthy 4 that takes the high road. The average 4 instead turns inward to understand themselves. In doing so they become trapped in "subjectiveness." Entrapped in their emotions, or the urge to understand and control their emotions, they withdraw and have an increasingly difficult time coping with the world. They have emotional difficulties more than all other numbers. They sense both the full human potential, and the depths to which we can descend; they view themselves as having missed their chance and potential and are destined to stagnate well below their station. The despair grows as they brood on what could have been or should have been.

The entire 4 process is driven by a search for identity. They want to sort out their emotions and answer the basic questions of "Who am I? " and "Is this all there is?". There is so much repression going on due to confusion or pain that they may not even be aware of their feelings until they are expressed through a medium. On first impressions they may seem shy or vulnerable, or you may see that they try too hard to fit in and that is their insecurity, but all of that fuels the inner conflict you'll see later. They will say "I'll live the way I want, and do things when I want", but that's an excuse to procrastinate because of uncertainty, or to be lazy, or irresponsible.

Most 4s lacked a role model. They didn't identify with either parent enough. There is a deep unconscious anger that one of the parents didn't nurture them. They are angry at themselves for being so defective that the parent left them. They could have had a feeling of aloneness in childhood, a piece missing by way of divorce, death, illness, alcoholism, or personality conflict with a parent. Usually the father is the negative influence. The child was forced to turn inward for their identity.

They feel that they were defective and this caused the parent's lack of attention. They may try to be better, take up the slack for the parent, make excuses for them, but in time they will begin to search themselves for the reason, and turn within. They feel powerless and frustrated. This causes tension, self-doubt, and aggression. If the doubt or aggression is turned within there will be compulsions, habits, "isms" such as eating, drinking, drugs or sex. These are the primary vehicles for escapism.

The ambivalence toward the parent can cause a rebellion in the child that is most clearly seen in the teens and twenties. They will defy authority, may even break the law, or drink to excess. They are acting out anger against a dysfunctional home. Some 4s come to believe their own lack of value. They tend to accept others for what they are without judging them.

Other 4s sink to a tough guy type of exterior, and even to a "thug." Mostly, 4s are needy people with a protective shell. They feel an isolation yet are trapped by a fear of intimacy brought on by a childhood feeling of not being worthy of stable loving closeness by both parents. The central cause of pain is an insidious type of emotional abandonment. The child always assumes that the parent is in the right and therefore they must be wrong. Their self-esteem plummets. They feel worthless and alone.

The despair that comes is partly due to the fact that they search for reasons as to why the parent doesn't love them when the problem is with the parent. They end up lost within themselves in despair trying to find a way to be good enough to make Daddy, or Mommy love them. This leads to despair, anger and fatalism. They may dwell on the past, wondering where they went wrong, and lamenting what might have been. It is melancholia, and is fought by outdoor activity and escapism.

Now and then there is a loop that is formed in which the despair, (which is unresolved anger), leads to escapism in the form of drugs or alcohol. The escapism reinforces their own poor self-image of being worthless, which drives them deeper into despair. Even if drugs or drink are not involved, they need to watch for such cycles of thought and habit. As blocked as the emotional Expression usually is, 4s can make the best artists, sculptors, chefs, or musicians. They seem to do it from the very core of their heart.

I want to encourage all of the 4s in the world to let go of their pain, and to view themselves as people of potential. Realize that no child is bad enough to warrant cruelty, neglect or abandonment, so lay the blame where it belongs. Be angry, then get it out and go on with your life. Be expressive and open with your newly felt freedom. You have much to offer, not the least is an ability to put ideas into form. 4s want to have close, intense relationships but are self-conscious, but you can overcome and be happy.

They may not be able to convey or demonstrate their love. Even to say "I love you" may be very uncomfortable for them. Their emotions are literally hog-tied, and remain that way until the despair overtakes them, or they learn how to express feelings through a medium such as music or art.

Many 4s have a rough exterior. They may work in a tough, blue collar job such as construction, trucking, farming, factory work or the like. This may be easier for them since no one expects a steel worker to open their heart and express their feelings (although no doubt there are exceptions). The superior function is physical sensing, the inferior function is intuitive.

Healthy 4s are inspired and creative. They are emotionally honest. Funny and serious. Emotionally strong. In touch with their inner impulses, and able to vent them creatively and without anger. They view both good and bad experiences as a growth process. They see all people as individuals, and let them seek their own path without judgment. Disciplined, practical, orderly, methodical, industrious, conventional, honest, and reliable. They fit in well with social norms.

In Numerology the very healthy fours are referred to as 22s. They have broken free of that trap of depression and anger. Unlike the average 4 who has landed and settled where the winds of fate have swept them, the healthy 4 (22) is an enlightened, goal- oriented, ingenious, masterful individual. The apex of a 4 is represented in the person of Leonardo Da Vinci.

Average 4s can be into art or music, and trying to express their feelings through a medium. Sculpting, woodworking, gardening, or just manual labor to relax is included. They can become self-absorbed, moody, depressed, self-pitying, and indulgent. This gives way to decadence, impractical actions, escapism, irresponsibility. Because this cycle is difficult to break, many 4s gravitate to blue-collar, mill work, construction, truck driving, labor intensive jobs to keep down emotional or mental pressures.

Unhealthy 4s are emotionally blocked. Self-hatred, depression, hopelessness. In being unable to get in touch with their emotions, they don't love or accept self. They abuse drugs, drink, eating, sex, even religion to escape. No

71

social values, no responsibility to society, or others. Undisciplined, procrastinates, stubborn, has a limited viewpoint, over-indulgent, crude, violent, vulgar, withdrawn, unable to express their feelings. It is a dichotomy that on one side 4s are so attracted to beauty, art, self-expression, and feeling; and on the other hand they are introverted worriers whose emotions are blocked and repressed to the point of self-destructive behavior in the name of controlling themselves, their emotions, others, and the environment because of insecurity.

4s will act out by anger turned against themselves. This leads to hopelessness, despair, self-destructiveness. Withdrawal from others through a tortured silence, drinking, drug abuse, overeating, and overindulgence are common for worst cases.

4s need to let go of hurt feelings turned inward: escapism, self-destructiveness, hopelessness, despair, feeling inadequate, being shame driven, fatigue brought on by depression, dwelling on past mistakes or what could have been, laziness. They need to focus on their ability for logic, order, method, good memory, hard work, putting ideas into form and action, working with their hands, their ability to accept others for who they are, and down-to-earth common sense.

4s will work things out by getting an aim, or path in life, and starting to walk it. Get a direction and start making a difference in your life. You are lost in your feelings and aimlessness. Be gentle on yourself. Don't think that you have missed life, or that it is too late to change. Decide what you want to do, then go for it without self-condemnation. Don't judge yourself by your past, just do your best each day, and before you know it you will have accomplished your goals.

FIVE EXPRESSION

Quick in thought and deed. The free spirit; impulsive, moody, and high-strung if tied down. They are curious and like travel and variety. They learn best from experiences of life. They are outgoing and somewhat sporadic. 5s are able to cope and adjust to new situations. They have high personal magnetism, sensual, and sexual appeal. They may confuse sex and love. 5 is a physical number so they will work in two different directions. Some will work with their hands in repair, installation, building, trucking; others will go toward selling, teaching, investing, speaking, writing. 5s are in constant need of activity and new experiences. They like to keep moving and doing. If the 5 is in a situation that does not allow them to express their free spirit, or if they are emotionally or physically squelched, they can become snappy, harsh, critical, or judgmental.

5s can be critical or temperamental in love. This usually indicates repressed emotions or needs. They may feel that something is missing in their lives, but not know what it is. This is cause for frustration and anger, leading them to lash out at times. A 1 Life Path may intensify this trait. 5 is greatly affected by the Life Path number. For example, a 6 Life Path may cause the person to appear more responsible than he actually is, or take responsibility to an extreme. This is probably because they absorb the environment and flow with it. But when these two numbers are in opposition, it can indicate that the environment repressed, or taught the 5 to truncate part of themselves in order to fit in, or to perform in a given environment.

5s are jacks of all trades. They are quick learners. 5s are good with public relations, writing, investigating. They convey ideas well. These people will be faced with choices between the world and the spiritual realm; that is, lust and habits versus love and spirit. Some 5s will become mystics or spiritual people, usually after they've run the gamut of the world and are dissatisfied. Some will have to fight addiction and lust for many years. The energy of the 5 may be intense but short-lived because they burn themselves out quickly. These people may renounce the world for the spiritual, or the spiritual for the world. One must remember that if morality is disallowed or spiritual law is disobeyed, it will be paid for (This is the Karmic law).

FIVE SOUL

Ability to cope, change and be fluid. They like to travel, and the experiences of life. Personal freedom is top priority. 5 is the number of sensual and sexual appetite. They are impulsive, critical, and can be irresponsible and given to excess. They tend toward immediate gratification. They adjust well. They are fickle, free-spirited, curious, and they like to investigate. They wring their hands if there is nothing to do. They had rather learn from life than from theory or books. They are generalists and will have many jobs and experiences.

They have a critical and/or temperamental disposition with their mate. 5 feels deeply but may confuse sex and love until spiritual growth or maturity moderates them. This may indicate a number of brief romances and/or affairs. If the 5 finds himself confined or in a stifling situation, he will become harsh, critical, judgmental, or moody. They can be quick to judge, but an underlying softness is evident with regrets if their actions are too rash.

The critical and moody attitude may extend into the job place. Because of the ability to adapt, 5s may appear not to stand up for their rights at times, letting others seemingly take advantage of them. This is because they know that they will adapt and they ask themselves, "Does it really matter or affect me?" And if it doesn't, they do not bother to correct it. If affected and not spiritually sound, the 5 tends to repeat mistakes and disregard values or morals.

The unbalanced 5 is uncertain in change, and has a fear of the unknown. They become nervous, overindulgent, and irresponsible. 5 represents a drive to express the self physically and through action. 5s may be teachers, especially in a technical field (because 5 is the number of mercury, and mercury is the conveying of ideas). 5 is the pivotal point of humanity, of growth, of direction. 5 may be drawn toward religion and religious teaching. It is the number of renunciation.

5 Souls, especially with a 5 Life Path, will be more apt to swing to the mystic and religious side. The 5 is both sensual and spiritual. They have charisma and an ability to make people feel better, happier, and interested. With a 7 or 5 NAC, it may add to promiscuity, and difficulty with faithfulness. This lessens the chances for a happy marriage because they may flit from one person to another. They may seem emotionally fickle. Part of 5s purpose is to understand and master their emotions.

ENMASS 5

Type 5 wants to be happy and to escape anxiety. They will do this by experiencing, and getting "acquainted" with as many things as possible. Because of this they are considered the "generalist." They have a wide range of knowledge and experience.

5s tend to act in the immediate. This usually leads to more doing since one action or search will lead to another. This type does not think about conscience very much. In extreme cases they could be somewhat sociopathic since they are involved with immediate gratification. Being the extroverted sensation type, their frame of reference is the "real" world of sensory data. Input is direct from environment to person more so than other types. This sets them up for becoming an addictive personality. They will consume more than they need, and need more than they can possibly appreciate, feeling that the world exists to fulfill their appetites.

If they are balanced, they will get great joy out of life and its experiences. Their thrust is toward productivity; however, if their focus shifts it will go from producing to possessing. This is where experience becomes consumption. They will then stay busy trying to keep their sensations high. But there is a type of narcotic effect which demands more, better, faster, longer. This will bring the 5 to overextend himself. Not finding happiness through these experiences, they become insecure, unhappy, anxious. At this point they will become enraged and desperate, claiming that they have been in some way deprived of happiness, unfairly so. They will lash out at those who deny them. In public 5s tend to be charming, and disarming.

As children they escaped into a world of imagination. 5s don't broadcast anxiety, they look happy and lighthearted. They love playing and planning. 5s are likely not to worry much. They are a perpetual Peter Pan. This gives way to a type of narcissism. They love new adventures. They view the world with infinite possibilities, and become nervous at the idea of losing an option or narrowing their possibilities. This is why they tend to make commitments with "back doors." They always want an alternate plan. They are masters at going with the flow, as long as the flow doesn't limit their personal freedom. This, to a 5, is the greatest sin.

5s have the ability to see connections between seemingly unrelated ideas, methods, and disciplines. They have unique abilities of problem solving. Inventive and imaginative, they possess the ability to synthesize unusual veins of knowledge. They must watch for rationalizing the escapism and boredom. Some 5s like escapism and having fun so much that instead of acquiring things they will use their money to get away, or just have fun. They approach relationships by sharing life's experiences, especially the good ones.

This seems to confirm their own experiences, memories, and feelings, and in some way validate them just that much more. The 5 seems to feed off the experience, and the other person's reaction simply expands the feast. It also reflects back to the 5 the way that they already feel. Here is a problem, however. With all of this living behind them, they are likely to become jaded and unflappable. At this point the 5 can get in trouble. They are apt to become apathetic or depressed, or, in seeking a better high, they can turn to drugs, drink, sex, or any high to break the monotony of the same old excitement.

If a 5 is in a restrictive situation, for instance a bad marriage, they will become moody, cranky, angry, even suicidal, as they blame others for holding back their freedom. If you can hold a 5 by keeping their interest, marriage to a 5 can be interesting. It should consist of a lot of activity, food, fun, travel, and sex.

They seem to be given to situational ethics as they go through life seeking what feels good. This is doubly true when it comes to love, which they can easily confuse with sex. They will rationalize their actions by saying, "But I love her, so what else counts?" It is difficult for 5s to be tied to needy or emotionally dependent people unless they are along for the ride and don't tie the 5 down. The 5, like the 1, finds it hard to take blame. Confrontation and accusations bring a loud inner voice of failure. Since they use others' opinions, or desire of them as a meter of their self-worth, this affects the basis of their worth in their own eyes. It is good they can divert their attention easily so that something bad can be covered up by something good fairly quickly so that the pain doesn't last long.

5s have good memories of childhood, but this may be because they tend to focus on the happy side of things. They don't usually cleave to hate or resentment very long. There is a slight tendency to be closer to the mother in childhood. There is also a rebellion against authority that would tie them down to work, or commitment. 5s hate boredom. They usually have several projects going on at the same time. They will go from one to the other seeing parallels and similarities between all of them. Casual commitments are made easily, but permanent commitments are hard. (They scare them a great deal)

5s want a little taste of everything that is best. They are gluttons for experience. They tend to think of more than one thing at a time. They do this by putting an unsolved problem on the back burner while working out a second problem. At some time the foreground problem will, in some way, spark a connection with the background issue, and the answer will bubble up to the conscious mind. This is just one way that one thing is in some way bound up or connected to another. They love talking, intellectualizing and brainstorming. If given a new fact, 5s will try to fit it into many different scenarios. This leads to a viewpoint that sees the interdependence and interrelationships of things.

They are editors, writers, communicators, linguists, philosophers, idea people. Eternally young, (and sometimes

81

immature), they love doing and experiencing, but fear having their projects judged. Because of their charm and ability to communicate, they can lead others to believe that their knowledge has more depth than it truly has. In fact, they have a wide base of knowledge, but usually not a lot of depth.

At their worst they can be charlatans. They are afraid of being revealed as less than what they appear to be. They are happy with situations in which no one is above or below them, and all are on the same level. They are good at promoting ideas, and networking with others.

5s were formed in part by a negative orientation to the mother image. Due to any of a number of reasons from poverty, war, illness, divorce, or simply her own nature such as neglect, smothering, or passive/aggressive control, she frustrated the child. The child found himself not being nurtured and secure. The child then tries to get his needs met and nurture himself. He did this from the world and its experiences. This substitutes for mother's love. The id is stuck in instant gratification, and they place no restraints on themselves, denying themselves nothing. The superior function is physical or sensing, the inferior function is intuitive.

Healthy 5s concern themselves with satisfying their true needs. They add to the world, not consume it. They are productive, have great memories and minds as well as large areas of knowledge. Healthy 5s assimilate reality and experiences into themselves. They affirm life and are joyous, full of wonder and reverence. The spiritual life becomes a reality to them. They acquire faith and look for the good in things and people. They will be swept into an awareness of the metaphysical. The inner world of the 5 is made up of impressions. It is a catalogue of experiences. They are multifaceted. They usually have refined tastes and a sophisticated air to them. Language and writing skills aren't uncommon. They are very observant and have quick, dry senses of humor. Adaptable, active, resourceful, versatile, curious, investigative, sensual, sexual, able to take a chance.

Average 5s have a vibrant love of life. They want to try it all. To perceive it is to know and enjoy it. They pay attention to the finer things of life, such as food, clothes, music, sex. They can be elegant people. They are "oral" people. Most of their activities deal with appetites and mouth. There is something of the comedian or performer in the five, usually driven by insecurity. They are sassy and irreverent. Their brashness may offend some but others find it refreshing and humorous. They are not subtle people, and can be tactless, simply speaking their minds. They tend to push activities and experiences past the bounds of good taste. They may be manic, high on their illusion of life as if on speed, full of grandiose plans, none of which are carried out.

Unhealthy 5s are jealous of what others have. They are wasteful. Excess rings in their lives. (You can never be too rich or too thin.) They started out getting high on life, but now life can't offer enough, not even in excess, so they turn to alcohol, drugs, debauchery. Not even T.V. or food is safe from this. They become jaded and insatiable. Unhealthy 5s stay in motion. Since all of their "reason" is turned extroverted, they can't figure out why they are unhappy. They become indiscriminate in their desires and consumptions; depravity is the order. They are unhappy and this feeling is directed toward the mother image who did not nurture them, so they act like spoiled children, since the id is frozen in that time.

They act out, doing and saying things to hurt others without concern or restraint. Having wasted their energy they slow down and become very depressed, even suicidal. Given to excesses, over-indulgence, addictions, impulsiveness, restlessness. Fickle, critical, discontent, noncommittal.

The 5 will act out by impulsive, consumptive behavior. They will accuse, blame and strike out at others to hide their own frustrations. The frustration and unhappiness of not being satisfied by anything for very long drives them toward more and more until they are stopped by addictions, compulsions, or exhaustion. Fear of losing their personal freedom can lead to lying, adultery, and lack of commitment.

The 5 needs to let go of recklessness, impulsiveness, addictions, not taking responsibility, venting frustration on others, burnout, need for instant gratification, impatience, escapism, lack of self-discipline or restraint, overextending self. They need to focus on their quick mind, ability to communicate ideas, charisma, spontaneity that energizes others; plus their ability to motivate and to investigate, their curiosity, sense of humor, and resilience.

5s will work out by realizing once and for all that any happiness that comes through the senses is transitory at best. All ups will have an equal down, so it is best to seek the center path. Commitment to someone you love will keep you from losing them and having to look for a "second best" for the rest of your life. To be willingly committed is not to be bound, it is only to love. You don't need a back door if you really mean the commitment.

SIX EXPRESSION

6s are helpers, homebodies, and minister to the needy. The 6 likes quiet pleasures. They are idealistic about relationships. They are always ready to help a friend. There is a love of music and arts. They also have a concern for fairness and justice. If this goes too far it will yield a judgmental, self-righteous, tyrannical person. The 6 needs to be coaxed in love to full sexual expression. The 6 has a peaceful nature unless home or principles are at stake. If they are insecure this number can be very jealous and possessive and they may have a quick and/or emotional temper.

This is a number of ministry, farming, law, teaching, medicine, counseling and music. If they are healthy, these people are the healers of society's afflictions. They are the parent image, loving the home life. 6s are down to earth and make good community leaders. If adversely affected they can become short-tempered, and meddlesome. They may try to dictate or be overly conventional. Although this number is called upon to be a shoulder to cry on, they may resent aiding and listening to others, if they are overtaxed. Most, if given a chance, can make good home bodies, parents, or spouses.

SIX SOUL

To ask is to know, and to know is to accept responsibility for it. Romance and family are top priority. 6s are very parental and concerned with values. The 6 identifies emotionally with things so they are opinionated. They are reliable. They are drawn to healing and teaching. The 6 listens well but they may meddle. They are crusaders, and can be obstinate. They may offer advice when it isn't wanted. They like taking responsibility for others in the role of a father or mother image. They want to be leaned on. They are idealists especially in home and love affairs. They are good at doing and fixing up around the home. They like to "nest." They are usually a conformist, good money-makers and homebodies. They have emotional tempers mostly when the welfare or tranquility of the household, family, or mate is in question.

Most 6s don't get depressed often. They tend to maintain at least an outward appearance of mental stability. Because of their reliability, they usually manage projects, money, and people well. Friends and family may lean on them. They tend to be happiest at home with the family. If they are affected or unbalanced there will be over-involvement with others' problems, and a self-righteous attitude. They can also be a dictator, or resent service to others. They will feel held down at home. The balanced 6 is concerned with doing what they perceive to be morally right. Purpose: to learn to love people as a whole, to find their place in the service and giving of mankind.

ENMASS 6

Type 6 respects loyalty. They will watch and test others and their attitudes before they will trust them. They have to watch their feelings of anxiety and insecurity. This is a type full of contradictions. They want trust but they test others first before trusting. They honor authority, yet fear it. They do not like aggression yet are at times aggressive. They search for security yet feel insecure. They fear being rejected, yet will reject others if they do not measure up to their moral and social value structure. Anxiety causes this vacillation. They feel more secure with "big brother" to watch out for them, be it the corporation, political party, or church. They need something to trust and believe in.

They want approval from others but resist being in positions of inferiority. They fluctuate from obedience to rebellion; likable to cranky and snappy. They are actually in conflict with both internal authority (superego), and outward authority. They tend to look outside of themselves for direction, yet don't like being in a subservient position.

They can be openly hostile to an authority figure if the distrust or anger at the father has built up. They will appear rebellious and defiant at the authority figure as there is a transference of feelings acquired in childhood. We should again point out that there are two sides to the 6.

We see conformity and rebellion; honor and anger occurring in the same person. Sometimes they happen at the same time causing fear and loyalty, love and hate to come into a dynamic balance in the 6, and it is all based around the father image. Almost always the child tried to love the father even though he may have been demanding or unfair. This did not leave a way to deal sufficiently with the negative feelings. As the child tried harder to reach a level of approval in the parent's eyes, anger built because of the harsh, disciplinarian, or unapproachable posture that the father operated from. It may have been a morally high or correct issue, but the way it was enforced did not convey love. This sends a double message to the child.

First it says that it is very important to do the right and just thing, to be loyal and good. But secondly, it forms an image of fear and suspicion in regard to authority figures. This forms a push-pull relationship. This tension forms the basis of their anxiety. When it builds they want the security they missed, but since they have come to trust in only themselves on the deeper level, they reject the authority on an inner level and either can become aggressive and belligerent, or try to serve and placate to assure the authority's continued goodwill and protection.

6s are an introverted feeling type. They, like the 8 type, want to be the protector. 6s are more parental in this quest than the bossy 8. Also, like the 8, they are looking for someone to be their protector. The 6 is looking for a guardian or father image to trust and rely on. Isn't it fitting and reasonable that the things that we seek to be are the very things that we are looking for in others?

So many times we could learn from ourselves if we would recognize that the simply stated truth of a song holds the key, "and in the end, the love you take will be equal to the love you make." We should carry it further and say that what we need, are missing, and hope to find is what we try to become for ourselves, and for others. It is just another way of trying to fulfill our own needs. When all is said and done, that's all we can rely on anyway.

6s emotionally tend to swing and are hard to anticipate. They may like someone, then become concerned about being taken advantage of, and withdraw in suspicion. This brings in their anxiety and the need for reassurance, so back to the person they may go for assurance.

The 6 child identified positively with the father image. They gained identity and security by being approved by them. Anxiety arose if approval wasn't forthcoming. They learned that by following rules, being responsible and obedient, they gained positive strokes from the father image, and this strengthened their feelings of worth and security. If they did not please this authority, 6s learned that retribution would come. This means that they have a very strong super-ego. In time this father image is transferred to other authorities such as law, business, government, husband.

They fear being left, so they place great value on long-term relationships. Family is the symbol of the emotional stability and commitment that 6 stands for. If they veer into disobedience they will worry about what others think. There is a fear that others will turn on them.

The superior function is emotional-feeling, the inferior function is mental-thinking. There is a need to be the authority, so that there is less authority over you, coupled with a need to serve and be protected by an authority image leads some 6s into being police officers, nurses, doctors, preachers, priests, or managers.

There are two distinct directions a 6 might choose based on which most affected them, the moral and loyalty issue, or harshness and authoritarianism. They can seek to serve and protect the moral standards, or they can rebel against authority and become lawless, or mafia types, serving another kind of group or family. It isn't surprising that 6s are likely to be involved in long-term relationships.

Their loyalty and tenacity can allow them to survive a long time even in a dysfunctional relationship.

Healthy 6s are reliable, trustworthy, loyal, trusting, independent yet cooperative. They take commitment seriously. They elicit strong emotional responses from others. They will fight for you as they would for themselves. Good natured, good sense of humor, friendly, a parent image (if they try to emulate their father image within). Capable of 50-50 relationships. They are good leaders since they know what others are looking for in authority. They can reassure others, and be emotionally open, loving and caring.

6s lost faith in authority as children. Something in the parents' actions spawned fear, feelings of being powerless, or overpowered. The parent may have had traits such as an explosive temper, or trying to hide some secret that made the child feel that they were untrustworthy. This is carried over to adulthood in the form of hesitancy to act, and suspicion of authority They tend to doubt their own ability. The anti-authoritarian stance forms a split path.

On one hand, it makes them gravitate to the underdog. They will go to extremes to beat the odds, from heroism or even martyrdom in the search to beat the system, pull together, and set things right that the authorities have screwed up. This is the rebellious stance.

It is fueled by feelings of oppression and anger of past misuse by authorities. This can be summed up by a "you and me against the world" attitude.

The other path is one of being devoted to an authority figure or group, as long as the 6 feels that the group or authority is going in the correct direction. They become loyal servants, able to follow a chain of command well. They are dutiful public servants, parental types. This is a strange type of self-protection. They like serving, and therefore affecting others. This is because they think that if they are on your side, they won't be harmed. 6s are afraid of being ganged up on, or harmed by an unexpected turn of others. So they serve the more powerful group or person in exchange for their protection. This type of 6 tries to do what is right in society's eyes. 6s do not give in order to get something back. They give in order to feel safe. They fear betrayal.

This is also a person who fears intimacy. They can easily project their fears and suspicions onto the partner, accusing them of not wanting to be close, or that they are in doubt of their true feelings and intentions. 6s need to know that the partner has respect and faith in them. They need to know that the partner feels safe in them. This is because this is what the 6 is in need of, so they will try to project their needs onto the partner. They will bask in the reflection of the feelings of the partner spawned by the 6.

These are feelings of "nesting" in a safe place. This is what the 6 wants to feel first-hand.

This should be a lesson to all of us that we all tend to live assuming that others feel, need, and want the same as we do. This narrow view can lead to misunderstandings and wasted time. We must all learn to see things from others' points of views. Real communication is to speak to people on their own level and from their own point of view. 6s should be careful not to project these feelings on to others to make them see ulterior motives that are harmful to the 6. This even goes for their mates. Because of the background of the cause of this number, it is difficult for 6s to trust and be intimate without fear. Yet they need and want closeness, and have the capacity to feel deeply.

Healthy 6s are devoted and protective without being meddlesome. They are interested in being patient and fair. Truth, justice and the American way is the battle cry for the healthy 6. They are domestic, reliable, tenacious, and conservative. They are good listeners, and therefore good teachers, counselors, and ministers. Education is important to them.

Average 6s identify with authority figures and follow their lead. They are traditionalists, family and company people. The 6 is dutiful, responsible. 6s on this level begin to show contradictions in personality. They are ambivalent and passive/aggressive. They want authority over them in order to feel more secure, yet they fight against authority and rebel at times. They may become defensive, authoritarian, partisan, blaming others if things go wrong. This is an overcompensation for their fear and insecurity. This fear may be seen in the 6 becoming dependent, even comfortable being ordered around. This vacillation between dependence and independent leadership urges makes them very unstable. When they make decisions they are likely to look for precedents such as rules, regulations, scriptures, by the book. This adds to their security.

Unhealthy 6s are insecure and dependent. Anxiety and inferiority is high. They are sadistic. They over-react due to insecurities. Archie Bunker types, fraught with prejudices, bigotry, blustering. Trying to recreate the security that they had in the past themselves, to no avail. They overcompensate their fear and insecurity to become tyrants. They deal harshly with the mistakes of others while letting themselves off the hook.

Everything becomes a crisis because of insecurity. Things are blown out of proportion. It ends in masochism in which the 6 seeks union with others in a twisted way by saying, "I've been bad, I didn't follow all of the rules, punish me so that you can love me again." If there isn't punishment, they will punish themselves in order to try and substitute their punishment for a punishment that they fear would be more severe from the authority. If this isn't enough they will provoke the authority by turning to sadism. Meddlesome, irresponsible, unyielding, self-righteous, a tyrant.

6s will act out through a rebellion and hardness that hides a fear of authority. The will have a quick, judgmental temper. A tyrant-like need to bully or control hides a fear of being abandoned, misused, or persecuted.

The 6 must let go of their fear of abandonment, feeling trapped by obligations, anxieties and worry about themselves and others, judging others, a tough facade to hide feelings, being negative about situations or people, the need to boss or mother others, and stubbornness. They need to focus on their abilities to guide and care about others, to serve the family or community, true concern for others, a nurturing heart, parental sense of fairness.

The 6 will work out by realizing that no one can take control or exert authority over them - that is something that has to be given. They are safe to be their own authority. Be secure with yourself, and you will find security in others.

SEVEN EXPRESSION

7 is the balance of what is precious and terrible about truth. It can be used to guide your path or it can be used against you. 7 is the number of analysis, aloofness, and secretiveness. 7s respect knowledge for its own sake. They may study, research, observe, or analyze in their daily way of life. A quiet storm is formed from the vortex created by introversion, and introspection along with a loneliness that is brought about by their own subjectivity. They need love and closeness, yet their introverted nature does not allow them to adequately express themselves. They must stretch in order to communicate their deep feelings to others. A 7 needs solitude, and a quiet home. 7s are observant, and have quick minds. They seek to perfect their beliefs and understanding. They tend to withdraw when in crowds. They hate noise and confusion. They become nervous.

Like the 7 Soul, the 7 Expression may indicate hidden sexual or emotional needs. 7s often hide their feelings, finding it hard to express themselves. They will probe to find out what their mate feels yet they are sneaky and deceptive regarding their thoughts and actions. Through the aloof nature of the 7 indicates a loneliness within and a need to be with people. 7s vacillate between needing time to themselves and the need to hide from their loneliness in the midst of people.

97

They can become stubborn if pushed. A 7 Life Path tends to mature emotionally slowly; they should not marry until 20-25 for maximum stability. Their quiet sensitivity can get them hurt by infatuations. A 7 tells things on a need to know basis. Their thoughts are abstract, but the 7 can use them, as well as their silence, as weapons against those with whom they are unhappy. They withdraw their attention and emotions and become a cold wall, saying nothing wrong, but hurting others in a sneaky, passive/aggressive way with silent aloofness and coldness. Faith in themselves is their challenge. There is an undertone of feeling less than adequate that haunts them. This adds to the fact that it is hard to express themselves. They would rather have an intellectual world than an emotional one. They don't trust their feelings.

The depth and aloofness of a 7 makes them an enigma to others. This mysterious air is a lure to many and they will be attracted to the "sexiness" of it. Because of their detached nature, 7 is life's strategist. They sit emotionally removed from the battles of life and plan the next step. Due to this view of life, they can use people and situations to their own ends. This is a rather devious trait that the 7 must guard against. They should remember not to use people or the secrets friends have told them in any selfish way. If you hurt, you will be hurt. Things always come back around. Be honest and up front. 7s may find it hard to open up; some may seem melancholy.

At times, they feel that the questions of others are distracting and irritating or a nuisance. This results in short, clipped answers. The 7 child may be hard to control because of a silent stubbornness. Some will take the punishment and not cry in order to do what they want. 7s are skeptical and find it hard to accept anything unless proven. They tend to live within themselves. Indecision is possible at times because of the analytical need for more data. With a 9 Expression and a 5 Life Path, watch for a violent tendency if outlets of self-expression and emotions are blocked. A type of intellectual snobbery is seen in an off balanced 7. Secretive, passive/aggressive, using their coldness to control others. Their purpose is to search and understand to gain maximum expression through learning and teaching, and to balance a reserved nature and a lonely nature. With a 2 Expression, the 2 and 7 are outwardly open but inwardly closed. On the outside they appear as a 5: outgoing, funny, able to communicate, yet they still won't show their true feelings.

"Maybe the "Faith" does better among its enemies than having to endure the indifference of its friends."

SEVEN SOUL

The mind is calculating and probing. Calculating can be applied to become devious, or insightful. Seekers of truth or dealers of deceit. A 7 Soul can turn truth to fit their needs, or examine the facts and seek the truth. The pivotal point of the 7 is knowledge, therefore there is usually an interest in science, medicine, nursing, lab work, psychology, technology, math, etc. If using truth with malice, the 7 will speak the truth at the chosen time which can crucify a person and leave the 7 without blame, because it was the truth... They will gossip and call it getting the facts. Information used wrongly is manipulation.

ENMASS 7

7s are observers and can be very private people. Their world is a mental world. Even if they are not "mental giants," they tend to think and not to speak. Financial interaction is uncomfortable, obligations feel coercive, relationships threaten their stance of emotional aloofness. Emotions are to be controlled. Intense competition is avoided. They remain in an aloof or self-protective posture. They are independent people who can be comfortable being alone for days at a time. Being an observer, they have a rather objective view of things.

They may seem emotionally cold or distant as they watch and observe people, or watch situations develop with an air of cool superiority, thinking that they'd never get involved in such foolishness. But the skeptical or cynical attitude that may develop is just a way of remaining emotionally removed. So is the mental snobbishness that some 7s have. The truth is they are uninvolved not because they are wiser, but because their fear of opening up and trusting is so low that it keeps them at a safe distance.

There is a saying in Judo, "to throw an opponent you must put yourself in a position to be thrown." It is the same with affairs of the heart. You can only be in a position to be loved, if you are in a position to be hurt. 7s have trouble taking that gamble. This same thought process and fear of being taken advantage of can extend into any situation in which there are heavy demands or expectations. Fears can be reduced somewhat if the limits, rules, and expectations of a situation or relationship are laid out at the start.

To prevent a chain of perceived intrusions and betrayals from growing into fear or paranoia, the 7 views life as a string of snapshots. They are all related yet isolated. What happens tomorrow may not be what happened today under similar environments. This type of outlook where nothing is taken for granted lends itself to the skeptical posture of the 7. The 7 wants to know. They want to understand everything. They wish to be able to interpret everything. This is a way of defending themselves from their environment. Genius is to fuse knowledge, insight, and reality. Madness is when these oppose one another and a split occurs.

The 7 can go to either extreme. 7s can see patterns in things, and gain insight. They are able to relate things in one context to another context. Genius sees and recognizes patterns in things; madness imposes patterns on things, which leads to distorted reality. In this they are like the 5. But unlike the 5 type, 7s may emphasize thinking over doing. Saying or doing reveals their position, and there may be a weakness there. It may be used against them. This is something that the 7 doesn't like to risk.

Many times this is because their words have been used against them by "trusted" friends or family. This balance has to be watched so that their mental world doesn't become all consuming. In the pursuit of pure ideas 7s do not want others to influence their thinking. (This seems to diminish their self-worth.) However, they tend not to totally trust their own ideas. If the 7 thinks that they are the only ones with the answers, they can drift into error by relying only on their unchecked ideas, and they can go further and further away from reality. They can project their anxieties and impulses onto their reality making them paranoid or off balance.

They are the Jungian introverted thinking types. This makes for too much subjectivity. The thoughts start with the subject and flow back to the subject. (This mean that facts are collected in order to form a theory, and not for the facts themselves.) A better explanation is that the 7 is a subjective thinking type. 7s were ambivalent toward their parents, who may have nurtured them erratically.

They may have received conflicting signals in childhood such as parents who drank, partied, were in and out of church, or off and on as far as dependability. Even the stress of an unhappy family would lead to this feeling of ambivalence toward the parents, and the world. The result is that the 7 lives in a constant state of alertness. They fear being controlled by others. They watch their environment and all in it in order to foresee trouble and protect themselves. Love/hate of parent and the world makes them detached; they retreat to their thoughts. There is a duality then between objective and subjective reality. This can lead to schizophrenia.

If the 7 is uptight they will have danger on their mind, but because they are looking for it they feel safer. 7s feel that if something can be seen (perceived), it can be understood, and mastered. They enjoy using knowledge. Ingenious, inventive, technical. Since there is always more to know, the 7 has trouble putting thoughts to action. They never feel comfortable with their level of knowledge since they realize that there is always more to know and learn. They fear the world yet are fascinated by it. The 7, like the 2, has a passive/aggressive streak. They will use silence and the withholding of their attention to control others. This is a good way of getting a point across and yet not disturbing their precious peace and quiet; they don't even have to display their suppressed emotions to do it. As a child they felt intruded upon. This could have been because they are very sensitive to noise and activity in their home, or because they could not get privacy because of a large, intrusive family, or small living space. They learned to "tune out" or hide out in order to find peace. The other family pattern is one in which there was abandonment so the child detached from his emotions and kept occupied mentally in his own world in order to survive. Their idea of controlling a situation is to stop reacting to it. Interaction drains them.

They take offense at having their time or energy put at others' disposal. 7s are often scholars of obscure fields. The expert in a field, having spent years compiling data, the 7s reclusive nature turns to feelings of isolation and loneliness if depression or enforced separation goes on too long. 7s have a feeling of superiority over those who like competition (as in sports), believing it to be a waste of time.

Since they are somewhat detached from their emotions, they need quiet time at the end of the day to sort out their feelings and wind down. They may calm down by thinking, reading, or working on projects. Since they are mind-centered, they connect with others through special interests or knowledge. They tend to interface with the world the same way. They are attracted to systems such as psychology, math, occult science, or natural science in order to explain and understand the world. At times they will realize how destructive this type of activity can be, especially to the insecure, but it is worth it to them to be able to secretly hurt someone without becoming actively emotionally involved. The superior function is intuitive, the inferior function is physical-sensing.

Healthy 7s are visionaries, profound and comprehending thinkers. They love discovery. They are able to concentrate and become involved with a project. Innovative, genius, secure enough not to detach from their environment, and not cling to their own ideas. They have an open mind, with intuitive foresight. They are closer to being contemplative than thinkers. They can convey ideas and information in simple, clear form. Wise, knowledgeable, dignified. They have a sense of the self and the universe in an inner-active role. Interest and research in philosophy, psychology, science, mysticism. Able to observe, analyze, draw conclusions and applications. Specialized fields, scientific and research writings. Needs time to be alone and to sort out the acquired data and associated thoughts of the day.

The average 7 is intellectual, analytical, specialized. Making a science of things, research, scholarship. Can be detached. Enjoys speculating on ideas and theories. They tend to interpret everything around a pet theory which may lead to extremes. 7s can be eccentric. They can make a "science" out of everything. They may break things down to study so much that the big picture is lost. They are bookish. Intellect is their forte'. There may have been a lonely period in their childhood which urged them to turn more toward their mind. They tend to be high-strung. Their thoughts flow in a stream from one thing to another in a chain of seemingly (to the observer) unrelated thoughts. This takes their conversation over a scattered, branching, detailed path at times. Their thoughts may be hard to follow.

The unhealthy 7 can be reclusive and isolated from reality. Cynical, aggressive, obsessed by strange ideas. Phobias, paranoia, schizophrenia, genius gone to insanity. Nothing is certain because every angle is examined, and all things are possible. They may think that one grand idea

106

holds the key to all answers. Or they may reduce things to such a point the awe is gone and the truth is lost. They love to take ideas to the limits, sometimes for the shock value. They can become antagonistic with anyone who disagrees with them since this actually threatens their reality. If you look you will find fault. They are rejected because of their ideas and self-righteous attitudes, and so feel contempt for others. Ignorance, skepticism, fear, dishonesty, melancholia, pessimism, false pride, sarcasm, mental disorders, uncontrolled anger.

7s will act out by retreating into a shell. A nervous recluse is hiding from the world. They escape into imaginations and fantasy worlds which have their foundations in the mind. Feelings of betrayal can drive them further in. A person that is hyper-sensitive to activity, noise, environmental disorder produces a snappy, grumpy, silent hermit. The basis is that of fear of not being able to take it all in and protect themselves from a hostile environment.

7s need to let go of isolating themselves, rejecting others, snobbishness, thinking that others cannot be depended on, cynicism, feeling powerless, violated or taken advantage of, suspicion, aloofness, deviousness, lying. The 7 must focus on their ability to find the truth, their fine mind, ability to reason, sense of class or elegance, ability to research, strategies, their spiritual insights, feel for the

107

metaphysical, science, medicine, math, the occult, and to teach others.

7s will work out by balancing physical and mental activity. Develop a sense of humor. Accept the fact that you can't know everything, or see everything coming so you might as well relax and laugh at it.

EIGHT EXPRESSION

8s are the organizer and disciplinarian. They like a challenge. They are capable and efficient. They have high ideals and drives. People are drawn to these individuals. They want 100% efficiency. 8s are businesslike, aggressive, and confident. They often take responsibility for the work of others in the position of a boss or supervisor. If used correctly an 8 Expression adds drive to a person's Soul number. 8s usually don't pamper or cater to a weak mate. They must strive for a 50-50 relationship since they have a natural drive to be in control. Many 8s will set a stage and demand that you accept them in the part they will play or get out. They can be ruthless. They may like psychology, law enforcement, management, business, money management, bookkeeping, quality assurance, inspection, or banking. They usually have sound judgment in affairs dealing with business. 8 is softened with a 9 or a 5 in the Soul. They may be drawn toward status symbols and/or expensive tastes.

With a 1 Soul it may be hard to read because of inward devotion of energy (mental) leading to a more quiet exterior. If the 8 is not healthy, everything is for them and there is no giving. The off-balance 8 is like their "mental sister," the 1 and leads the 8 to be egocentric to the point of having a subjective viewpoint in life that doesn't allow them to see what effect their decisions have on those around them. This can lead to them hurting or angering those closest to them and not accepting any responsibility for it. What is worse, they are very proud and usually would not apologize even if they do come to realize that they were wrong. Obviously, to overcome this problem the 8 must be objective enough to put themselves in the other person's position, and understand that they can be wrong about many things. Since this is one of the 2s strong points, a negative attitude can be lessened by a 2 Life Path or a 2 Soul.

The balanced 8 can make an excellent supervisor, or self-employed person, and has good potential in business or as a company owner, real estate broker, or stock market investor. 8 also relates to sports, athletics, or martial arts. This is because they strive to compete and be the best. Winning and achieving is important to them. They may think that they know all the answers. They may consider a mate on the basis of income if they are too materialistic. 8s are devoted people and are capable of much love and caring, yet they are also a people of appetite. Since they value efficiency, strength of will, and control, they tend to suppress their emotions and put on a hard exterior. They may be more interested in the quality of life rather than the love in it. Although they seldom show it, there is an underlying softness and need for love.

EIGHT SOUL

Money, finance, control of self and others. Although 8 is the balance of the physical (or material) and spiritual, 8s are usually inclined toward the material. They are confident, businesslike, authoritarian, and are drawn to efficiency and quality control. They can be in law enforcement, and positions of authority. They may look at people as "what can this person produce or do for me?" The executive number, given to management, bookkeeping, and ownership position. They take responsibility for the actions of others in the way of a boss. They can be intimidating and may come across as a know-it-all. They can be aggressive or outspoken. 8s are stable but not demanding mates. Because they tend to dominate they need to strive for a 50/50 relationship; otherwise they may take over the household.

The 8 doesn't like to pamper or cater to a weak mate. They can be materialistic, but very giving to loved ones. 8s are usually strong-willed. They like the finer things of life. Quality is very important. Things must be systematic and logical. 8s like big houses and nice cars. Finding the best system and putting it to use with money and/or people is a forte'. 8s are ambitious. Material success and money are important. They could own a company or hold a high position. Accumulating material items may be important. 8 women need to marry strong-willed mates since they will be inclined to try to dominate them, yet they will not respect them if they can dominate them. 8 men will need to marry a strong, stable woman so that she would not be outmatched and dominated to an oppressive degree. If affected they do not respect authority and can be dishonest. Callousness and materialism will set in.

They are status symbol and wealth driven. Many times, 8 relates to sports and/or simply being the best and most efficient in what they do. The material outlook leads many 8s to put a price on feeling secure. They need money in the bank and the bills caught up to be secure. They may even take the income of someone into account before allowing themselves to care. Being overly concerned about the quality of life instead of the love therein.

The 8 female tends to break the mold of most women. They are more "male" in their thoughts and ways than most. They are strong enough to "get ahead in a man's world." Some 8s, especially with a 4 or 8 Expression may have drinking or motivation problems because of the intenseness of the Vibration. It is like an overload. 8s like to have power over people. The more rigid 8s view children as an inconvenience and would rather not bother. These people have a lot of money pass through, but a lot will be given if these people are advanced.

8s vacillate between philanthropy and greed. The 8 who is out of balance will be self-absorbed to the point of ignoring or not considering the feelings or views of others. They will be blind to what their expectations, demands, or decisions do to anyone else. If it is brought to their attention, they will usually have too much ego and false pride at stake to admit a mistake, even if it means the loss of a friend. To guard against this, the 8 needs to practice looking at things from the perspective of others and always remember that they are working from a subjective point of view, so they can be wrong as easily as anyone.

ENMASS 8

8 types want to be self-reliant, to act in their own self-interest, to have impact on people and their environment. Love of power is the love of self. They attempt to conform the environment, and those in it, to their aims. They relate to the environment in order to prevail over it. They take charge, imposing their will. Getting their way is very important to them. The 8s sense of self is stronger than their sense of others. They are steely and single minded. They are the extroverted intuitive type.

They have a keen sense of things in the making. They are always seeking new possibilities. Stable

113

conditions suffocate them. They cannot be frightened away from a new possibility, even if it goes against previous convictions. They are the champion of the underdog. They are confident that by their will they can reach their goals. Although this presentation may sound harsh, if motivated correctly it will yield experts, athletes, and gold-medal contenders. However, if they go astray, they usually get caught up by their own egotism. They can't see or believe that there is anything wrong with them, even though they may not take the needs or wants of others into consideration.

One possibility of the formation of the 8 type is as follows: the 8 may have learned that one parent in their life did not respond to them unless they asserted themselves. This assertiveness may have had to increase to aggression from time to time until the child got his attention and his way. They learned that a strong-willed child could dominate even an adult.

Soon this same process was used in other areas of their life in ways of being aggressive and strong even if they were wrong in order not to face the fact, or punishment for doing wrong. They then began to walk on other's feelings. If the ego is unchecked they will view life only as power and its use, so they will take advantage of any weakness they see. The preferred position is to charge in, take control, and maintain it. 8s believe that the truth comes out in a fight. A clean fight is exhilarating to them. They feel that anger, fighting, intimacy, and truth are all related.

The 8s tough exterior covers a heart of a child that had to fight for his space. They would like to stop fighting, but they don't trust others to take control and be just. Blame, and punishing the wrong-doers is a preoccupation with 8s. They have an all-or-nothing way of approaching things. Security to a 8 means knowing all of a situation, and having power over things. The 8 may say that if they know all of the facts they can have the proper response and emotional posture for it. The 8 is intent on power or control. Power can be in the form of money, possessions, people or simply control.

Another possibility of the formation of an 8 is one of hard knocks and simple survival. Because of a parent who was a disciplinarian, harsh, or emotionally distant the 8 may have difficulty in expressing the vulnerable side of themselves. This is a childhood scenario of being pushed around, treated unjustly, ignored by a parent, sibling, or friends.

A bad school, tough part of town, or a poor childhood could exacerbate a survival instinct. The feeling was that the person in control did not act with the child's best interests in mind. There could have been a divorce or other situation involving a parent's harshness or anger that the child took personally. It damaged the child's faith in their authority and security figures. They learned that the world was not safe. The 8 child had to be old enough to stand on his own or think for himself in order to become self-reliant. This means that at least part of the mistreatment should have occurred between the ages of 6 and 16. There could have been a simple but definite disagreement and an emotional parting of ways.

Another possibility of the formation of the 8 type which can, at times, exist side by side with the other patterns is as follows. This type can be caused by one parent turning the child against the other parent by having no faith or anything good to say about them. This suspiciousness can also be caused by a parent or adult abusing, neglecting or molesting the child. This disregard for the child's welfare makes the child suspicious of them. So now the 8 feels that he should be in control because he has been taught not to trust the authority figure. They think that they can do it better than others, and they will protect not exploit others. Yet, due to their strong personality and will, at times they can do just that by running rough shod over those of less strength.

No matter how the 8 was formed they can become so focused on a goal that they can deny pain, fatigue, opposition, even the odds that are against them. It does not

116

let them see what is enough, or even their own limits. At times it can go so far as to create a type of tunnel vision. The 8 will not see the full picture. They can repress feelings and even incoming data until the truth overtakes them. When they are knocked down by it, they realize that the signs were there all of the time. They may even find that others' ideas, opinions, or views simply annoy them.

The 8 is the type of the judge since they demand justice. They always want the wrong doers to be punished and vengeance to be done. It is always their justice that they try to impose on others so they appear to be judgmental. They can be irritable and dogmatic. If the 8 is not balanced, the right and wrong of a situation will get totally lost in the goal to win the argument. 8s are very competitive, even in discussions. It is difficult for them to restrain their expression, whether it be anger, sex, or competitiveness. They are a consumptive type. They can be classified as loners. Although it might not be their preference, it is what is easiest for them. They become attached in slow painful steps; steps of testing and trials for the mate.

They value open honest arguments. If you can't take anger expressed in your face, don't pick an 8. They will test the mate to see if they can dominate them. If they can, they won't respect them as much. (This is much like the 1) Once trust is established, there is a bonding that is

117

very deep. We can see why 8s would not be so good at diplomacy or "sweet-talk." They aren't emotionally attuned, and if they think that you aren't being up front about everything, they will attack. The attack comes from an insecurity that they are being blind-sided or manipulated, and a feeling of frustration of having to waste energy on things as frivolous as emotions. Especially when it can all be avoided if all of the cards were really put on the table.

The 8, like the 1, hates being wrong. One of the favorite tricks of the 8 who has been caught in a situation where they are wrong or have made bad choices is to attack first. Accusations will be directed to the innocent party. They will often pick an area of the other party's behavior that can be brought into question so that the discussion will be re-directed away from their weakness. The sad thing is that the 8s pride may be such that they refuse to inspect their own behavior. 8s will let you know exactly where you stand, and they expect the same. They are possession, power, and territory-driven, and that goes for work as well as romance.

The mature 8 will have learned to give a little and meet in the middle. They have an overriding fear of having to submit and depend on others, probably because they did not think that they could depend on one of the parents

118

without a fight of wills, or being taken advantage of. 8s grew up in a situation of having to fight for their rights. It could have been a physical fight such as with siblings or other kids. Or it could have been a fight of wills. The child may have had to simply set his mind that the situation would not break his spirit.

8s don't like compromise. They tend to view things as black and white. The middle ground leaves them feeling vulnerable. The superior function is mental thinking, the inferior function is emotional-feeling.

Healthy 8s are magnanimous, self-restrained, courageous, self-assertive, confident, inspiring. A leader and authoritarian. Self-restraint means not kicking people when they are down; knowing what and when things are appropriate and restraining self until then. They can better the lives of others. Benefactor, visionary. They can thrive on and learn from adversity, turning setbacks into opportunity. They can create and maintain social order, material success and personal achievements. They are fair, ethical, and responsible for their actions, especially as others are concerned.

Average 8s are enterprising, rugged, forceful, aggressive, dominating, willful, intimidating, combative, belligerent. Builder, power broker. They think that there can only be one person on top, and they are it. They are not team players. They are the entrepreneurs, business and political movers and shakers. They are the self-made man. Money is the means to the end of being self-sufficient so as to not depend on others. They are negotiators (buy, sell, trade, make a buck).

They love risk, danger, and excitement especially in the financial world. To make money is to make more of themselves. Female 8s tend to dominate their mates since they have the same ego structure as the male 8. Cultural restraints stand in their way however. 8 men are ambivalent toward women, seeing them as they had their mothers. They tend to dominate them, even becoming aggressive. They can easily become womanizers. 8s describe a combative childhood, a situation where the strong survived. They learned to protect themselves by becoming sensitive to the intentions of others. They grow to ignore the odds, and even become blind to the issues at times, as they pursue a goal single mindedly. They come to think of themselves as the righter of wrongs, the enforcer of justice. Fairness, justice, and control are the central issues.

Unhealthy 8s are relentless, ruthless, vengeful, violent, megalomaniacs, intimidating. Only money seems to be reliable to them; even the love of friends and family is secondary to power, control or money. Their view is so narrow that they are blind to what they and their demands inflict on others. Their pride will not allow them to even examine the possibility of being wrong, much less to admit it. This same pride and need to be in control makes them refuse to ask for help from anyone. They have very poor judgment when it comes to others and their emotional needs. They use and hurt people and are blind to everything except that the thing they wanted done was done in their way.

Unhealthy 8s are viewed as unstable. They begin to believe their own bloated image of themselves. They swagger and bluster and are self-important. They hate softness (weakness) in themselves and even more so in others. It is viewed as weakness. Might makes right. Treacherous and immoral, they will do whatever they have to do to reach their goal, including violence. The more power a person has the less need a person has to justify themselves; therefore, the acquisition of power is a means of combating guilt. The more the 8 sinks into megalomania the more they are likely to think that they are above the law, and even the instrument of God, or God himself.

8s will act out through aggression and a bid to control the environment and all that are in it. They will be bossy to the point of rage and physically compelling others to obey if necessary. If a person resists, they will escalate their effort until someone gets hurt, all in the name of control. 8s need to let go of abusiveness and anger toward others, trying to control or bully others. They need to stop the bossiness and thinking that theirs is the only way.

They obsess about perfection in performance to the point of becoming angry if someone falls short. They are hard hearted, thinking that everyone is incompetent. They fear of being controlled by others, letting pride, ego, or coldness come between them and the ones that they really care for. They force their way on others by greed and intimidation. The 8s need to focus on their ability to know the potential of people and help them achieve it. They have the ability to organize to make people's lives easier. They know how to make and manage money in order to give and share. 8s can be very philanthropic. They have the ability to inspire confidence and leadership. They have the ability to manage and direct.

8s will work out by allowing themselves to feel, and put themselves in the shoes of others. They should ask themselves if they would they like to be hurt, yelled at, hit, demoralized, or abused? Then why do it to others? They don't have to be correct and in control all of the time. Do unto others as you would have them do unto you! Remember?

NINE EXPRESSION

9s hate being cooped up. They may have an explosive temper, yet they have compassion and understanding. They are givers, often giving too much of themselves. This can lead them to lose a part of themselves, much like the 2 can. They may have too many irons in the fire. The 9 may judge on first impression too much. If they have a point to make, they won't stop until it's made. They may be too generous and are warm people. 9s can be emotionally needy. Reassurance in love is important to them. The 9 likes pampering.

They must guard against self-pity. They tend to be governed by heart rather than the head. Some of them are given to theatricals and to dramatic scenes. They are a type that may at times appear in plays and movies. Because of their wide and altruistic viewpoints, they want to be impersonal in the way they love, but they become distressed if they are not receiving a personally directed love. They have the ability to inspire trust. 9s are able to put themselves in the place of others. They are a helper, artist, minister, nurse, doctor, psychologist, social worker. They can be generous, passionate, and compassionate. They may over-reach themselves at times and spread themselves too thin. They can also hold a grudge for longer than most people live.

There is another side to an unhealthy 9 not often mentioned, and that is the need to keep the peace and to preserve the status quo, even at the expense of happiness. 9s will tolerate many things in order not to move out of a given situation and into the unknown. It looks at times like a slothfulness, but it is not. It is based in the fear that what they have is the best that they can obtain or what they deserve. The sign of this is that the 9 will go through a list of "good points" about a situation, then still state how unhappy they are. This is akin to making a comparison between apples and oranges, because the first list was facts and the second list feelings.

The ability to weigh their feelings against a list of tangibles seems to confuse the 9. They may feel like there is a bad situation but there is always another reason to stay. So, the struggle remains to preserve even a living hell. With an 8 or a 1 soul they may manipulate through dramatics. With a 3 soul in conjunction with a 3 Challenge they could be quiet and insecure.

9s need to maintain an aim in order not to become scattered. Their concentration tends to wander if they don't keep focused on a given objective. At the same time, it is their nature to keep a wide vision of humanity. Even though they feel guilty when they put themselves first, they must learn that at times that will be the proper thing to do.

There will probably be hard luck in love. Although it is hard to say which causes the problems of the 9 first, their choice of mates or their actions toward the mate, it is likely that the 9 will have some times of disappointment in love. No, this is not the cliché that can be applied to most people on the planet - this is a type of trouble that you get yourself into by your choices and interactions regarding relationships. The 9 is subconsciously drawn to people who mimic dysfunctional problems in their childhoods. This is true for all of us but is much stronger in 4s and 9s.

NINE SOUL

This Vibration is one that the Soul has either chosen, or was delegated to, so that it may be subjected to trials and, hopefully, may grow more quickly. Painful childhood or very strict or alcoholic parents. A broken home from dead or divorced parents. Emotional, generous, idealistic, compassionate, understanding. A giver, intuitive (trusts first impressions). Bull-headed (sneaky), may be given to self-pity. They have had hard knocks. They worry about failing in love. They are insecure and need continual reassurance. 9s do well in the medical field as physical therapists, lab technicians, nurses is .due to the humanitarian aspect of the number. They tend to have too many irons in the fire.

This Vibration adds softness to the Expression. This is proven for a 4 or a 1 Expression. It adds warmth, depth and emotion. Giving, humanitarian, idealistic, motivated in too many directions with few results. Partly due to their idealism, and partly due to the choices of their emotional involvements, the 9 may seem to get hurt or used in love more often than most. It may seem to them that they come out on the short end of things, as if the other person always gets more out of the relationship than the 9 does.

I would like to remind the 9 that they cannot "fix" anyone. It is up to the person to fix themselves. This goes for the 9 looking for someone to make them feel "complete and happy," or for their efforts to try to help that dysfunctional person that your heart may have gone out to. If you came from a dysfunctional home, you may be drawn back to a dysfunctional home. Your mind may know that it is wrong, but that little child in you that was hurt or stunted in that environment is stuck there trying to figure it out. So that situation feels familiar to you. Be careful not to be drawn to cold, abusive, or emotionally unstable mates if your parent was like that.

Parents may have been very strict, religious type. Father may have drunk too much. With a 4 Expression they have a gift for painting, art or music. Refinishing furniture and expressive ability, antiques. Probable alcoholic parent, overly strict, or emotionally cool father. With a 7 Expression they can be rebellious because of strict parents. With a 1 or 3 Expression they may favor psychology and writing or be a scattered party person. With a 9 Expression they probably have divorced parents. 75% experience personal divorce. With a 1 Expression they can have divorced parents. If affected, impractical, fickle amblers (too many irons in the fire, indecisive (gives too much). Dramatic, especially in fights. 9s seem to be heavily influenced by the year Vibration.

ENMASS 9

9 wants union, harmony, peace. They want to preserve the status quo. Tension and conflict are to be avoided. They tend to ignore things that upset them. Their sense of self comes from being in union with others. Their view of life is open and optimistic. This causes an easy-going attitude that doesn't see the need to change things. They may even ignore the wrong that is staring them in the face. They are a relating type but they have a hard time relating to reality. 9s tend to blur their own identity because they want union with another. They may not reach their full potential because of this.

To better conform to others the 9 represses part of self. They equate self-assertiveness with aggression, so they have difficulty in expressing self as they should. They are the introverted sensation type. They are conspicuously calm and passive. This is because there is a kind of detachment with reality.

The formation of the 9 type seems to have two patterns that run sequentially. The identification with the parent image was comfortable for them. Early childhood was a comparatively idyllic time which the person would like to recapture. In the second part of the sequence, or the second scenario, the later period of childhood could have been shattered by illness, death, or divorce of a parent. This propels the id to try to hold on to its better days where union and reliance on another met all of their needs.

Many 9s may have been close to their grandparents and felt a parental bond with them, especially in their early childhood. This love could have filled the void of a missing parent and provided for the emotional needs of the child. (I have noticed a very high percentage of 9 Souls come from broken homes.) In many of these instances the grandfather took the place of the father. If there was not a divorce there may have been abuse (either emotional or physical). This to the child, is tantamount to an emotional divorce. (Normally these emotional changes would have occurred between ages 4 and 9.)

In another scenario the 9 child was overlooked. Their needs, opinions, and point of view were not taken into account. At times, when they expressed a view they were told to shut up, or that their opinion was stupid. Their ideas were ignored. After too much of this, the 9s began to repress their feelings, preferences, and feelings.

They let others make the choices for them. They developed a keen sense of what others want. A type of emotional diplomacy keeps them from going against the flow and being reminded that their opinion doesn't count. That is always very hurtful. They take comfort in small physical comforts. They began to emotionally withdraw as they learned that nothing helped their cause, not even anger. They try to set up ways of not having to choose by setting up routines and operating on a kind of ritual.

9s try to operate through this numbness to the effect that they have trouble keeping their minds on things or sticking to things. 9s "feel" their memories, they are so strong. Therefore, they are not likely to fade, and neither are any grudges they may have. They are not fully in touch with any feelings they have. It is almost as if a partial filter is set up. Anger is one way that the wants and wishes become revealed. They may say, "I didn't realize that I felt so strongly about that." Without this direction it leads to scattered energy, teetering, not being able to direct and motivate themselves over a long period.

9s are very susceptible to inertia. They have trouble with commitment and follow-through. They feel a need to keep the status quo. They will go to extremes so as not to act or change things. This goes for relationships, situations, and even things about themselves. This can cause serious problems in relationships as the 9 "flakes out."

They can't come to a firm decision because they were emotionally punished for it as a child. In one scenario of a 9s childhood, the parent viewed the child's wants as an intrusion or an interference with their desires. The parent then ignored or chastised the child for having desires that might conflict with the parent's wishes. The parent could have been selfish, or given to "martyrdom." Yet, on the positive side, this has forced them to develop the ability to see all sides of a situation. We must realize that repressed feelings and preferences are like water - they will always seek a way out. This lends itself to a number of passive-aggressive strategies. One is to take control by being late. This puts others on your time schedule. Another is to refuse to make up your mind or make a commitment. This puts others temporarily under your control since they are waiting on you to decide. (That is, until they get mad and give up in anger.) 9s can use their diplomatic sense (which allows them to know what others expect) against you, by simply not performing.

Healthy 9s are self-possessed and fulfilled. They are content, optimistic, emotionally stable, supportive, good natured, and unpretentious, having overcome their fears of becoming an independent person, at one with themselves, even their aggressions. Able to bring more of themselves to others. They do not idolize others but are able to love realistically. Love of self and others can bring a mystical overtone. They have no guile and do not understand lying or cheating in others. They are positive and generous. They actively play a part in the cycle of life, growth, and death. It is embraced, and they age with dignity. They are idealistic, tolerant, giving, forgiving, compassionate, generous, and universal in their frame of thought. They are artists, thinkers, romantics, and universalists.

Average 9s are self-effacing, accommodating, passive, minimizing problems to appease others. Fatalistic, resigned to the fact that nothing can be done. They love to commune with others and nature. They love the outdoors: hiking, sailing, camping. They have a mystical side, a magical, mythical sense of the world. Elves, fairies, and such are shown to others through them. The average 9 sees themselves through the eyes of others. This may cause them to subordinate themselves. They fear asserting themselves so they don't disrupt the perceived communion. They can begin to live for the other person.

They take the middle-of-the-road stance, morally and socially in order to be accepted. Respectability is very important to them because of this. They love the past and the old fashioned ways. They are nostalgic, sentimental, and take things at face value. They never want to upset the status quo. This is taken to such a degree that they tend to ignore negative things and say "Oh, we don't have to worry about that." They develop a happy-go-lucky outlook.

The next step is to detach themselves from reality, and form a take it or leave it attitude. It is an easygoing style gone one step too far. They diminish their feelings and keep things on an even keel. Things don't sink in. This makes them part of the problem and not the solution. In relationships they idolize the other, then begin to substitute the idolized person for the real person. This makes them put less and less energy into the real relationship. They will do or promise whatever it takes to resolve a problem with others to appease them, but since they really do not want to deal with the problem, it isn't resolved and will show back up. The discussion has simply bounced off their heads. They have sacrificed their loved ones and friends to the need for peace, the status quo, and not dealing with reality. The superior function is intuitive, the inferior function is physical-sensing.

Unhealthy 9s are repressed, neglectful, obstinate, disassociated from reality. Catatonic. Multiple personality. There can exhibit a strange type of obstinate passivism in that they go too far to avoid conflict. They repress their aggression, and become adamant in not facing problems. They flake out and sacrifice relationships, making others angry when they try to force the 9 to do anything about fixing a problem. They may strike out at the person, but more than likely, since they wish to maintain the status quo, they will be passive/aggressive. They will accuse the other person of causing trouble and making waves. They will use lines such as, "Everything will work out", or "We've made it fine up to now", or "You're making too much out of it", and "You're causing trouble and putting too much pressure on me." For people who do so little, 9s have less energy, probably because it is spent in internally walling off reality. When reality does show its head because of their neglect, or having hurt someone through it, they will be plunged into despair, denial, even suicide. They can become bitter, fickle, selfish, irresponsible, and given to emotional extremes.

9s will work out by realizing their passive/aggressive behavior. Like the 2, you must dig to find your real motives. They will have a fiery temper if they are not in touch with their feelings. They need to see themselves as the peacemaker and altruist so badly that

133

they will deny anger or its results. They will control by passive means, even to the extent that they will get satisfaction in seeing someone struggle. While they could help, they will stand by and do nothing. 9s carry grudges. Being flaky and forgetful when they don't want to face reality, even if it causes others to carry more than their share of a load.

The 9 should let go of believing that bad situations will just go away, ignoring unpleasant situations, being afraid of changing things, being emotionally detached, denying their own aggression and temper, not being in active control of their life, dependency, getting lost in doing the same routines and habits (this prolongs and promotes the numbness of life), living vicariously or pouring themselves into others in order not to face themselves or a situation, and having too many irons in the fire so that they don't have time to focus on themselves or problems.

The 9 should focus on their talent to give, altruism, intuition, far- reaching views, humanitarianism, art, acting, passion, ability to get in touch with feelings and truly live life, psychic ability, emotional content, the heart light. 9s will work out by getting a grip on how they really feel, and not playing silly games with others. Fight cleanly. Take an interest in the reality of things. Approach the world head on. Be dependable and straightforward when dealing with others. Above all, don't scatter your energy. Pick one thing and do it, then go to the next item.

NOTES ON THE QUIESCENT SELF

In the past I all but dismissed the Quiescent self. I felt that our dreams of what we wished that we were accounted only for vague day dreams. This was a great mistake. After doing a number of charts for couples, I noticed a strong correlation between the Quiescent Self of one mate and the Soul or Expression of the other. It just makes sense that we would choose a companion that has the qualities that we wish for ourselves. After all, the Quiescent Self is the perfected qualities that we desire to obtain.

The Quiescent Self defines the super-ego - those attributes, personal qualities, judgments, and values that were impressed on us by our parents and society that we use as a measuring rod toward what is good and correct. The super-ego is an unconscious function and works to restrain the id, which is the child within us all, from being as selfish and destructive as it would want to be.

We manifest our actions and thoughts to the outside world through the ego, but the heart's desire, basic drives, instincts, all come from the id. We seldom are able to act out what we really want since it is usually selfish, destructive or socially improper. The super-ego (Quiescent

136

self) takes the ideas of what is correct and good, and tries to restrain the ego to those boundaries before the ego acts them out. A malformed super-ego, or lack of intervention between the super-ego and ego is one of the main causes of sociopathic behavior.

The Quiescent Self is the number derived from the consonants in the full name reduced to a single digit.

QUIESCENT 1

Spouse/lover: A pioneer, strong individual. They give new direction. 1's are leaders. Willfully persuasive. Ability to sell people on an idea.

Parent: You could have had a critical or hard to please parent. They may have had unreasonable standards set for you. You could have felt like you didn't fit in to the family. The lack of balance is in the area of acceptance, will, and being self-centered. The parents may have been blind to their own conflicting and arbitrary ways or ideas.

QUIESCENT 2

Spouse/lover: Patient, understanding, peaceful, tasteful, cozy home, close Friend, neat, clean, quiet, elegant. Sensitive, able to "read" people. Able to sense the feeling and ambiance in a room or group of people. A need to couple and to be close. Wants to share their feelings.

Parent: You could have had a parent that was sensitive, patient, kind, or tactful. They tried to be like a friend. They could have complained and been nervous; or a manipulative or passive/aggressive parent. The parent may have appeared weak so as to put the child in the position of being a necessity to the parents well being. The child may have felt that the parent was childish and the child became the parent to the family. The lack of balance here is in diplomacy, tact and helping others, being the boss.

QUIESCENT 3

Spouse/lover: Popularity is important. Strives to be socially acceptable, friendly, outgoing. Loves to be the center of attention. Vibrant, able to meet people and sell them on yourself. Prideful, appearance is important.

Parent: Your parent may have been concerned with looks, appearances, and fitting in. They may be light and happy, or jealous and envious. Art and self expression, fashion, sales, and meeting people could have played a role in your parent's life. The lack of balance here is in jealousy, pride, and concern with fitting in and being accepted or admired. The parent may have been a perfectionist. The parent may seem to say or do one thing in public and another when away from people they know.

QUIESCENT 4

Spouse/lover: Plain, realistic, stable, the builder, settler of systems. Down to earth. Practical approach leading toward solutions. In emotional control, disciplined, orderly, methodical, systematic, logical approach is important. Working with their hands.

Parent: Your parent could have been stern, unemotional, logical, and method driven. A disciplinarian. They may have had addictions to food, drugs, alcohol or religion. Depression or self pity may have been involved. In a small percentage of parents the work habit may be off balance being either lazy or a workaholic. The lack of balance here is in the expression of emotion, addiction, depression, and work ethic.

QUIESCENT 5

Spouse/lover: Lively, magnetic, able to cope with change. Mystical and free. Life is a sensual adventure. Casual. Teaching and communicating ideas is important. Loves new experiences. Gets bored quickly. Likes travel. Able to think quickly even if on the move. New ideas excite them. Inventor, investigator.

Parent: Your parent could have been quixotic, changeable, sexual, sensual, or overly prudish. They may have been critical or sarcastic. The lack of balance here is in self gratification, appetites, and responsibility. The parent could have been quick witted and impatient.

QUIESCENT 6

Spouse/lover: Family and justice are important. They are good teachers, guides, counselors, doctors, nurses, social workers, or authority figure. Sympathetic, jolly. Devoted, parental type. A solid individual, this type is an emotional yet reliable person. Dominating with a need to have at least the look of an all American family.

Parent: The parent could have been very concerned with "doing the right and honorable thing." Concern about what people think. A nurturing and strong influence that tends toward meddlesome, gossiping or nosiness. The lack of balance here is in the area of being meddlesome, judgmental, and begrudging service to others. There could have been a need to place blame and punish the guilty.

QUIESCENT 7

Spouse/lover: Reserved, cerebral, elegant.. A thinker, philosopher, refined. The use of the mind, knowledge, and a quiet environment is important. These people value truth and straight forward, objective ways. At the same time they can be elusive or two-faced. The lack of balance here is in the area of emotional aloofness or expression, suspicion, lack of trust, and stress on education or resistance to it. They are cynical, sneaky, or devious.

Parent: The parent may have been aloof. The ideas regarding sexuality could have been out of balance in either direction.   Learning and school were areas of concern. The parent could have encouraged the child to hide or not discuss feeling of a personality.   Lack of balance is in the use of knowledge, secrets, and deviousness.

QUIESCENT 8

Spouse/lover: Success is important, showman, boss, organizer, loyalty is looked for.   Ability is admired. Needs to be in a position of authority. Executive.   Thrives on pressure. Staying power, perseverance, drive, tenacity. Status, money, and power driven. Intelligent, efficient, in control.

Parent: They may have been materialistic. Order and efficiency were too important. The lack of balance here is in control of others, and materialism, emotional abuse. This parent fears being controlled or influenced. They see emotions as a weakness so they tend to be cold and harsh. Some parents wouldn't change their mind or admit their mistake if it killed them.

QUIESCENT 9

Spouse/lover: Compassionate, giver, warm, understanding, artistic, generous. Altruistic, philanthropic. Emotional. A Dear Abby type. Loves to help others and needs to be needed. Self expression is important. A tender heart. A passion for life.

Parent:: The parent could have been viewed as unstable or overly emotional. They could have been creative or artistic. They could have had a bad temper. They were probably too fickle or changeable. The parent may have denied their temper and aggression and blamed others, even the child for them. The lack of balance here is in the area of being emotional, hiding from reality, refusing to act until things get bad. They tend to spread themselves too thin.

SECONDARY CONSIDERATIONS IN A NAME

CENTERS

As we read through the numbers and their meanings, we will see parts of ourselves in several numbers. This is because there are different levels of the self. There is the self that we really are. This is usually hidden or lost in the traumas of childhood and the demands to conform that were brought to bear in this time. In numerology this is called the Soul. Although the original and primal self is still very much alive, it has been bound and gagged by the demands to truncate actions or thoughts deemed to be socially unacceptable in order to fit in and not invoke the anger of our parent-gods. With the abolition of the real self, a vacancy was left. This hole we have filled and it is called the Expression.

When describing the personality, the Expression must be dealt with as if it is real. After all, most people think it is. The Expression is a combination of what we are and what we wish that we could be. This self that we want to become is a picture of some things that we feel that we

143

need to balance our personality. When we come into contact with a person with this list of attributes, we are both attracted to and confused by them. We are therefore alien to our thought processes and understanding. We usually marry this type in order to make their attributes part of us. We will probably fight with them due to the fact that we just can't understand them. As usual, our strength is also our weakness. This self that we want to be is called the Quiescent Self in numerology.

There are ways of classifying and grouping numbers that will make this and other phenomenon easier to see. One type of classification is called the Planes Of Expression, or POE The POE divides the numbers into four functions. They are the mental, physical, emotional, and intuitive. The meanings and use are covered in the section titled POE

Another method way of classifying the numbers is through the centers. These centers break the numbers down into three categories. The effective center includes 8, 9, and 1. The affective center is made up of 2, 3, and 4. The theoretical center contains 5, 6, and 7. These centers define our primal responses and the way that our instincts function. Since it is the instinctual responses that are the last to be subdued by parental and sociological pressures, not only will it become obvious long after others parts are repressed, but it will give us an idea of what the primary center is. And if we can identify the primary center, we will have narrowed down how the Soul, Expression, and Quiescent Self will operate.

The affective center (2, 3 and 4) deals primarily with emotions and relationships. Their drive is to commune with and understand people. They think of things with reference to the "human equation." Interaction with others is important to them. They tend to ignore facts at times. They rely more on feelings in making decisions. They are more concerned with their image than the facts. We find that these numbers vacillate emotionally. If they come into a situation in which their feelings get hurt or confused, they withdraw emotionally. This causes loneliness and anxiety on their part and is contrary to their basic makeup. This seems to happen more to the 4 type than any other. That is because the 4 is the most likely to be emotionally repressed or out of touch with their feelings.

The affective types are manipulators. They do this both consciously and subconsciously. This means that at times it is not fully realized by others or themselves. They can manipulate in order to instill love, trust, or any emotion that they feel is needed. These types struggle with a feeling that they are not good enough to be loved.

The theoretical center are types 5, 6, and 7. They are based in researching, calculating, deliberating, information and objectivity. They gain security and pride from knowledge. They believe that the more they know the more they control, and the more secure they are. In their search for an objective point, they emotionally distance themselves from a situation. This allows them to watch it as if it were a movie. The theoretical types lean toward abstract learning processes such as books, tapes, videos, and courses. They seek relationships, systems and connections between things. In their detached viewpoint they see the illogic and humor in the human condition.

These people are skeptics, partly because they don't trust information that is not from the theoretical center, and partly because they don't trust people very easily. They feel superior due to the fact that they are detached from what they see others as being entangled in. The more information they have and the more reserved they are, the more secure and superior they feel. These people fight against feelings of being incompetent.

The effective centered people are 8, 9, and 1. They measure situations and people by power, influence, and energy. They believe it is important to be in control. The focus is on security, survival, and influence. They will endeavor to control their environment and all that are in it. This is usually done openly, but if they come up against a strong personality they can become passive-aggressive in their quest for control. They put demands on themselves and others. These demands can be high and they may not be acceptable to others. If that is the case the effective-centered person will become dismayed and even angry. They have a rooted, secure, confident, immovable air. They are not easily intimidate by authority or power, but they can intimidate others.

The thing that drives them is a sense of an unknown but impending threat. This is sometimes caused by what the child perceived as an unexpected and sudden change within the family, a parental situation that upset the child's sense of stability and trust. They have a deep and hidden sense of being unimportant.

As we can see, the obvious strong suit of all of the types is the overcompensation of the real weak points. When we look at the centers we see that in each center there is a number that seems at first not to fit. This is because they are repressed. We cannot forget that a type or number relates to a specific set of character traits. It could be the openness of these traits, or the repression of them. That depends on the number.

The 3 is out of touch with reality, preferring instead to live with an illusion. This illusion is that they are all things to all people. It lends itself to an outward show of accomplishment and competence in life. They weigh and balance their actions and opinions so as not to harm their image with others. The aim is to get ahead, and to achieve that necessary to fulfill the feeling that they must impress others. They sell their personalities to gain entry into the clique. This is a rejection of the affective center. They truncate their feelings in order to blend in with the crowd and thereby not be rejected.

6s repress their ability to calculate and decide. Instead they turn over this act to an authority figure and let them set up the rules which the 6 will live by. This is a rejection of the theoretical center. The only time that the ability to think in a theoretical way will come into play is when the 6 uses it to see a situation as it relates to the group, family, or authority figure that they have attached to.

The 9 wants to preserve things, even if it isn't working well. They tend to be passively stubborn when it comes to staying in tough, sometimes dysfunctional situations. They will think and brood over a problem or relationship and do nothing about it. They had rather use their energy to create a peaceful environment and ignore the problems, than they would alter the situation. This is a repression of the effective center.

PLANES OF EXPRESSION

The parallel between the Planes Of Expression (POE) and the Jungian types is impressive. There are two "archetypes," (extrovert and introvert), and four types which closely resemble the planes.

THE EXTROVERT is very comfortable in the outer world, with objects, people, and situations. His attitude is romantic, and can seem flighty or shallow and adventurous. He is ill at ease with subjective and subconscious matters. He is likely to jump into things without a lot of forethought.

If they make a mistake, it doesn't effect them as deeply as the introvert, and since it doesn't sink in, they are likely to get caught in the same situation more than once. His contact is, or wants to be, immediate. If unchecked they can become compulsive, infantile, or egocentric. Because the body, soul, and mind communicate with its owner in a kind of subjective way, the extrovert can neglect them. Therefore they can push them too far at times. They may spread themselves too thin, work too hard, suffer from physical or emotional stress.

They view the world and things that happen from the outside in; that is, they see the world influencing them, more than their influence on the world. This was the way

149

that Freud looked at things. He saw the person being molded mostly by what they experienced as a child. Privacy is not a big issue for extroverts. They may tend to be superficial, and take words quite literally; for example, "You must come to tea one day," which isn't meant at all.

THE INTROVERT takes choosing friends very seriously. They usually have fewer and deeper relationships than extroverts. They value self-knowledge, and understanding. They insist on privacy and they respect others' privacy. The energy of perception flows away from the object to the subject. They see the interaction of people and things. They understand that their internal view of the world matters most to their comprehension of it. Jung viewed the world in this way. He saw that the personality sees things from an individual standpoint and that this subjective approach greatly influences one's interpretation of the world.

The introvert's subjective reaction to the outside world is the most important thing to them. They may deal in abstracts. They are uncomfortable in the outside, objective world. Peace and quiet is important. The four types can be understood by saying that a person can see things with his sensations, can classify things with his thinking, evaluate things with his feelings, and estimate

150

possibilities with his intuition. We know that all people have all types; it's just a matter of emphasis.

It is important to note that there are inferior and superior functions. The superior function is the one that you function with. It is the function that you can control and focus. The inferior function is the one that controls you. If you get hurt it is on the inferior level of that type.

The inferior and the superior are opposites. You are more likely to marry people of your inferior type. The thinking type is vulnerable on his feeling side. The feeling type is vulnerable on his thinking side. When a person is hit on his inferior side he gets emotional, and out of control. Sensation is the opposite of intuition. Thinking is the opposite of feeling.

In the Planes of Expression there are four types. Parallels can be drawn between the POE and the Jungian types.

MENTAL POE - mind, reason, thought, leadership, a picture of reality, what we perceive. Objectiveness, directed mentality. Hates to be criticized. 1-8: related to the thinking type.

PHYSICAL POE - tenacity, senses, responsibility, conformity, patience, practicality, common sense, observation via the senses. Experience, realist, able to remember facts. 4 and 5 relate to the sensing type.

151

EMOTIONAL POE -- feeling, imagination, emotion, sympathy, creativity. Has likes and dislikes based on feelings; this means that they are likely to be strong willed and arbitrary at times. Social, can be generous. 2-3-6 relate to the feeling type.

INTUITIVE POE - inner guidance. Analysis is done with an inner sense. Insight, a feeling of where things will lead. May not relate to the physical world or their bodies very well. Apt to jump from point to point in a conversation; this is because they tend to forget that people aren't following their inner thoughts. When they speak their minds it may be in the middle of a thought. 7-9 relate to the intuitive type.

SPIRITUAL POE - ability to recognize and control the good and evil within. Compassion versus egocentricity. Self verses others, conscious. If this plane has no numbers in it the person is likely to be sociopathic to one degree or another. 2-7 -9

The first and easiest way to interpret the data is to add the number of times that the numbers is a particular plane occur in the name. Then compare the numbers of the different planes to see if there is one plane that is substantially higher or lower than the others. This will give insight into the strongest and weakest planes and their functions. Because the letters of "E" and "N" occur often in the English language the amount 5s must be 3 or 4 higher than other planes to matter.

The other way is to calculate the numbers in each plane and then refer to their meanings in the chart on the POE.

Example: Robert Steven Cox
                962592 125455 368

Mental (The number of 1s & 8s in the name) = 2

Physical (The number of 4s & 5s in the name) = 5

Emotional (The number of 2s, 3s and 6s in the name) = 6

Intuitive (The number of 7s and 9s in the name) = 2

Both the number and the amount of the letters should be considered. If the person is "heavy" with emotional numbers he or she will behave more emotionally. If the emotional plane exhibits a emotional number it will act more emotionally. For example, Mr. Cox has a 6 in his emotional plane. This means his emotions will be directed in a familial and disciplinarian way, owing to the fact that six is the number of family.

There are Planes of Expression within the birth date also. These planes are considered active when the numbers that are needed for the plane are all present. The more of these numbers that are in the birth date, the stronger the plane in its influence. This, like the Table of Inclusion and the Planes of Expression, are weak influences that are overshadowed by the Soul, Expression, and Life Path .

These weaker influences should be used to fill in and shade the bigger picture of the three main numbers. To see if a plane is active first write down the full birth date. Example: 5-25-1955 has 1, 2, 5, and 9 in it. There are four 5s in the sequence.

Then check the chart below to see which planes are active. The explanation for what influences and strengths the planes hold in store are also listed. Remember that all three numbers must be present for the plane to be active. They indicate only an increase in these areas. The above example (5-25-1955) has the "enterprise" plane active.

3, 6, 9   Caring - Intelligence, higher education, compassion, teaching, counselor, minister, doctor.

2, 5, 8   Driven - Passion, conviction, intensity, strong-willed.

1, 4, 7   Dexterity - Affectionate, demonstrative, manual dexterity, clever, skill.

1, 2, 3   Mental - Can get absorbed in their own thoughts. Verbal, creative, moody if stifled.

4, 5, 6   Persistent - Resolute, stubborn, obstinate. They have endurance and can remain in difficult situations in order to reach a goal.

7, 8, 9   Active - Great amounts of physical and mental energy. Reckless, fidgety, nervous. They can be aggressive at times. Possible allergies and hyperactivity is indicated.

3, 5, 7-Discernment - Mental penetration, insight, music or science are strong points.

1, 5, 9-Enterprise - Determined, purposeful, enterprising. They have a natural incentive to accomplish things.

MORE INFORMATION ON THE PLANES OF EXPRESSION

EXTROVERTED SENSATION - realists. Able to retain facts. They experience the concrete world, but they don't assimilate it into themselves. Love new experiences, being physical, sensations. Given to materialism or pleasure seeking. Can over-exert themselves. They are likely to get bogged down by facts and details. Sensation type relates to the physical POE number 5.

INTROVERTED SENSATION - highly tuned and spiritual. They have an inner physical attitude. They can sense the unseen. They take the information coming in, and then go away to boil it down to abstracts, file their findings away, and do it again. They may spin their wheels if they dwell too much on details. Relates to POE 4.

INTUITION EXTROVERT - intuition is an unconscious perception. For the extrovert this perception is directed outwardly. It appears to be an attitude of expectation. It is concerned with seeing possibilities and hunches. It is great for pioneers since it works best when there is nothing to go on.

In conversations they leap from point to point, much to the confusion of any sensation people that may be listening, who must fill in the gaps. They live in the future or the past and are most uncomfortable in the present. This means that they react in retrospect or anticipation, but draw a blank on the immediate experience. They hate repetition. Since they are weak on the sensation side they tend to neglect their bodies and end up with fatigue or ulcers. Their thinking is speculative. They can see the potential in people. This makes good educators, teachers, counselors, and psychologists. The intuitive type relates to the intuitive POE number 9.

INTUITION INTROVERT-- they draw from deep levels of the unconscious. This is good for pioneers and dealing with the intangible. They have vision, and don't get bogged down in facts and details. If their other sides are neglected they will have their head in the clouds. Relates to POE number 7.

THINKING EXTROVERT - intellectual reconstruction of concrete actuality and accepted ideas. Engineers are the thinking extrovert type. Things must relate to objective facts, scientific data. They try to condition and construct their whole life, and the lives of those around them by formulae constructed from objective data. They try to work in absolutes; this can make them rigid. Beware of critical, domineering, disgruntled mind-sets. If they ignore their feelings, they can take up a particular belief, (even a religious one), and become a ruthless tyrant. The normal, balanced extroverted thinker strives to replace old ideas with a correct new one. Darwin is a good example. The thinking type relates to the mental POE Numbers 1 and 8.

THINKING INTROVERT - unlike the extroverted thinker, the introverted thinker's thoughts are aimed more within. They are the philosophical types. They often have trouble finding the right words because they are trying to present images coming from the unconscious. They do not directly relate to objective facts. They may seem distant, naive, or detached, but they are trying to remain separate in order to understand others. They hold you at arm's length to placate you. If they are exposed to objective situations they can become timid, anxious, even aggressive. They are likely to throw their ideas out to others as is, not realizing that they might not be clear to others. If it isn't clear they can get annoyed and think less of them for not understanding. They don't make good teachers. They will take their theories apart and examine every detail, even thinking of objections and opposing thoughts. Relates to POE 7.

FEELING EXTROVERT - These people are likely to have traditional social standards. Its design is not to upset the feeling situation. It is an act of accommodation. Fashion, culture, sociability is the thrust. More women than men fall into this category. If it is unbalanced, they can become vicious, cold, untrustworthy, and materialistic. They do this by putting people down while trying to make themselves look good. This is done with subtlety, in a socially acceptable way (knife in the back while smiling). This is a kind of passive-aggressive action whose anger, aggression, and intentions are hidden behind a socially acceptable façade. You must judge their intentions.

They have definite likes and dislikes, and the ability to appraise things and people. This makes it a rational function. Because it is a rational function it can be applied to ministry, counseling, social work, and/or manipulating people, especially the intellectual types who are vulnerable to the games of their opposite type. Because men are stereotyped as thinking types, the feeling man is in for a socially rough ride. The feeling type is related to the emotional POE Numbers 3, and 6.

FEELING INTROVERT - feelings are derived from an inner premise. They may be hostile to the object, or person with which they are dealing. They may seem inaccessible and silent. They protect themselves from the outside world by removing themselves from it and belittling it. They retreat into themselves or some place to feel safe. They have an insecurity about their environment,

159

and at times present a child-like appearance, hiding their real personality. They are in a world of their own. Feelings are not extensive but are intensive. Relates to POE 2.

CONVERTING THE BIRTH DATE

The name contains the major personality traits which are "hard wired" into our psyche. This is our heredity. But the interplay and influence of heredity and environment is a fine line to drawn. The numbers deducted from the birth date shines light on the environmental factors of our life. They certainly become part of what makes us who we are, but the origin of the molding process is from without and not within.

Like the name, the birthday is also converted to a mathematical formula using the number of the months as follows:

Jan. = 1   Feb. = 2   Mar. = 3   Apr. = 4   May = 5
Jun. = 6   Jul. = 7   Aug. = 8   Sep. = 9   Oct. = 1
Nov. = 2   Dec. = 3

The entire birthday is written down. All digits are added together and reduced to a single digit. This digit is the Life Path.

Example: 05-25-1955; $5 + 2 + 5 + 1 + 9 + 5 + 5 = 32$
$3 + 2 = 5$ 5 is the Life Path.

INFORMATION ABOUT THE LIFE PATH

The Life Path is the path traveled by the Soul. It gives us an idea of the environment, situations, types of circumstances, and people encountered along the way through life.

It is an indication of abilities, aptitudes, vocations, hobbies, and a way of tackling life. This is because it is what the person has been exposed to. When looking for interests, abilities, or vocations it is best to take Soul, Expression, and Life Paths into account as a complete picture. The Life Path has within it abilities and challenges. It is obvious that if a person runs into certain situations which are indicated by the Life Path, that the handling of these situations will reveal strengths and weaknesses.

An example is the 5 Life Path. The 5 will mean that a person will have travel, variety, and sexual, or sensual experiences in life. One could learn to think on their feet, learn from life, be educated by experience, enjoying the ride; or they could become addicted to new or sensual things, resist change, or become cynical about life. It is up to the person and their personality.

LIFE PATH 1

Your path lies in working alone or in a lead position, and living an independent life. Your choices and lifestyle may not fit into the established norm. That's okay; you're a pioneer of sorts. If you learn to trust yourself and your own opinions you will do well. Headstrong, a leader, positive in nature, you tend to drive yourself. Original, creative, critical (yet easily hurt if criticized), demanding of yourself and others. A talent in music, singing, or art is common with this Life Path.

Parents may have been overprotective. You are domineering and at times you seem indifferent, (although this is canceled out with a 2 in the Soul or Expression). This Life Path brings with it times of loneliness and independence even when you don't want it. With this number, the child was made to feel inadequate and criticized. This sets up a "sore spot" in the child in us that makes us drive ourselves too hard in order to overcome or quiet the voice of the parent. Individualistic, ambitious, sarcastic (when angry), opinionated, outspoken, dislikes compromise, resists conformity (resulting in feeling alone). Learn to be less selfish and have less self-importance to compensate for a hidden feeling of inferiority.

Once they set their minds on something it is very difficult to change their minds or their plan. Dislikes being wrong and hates admitting it. 1's can be a stubborn lot. They have talent in music, writing, painting, selling, or inventing. Many of these talents go untapped and unacknowledged because of feelings of insecurity, and the need to be perfect in their endeavors. The 1 must realize that they are forceful in the pursuit of their goals; therefore, they must learn the balance between leadership and diplomacy.

May be directors, department heads, self-employed, sales or group or church leaders, company owners, inventors. There's a hidden rebellion here. Family may have been critical or expressed contrary opinions. This undermined the child's confidence. Parents may have been impatient with the youth. 1's have the will to survive and are capable people. Competitive, they need bright minds to interact with; otherwise, if they are not challenged they may become melancholy or disinterested. 1's have a choice of being critical, demanding, domineering, and obstinate; or determined, original, creative, pioneering, ambitious, and leaders. These represent the two sides of the life choices in the 1 Life Path.

LIFE PATH 2

Your path lies in being cooperative, sensitive, and working well with others. You are a helper; considerate, diplomatic, and a peacekeeper. You can be shy or reserved at times. You will be put in situations where you must put the concerns of others before your own needs or wishes. The major warning associated with this Life Path is not to be taken advantage of. Although you dislike confusion, noise, and too much activity, you also dislike having to be alone. You have needs that include affection, bonding, and being appreciated.

If you become unbalanced, you will need motivation and to watch your indifference. As details start to get you down, you will procrastinate, so you need to relax and pull back if you feel yourself getting too involved. You may wear your feelings on your sleeve. This means that you are likely to be overly sensitive, even to the point of taking things personally when they are not meant that way.

On the positive side, you are able to work with details. This is because you are a patient person. You are sensitive to the feelings and needs of others and may be a quiet person. The shyness and quietness may be overridden by an 8 or a 1 Soul. Partnerships in love, life, and business are your path. You must learn to be cooperative and tactful without becoming dependent or weak. Refined music, things harmonious, exacting, precise, and balanced soothe you. You may seem timid at times. You like the more precise and accurate things, such as mechanics, logistics, secretarial tasks, religion, photography, painting, and decorating. You can understand both sides of a situation. You have the ability to manage people and develop concepts and methods. If you are driven too hard there is a tendency to become tactless and vain. Guard against the laziness that comes from letting others take control too much.

You may have been dominated in early life and/or childhood. This has put you in situations where it was hard to assert yourself, but overcoming this will strengthen you and give you insight into diplomacy, tact, and timing. It also develops the ability to sense the "emotional climate" around you. You seem to know when to hit people at just the right time in order to make a point or get what you want.

You must keep directed and intent, otherwise you may become aimless. Watch for being overly apologetic. It may have been hard to live up to your family's expectations. There could have been a moody or unpredictable parent who taught the child the use of timing and diplomacy the hard way. In your attempts to be diplomatic you may tend to ride the fence so as not to displease. But many times this means that you will not please either side, not even yourself.

Many 2s come from broken homes and may have lived with their mothers. If you are tactful, sensitive, and observe the details you will do very well. If you are demanding, manipulative, or spineless you will not, because you will be fighting your destiny and you will be manifesting all of the negative traits of this path. Be strong and keep a balance between details and the big picture. Also, balance your needs and the needs of others. You will find that sometimes you will come first. There is no need to feel guilty if you put yourself first from time to time.

LIFE PATH 3

The fullest form of this path is lived out in the public eye as an actor, artist, speaker, entertainer, or writer. 3s are mentally quick, social people who are capable of motivating others. They are versatile and show an interesting split of a hard working and somewhat picky person, one who could be a perfectionist; and a social, friendly, open person for whom love is a necessity for happiness. On the negative side they may seem shallow, superficial, jealous, possessive, intolerant, proud, and may spread themselves too thin. On the positive side, their creativity is strong. They are capable of meeting people. They are neat, hard working people. Possessions are important to them. They are optimistic, happy people. They will find their happiness through self-expression. They have a good use of words. They are good speakers, with a sense of humor. Selling is indicated. They must learn to be expressive and work with others without becoming verbose, overly proud, or superficial. They usually have a sense of art, fashion, decorating, and how to meet the public. There are three categories of 3s:

1. The expressive 3: inspiring, able to meet the public, intelligent..

2. The artistic, creative, sensitive type.

3. The shallow, partying, drinking type.

A fast talker, likes to be the center of attention. Groups 1 and 2 can be combined in some way, but group 3 is usually not combined as easily with the other two groups. With a 4 or a 7 Soul or Expression, the 3 may overcompensate and end up as the third kind of 3, only quieter. As children, many 3s may have sung and danced. They are usually creative as children. Sex is usually very important to these people. It has a strong influence in their life and could be either positive or negative. 3, when backed up by a 6, 1 or 8 Soul or Expression makes for very good management and executive ability. Good sense of humor, and wit. They need companionship but if they reject this they can become bitter and introverted. The negative 3 usually exhibits a false pride, fault-finding, gossiping, vanity and stubbornness. 3s are generally a very socially answerable number there are fewer 3s convicted of crimes than any other number.

LIFE PATH 4

Your path is one of work, planning, and methodical approaches. You are capable of great endurance and tenacity. However, the reverse is also true, so watch your laziness. Don't begrudge labor. Keep on the light side. Take time to relax and don't get too dull or in a rut. Don't try to escape, either. As you can see by this "back-and-forth" pattern, 4s can be a number of extremes. You have the ability to work in a blue collar environment where labor is hard and repetitious. At the same time you tend to escape into your own world. You would make a good construction worker, mechanic, carpenter, builder, butcher, soldier, farmer, engineer, mill worker, plant worker - you can handle routine work well. Along with the ability to work with one's hands goes music, painting, and sculpting. You are probably a skeptic about religious or philosophical matters until you have experienced their application in your life.

4s may hide their feelings and they usually don't express the feelings that they are in touch with very freely. This can lead to outbursts of temper or depression. Some of your strong points can include repairing, employment and personnel, buying and selling, building, contracting, logistics, inventory control, and plant work. You tend to have a good memory. You are logical and methodical, and you express yourself through form. You tend toward the systematic and practical lines. You are careful with money, loyal and down to earth. You must learn to stick with and endure job trouble or hard work in your life.

This is not an easy path. There are usually no big breaks; instead it is one of slow progress. If you are balanced and healthy your life can be one of a slow but sure upward mobility. If you drink too much, or repeat your same mistakes regarding your relationships and choices of dysfunction anomalies, you could lose everything.

On the negative side, you may be discontented, drink too much, become undisciplined, or an escapist. The escapism usually comes in the forms of drinking, drug abuse, food, or sex addictions. Escape into books and movies is common and not unhealthy. 4s must learn moderation in both verbal and emotional expression. It is very possible that the 4 has abilities such as music, working with their hands, sculpting, painting, gardening, refinishing furniture, sewing, or hairdressing, many of which are undiscovered and desperately needed to allow the 4 a fuller expression of their bottled up emotions.

4s should learn to evaluate ideas and lay lasting foundations. If too firm, the 4 can give way to narrow-mindedness, stubbornness and a dislike of change. Stinginess, selfishness, vulgarity, or rudeness can also

171

result. In the 4s childhood their family may not have expressed themselves emotionally. There may not have been much touching or verbal expressions of love. Watch for venting your frustrations properly. Otherwise, violence may occur. Try to express yourself in a complete, systematic, and reliable way. Be careful to understand and work through the family problems that may lead you into destructive patterns in your adult life.

LIFE PATH 5

Wit, energy, outgoing, curious, critical. You may misuse your personal freedom which can lead to overindulgence. Your life is fluid and likely to be full of changes. Every day is a new adventure and you shouldn't plan far ahead since things will change anyway. God loves variety, and life is a kaleidoscope of change; the 5 embodies this understanding. Your family may have moved a lot which gave you a varied environment. It will be hard to adjust to changes which include strong ties. There is likely to be travel and several lovers or marriages.

The 5 may change residences often. They may have many interests. They are given to teaching (occult or eastern philosophy), writing, speaking, and the conveying of ideas. 5s can't keep still. They have a large amount of nervous energy and must keep moving. A 6, 7, or 4 in Soul or Expression "weighs down" the 5 and allows them to slow down enough to focus the energy; otherwise they can experience burn out. They must learn responsibility by overcoming impulsive and self-indulging sensual acts. The 5 communicates well, speculates and speaks, follows hunches, and attracts publicity through writing, politics or acting. The 5 could be analytical and sometimes unsympathetic. Like the 7s, 5s also tend to remain aloof while viewing a situation and gathering information.

173

Anne Burton

Building, selling, installing, repairing, or researching are all open for the 5. With a 9 or 7 Expression, the 5 must decide between good temperament and a sarcastic wit. Remember, this is a swing Vibration that is caught between renunciation and indulgence. They have a religious and mystical side, as well as an earthy sensual side. Involvement could be very diverse. Construction work, farming, languages, religion, philosophy, teaching, ministry. They can be sarcastic, magnetic, witty, funny, and sexual in thought and action. There may be a spiritual swing between a mystical and religious understanding, and an earthy, lusty attitude.

With a 9 Expression, the 5 will lean toward writing, acting, publications, or advertising. Although it is sexual or sensual, wanting and needing to experience, 5 is the number of moderation, (or lack of same). It is not at all uncommon to find 5s teaching, preaching, or conveying spiritual ideas. Unless you have direction and commitment, you will have unsung ideas and have trouble sitting down and taking the time to implement them. It may indicate a wild or free childhood, with a morally settled religious period following. 5 works best without immediate supervision.

If confined or restricted they will become sullen and resentful. They can rebel against authority. 5s need to try to develop an eye for detail, since they have trouble in taking things slowly and they have a habit of jumping into their latest project with both feet. They need to learn to slow down and take more notice of the minor details. 5s have to learn that to consume something is not necessarily to taste it. This goes for sex, food, and life in general.

LIFE PATH 6

Your path is in taking a balanced, parental responsibility and concern for others. This could be as a devoted spouse, a devoted and concerned employee, or employer. Your perfectionism may lead to trouble in relationships. 6 may indicate domestic troubles. You must always consider family before self in order to perfect this path. Learn to settle down with responsibility and try to work with imperfections in relationships. You have a gift of responsibility and parental concern. This is a good money number and a good vibration for ministering to others. It may include the healing arts, counseling, care-giving, teaching, child care, church or community work. According to your Soul number and Expression number, you may not even like to deal with other people's problems, but with this Life Path number, you will. People will come in off the street at times and end up telling you their story. You must learn to listen but not get caught up in worrying about them. You can't accept responsibility for everyone.

If unbalanced, you will be meddlesome and a busy-body. You don t like to take "no" for an answer. If you are on the right path, your home is your refuge and your castle. Your main concerns are justice, beauty, harmony, and a solid devoted home and family. Your home is your show place. If you run from your responsibility or commitment of your heart, there will be trouble, especially at home, marriage, and love situations. You could become a worrier or possessive. The 6 can be drawn to being an actor, singer, social worker, care-giver, healer, or a parental image. They are often found in middle management positions where they tend to treat people as if they are in a family, with the 6 in the parental role. This is not bad, as long as the parental image is one of benevolence, and not that of tyranny.

LIFE PATH 7

The path of the 7 is one of inner thoughts and solitude. Learning, searching, and wondering why things are the way they are. The most troubling thing about the 7 in any of the primary positions in the chart is that it seems to be a type of thought pattern that deals with both analysis and intuition, such as psychology, theology, scientific research, or metaphysics. This type of thought process can lead one into daydreams. They can believe what they want to believe in spite of the facts.

This combination of thought processes can hamper the ability to express oneself. There simply are no words to directly communicate some things that the 7 feels or thinks. Melancholia can be the result. Certainly a quiet, aloof, or introverted demeanor may result. This is especially true for the 7 Soul or Expression. 7 is a number of the mystic, and like all mystical experiences, there is joy in the knowledge, and frustration in the attempt to explain it.

7 seeks reasons behind things, but because of the qualities of research and observation, they may tend toward being a skeptic. They are analytical, quiet, and moody. Research, investigation, teaching, and philosophy are some of your strong suits. There are often feelings of being

unfulfilled and an underlying question as to if this is all that there is to life.

Life may disappoint. The 7 feels alone and needs love, but they may have trouble with expression. There is a search for faith and enlightenment. With a 7 Challenge, they could be deceitful and sneaky. 7s can be secretive about themselves and tend to tell things on a need-to-know basis. Since open communication is the first rule of marriage and one of the things the 7s must try the hardest to do, there is a high percentage of divorce during the first stage of the 7s life. This is true up to the age of 36.

7s must learn faith in self and God. They must learn not to hate being alone. They like to learn, but they don't like to be taught. They don't understand finances, and may not understand the law, since it is legal and not ethical or moral. In so many words, 7s tend to complain the loudest about the moral space between the letter of the law and the spirit of the law.

7s love teaching the higher things of life. They are also found in the areas of bookkeeping, technical fields, or fields requiring calculations. They are somewhat reserved, quiet, and need to know the whys and wherefores of things. They tend to be introspective, cultured, mental, and philosophic. The 7 strives for mental and spiritual perfection if they are healthy. At times, their silence will seem stand-offish to others. Others may see the 7 as unemotional, moody, and secretive. Because of their introspection and quiet needs, they may do better living by themselves. With a 3 Soul or Expression there could be stress within the psyche causing outbursts or aggressive moodiness. You must apply your gift for study and getting to the bottom of things. Philosophy and psychology interest the 7.

Jobs may include working with government or a big company. They are usually conservative and logical. This number is somewhat soft and gentle, but they can use their aloofness and apparent coldness as a tool to punish others if they have displeased them. This is a passive/aggressive action in which they can strike out and still claim that they have not done anything wrong. In this act, the 7 is wrong and destructive to the relationship. Talking can be painful to the 7, but silence is deadly to a relationship. We must decide which is more important to us.

LIFE PATH 8

Their family may have thought too much of status and religious or materialistic dogma. 8 Life Paths are usually somewhat conservative, materialistic, and a little stingy. They could be forceful, intense, deceptive, or self-interested. They make good engineers, heads of departments, supervisors, owners, or administrators. 8s can be strong-willed and aggressive people, but they just want someone to love them and accept them as they are. The 8 needs to attempt to show more of their soft side.

The Life Path of 8 will lead them into situations where they have to deal with a parent, boss, big business, or government which is considered absolute authority or tyranny. 8s demand efficiency so they may be picky, precise, or hard to please. There is compassion for the needy but help is given from a distance so as not to get involved. 8 could be a strong faith number with political interests. A choice between positive and negative sides of the 8 is based on spiritual and material choices and attitudes. They are generally successful in business. They hate being dependent on anyone, and they look down on those who depend on others.

They have trouble in finding the center path, so they can go from indulgent to rigid in their lives. 8 deals with finance, real estate, and organization. It is an

181

executive number. They can drive themselves too hard, and may nag or judge wrongly. They may be put in a position of authority. If this happens, they, more than most, will have to be reminded that power corrupts, so don't get greedy, materialistic, or ruthless. Use your executive cool, organizational and financial skills, and judge others on efficiency and quality. They must learn the proper views of material wealth and power. They must learn to be boss but not dictator. Lawyer, judge, efficiency expert, researcher, engineer, quality control. With a 7 Expression they will be less materialistic and more spiritual.

LIFE PATH 9

Generous, perfectionist, idealist, healer, sensitive (psychic). They may swing from happy to sad quickly. They are givers, but they need to learn to control temper. 9 is the number of passion and compassion. They have a humanitarian outlook. They should continue to develop this throughout their lives. Idealists can become disappointed and withdrawn when the world goes counter to their beliefs. They must learn to give but not to be taken advantage of. They must learn the proper place and time for generosity and emotional expression. Expression may be through music, art, sewing, decorating, acting. They are good at working with people, entertaining, and being a lecturer, receptionist, company representative, teacher, counselor, or travel agent. 9s usually have trouble with romantic relationships. They have an ability to love many. Must strive for universal love. A high sensitivity can make the 9 have mood swings from happy to sad quickly. There is a tendency to be dramatic. It shows itself through writing and acting abilities.

Because of the compassion and need to give, medicine or healing may be considered. In their early years, they probably had to deal with harsh realities of life. This dealt with family dysfunctions, broken homes, and a love life that was less than happy. They must balance the ability to inspire and help mankind with the idealism and knack of being taken misused. There is a high percentage of divorce if they married before age 28.

NOTE: The "undertone" of the Life Path is formed from the month, day and year - the base line numbers. Each number is in effect for approximately 28 years and continues to cycle until death. (Refer to product and harvest cycles for meaning). Example: $5/25/1955 = 5 + 7 + 2 = 5$. 5 from 0-28 years, 7 from 28-56 years, and 2 from 56-84 years of age.

FIRST CYCLE

The First Cycle is also called the Natal Attainment Cycle, or simply NAC It starts at birth, (surprise!), and is felt all the way to 36 years old. Its effects start to decrease at 28 years old and fade until aged 36. The NAC is the addition of the month and day of the birth date.

The NAC is a strong indicator of the conditions under which a person grew up. This cycle gives insight into the childhood. It also is an indicator of how the child viewed his parents, environment, and the feelings of the years that molded the child.

This cycle has a lasting impact throughout the life of the person since it represents the formative years. However, the strongest influence is felt from birth to approximately 28 years of age. This number is an attainment number. Any number that is derived from the addition of any two numbers in a birth date or year will be an attainment. This does not mean that it will not have its negative influences, but it does mean that because of the conditions it represents, and the stresses thereof, the person will have grown, learned lessons from, and have been strongly impacted by the respective area that the attainment number represents.

Example:

Birthdate 05/25/1955 = (5)

(2 + 5 = 7)

(1 + 9 + 5 + 5 =20; 2 + 0 = 2)

    5 + 7 + 2 = 5 Life Path

    5 + 7 = 12; 1 + 2 = 3 First Cycle or NAC

FIRST CHALLENGE

Like the First Cycle, this vibration is also calculated from the month and day of the birth date. It is the subtraction of them. Its meaning allows us to look at the problems, challenges, and deficits of the formative years. Like the First Cycle (or NAC), this NAC Challenge lasts from birth until the age of 28, when it begins to fade until 36 years of age.

This is one of the most important numbers to understand since it represents the negative and possibly crippling influences exerted by parents, environment, and society in the most vulnerable times.

The NAC or First Cycle Challenge should be read in conjunction with the Major Challenge. The Major Challenge represents those anomalies that are deep enough to follow us throughout our lives, and even seem to become worse at the midway point. Thus, the Major Challenge can indicate how and in what direction the mid-life crisis will overtake us.

Example:

Birth date 5/25/1955 = 5

2 + 5 = 7

1 + 9 + 5 + 5 = 20 = 2

Reduced Birth Date   5 7   2

5 + 7 + 2 = 14 = 5

> First Cycle Challenge = month minus day 7 – 5 = 2
>
> Second Cycle Challenge = month – year 7 – 2 = 5
>
> Major Challenge = 3

In simplest terms the formulae are as follows:

> Month + Day = first cycle
>
> Month - day = first Challenge
>
> Day + year = 2nd cycle
>
> Day - year = 2nd Challenge
>
> First Cycle + 2nd cycle = 3rd cycle
>
> First Challenge – 2nd Challenge = 3rd Challenge
>
> Month + year = 4th cycle
>
> Month - year = 4th Challenge

The duration of the cycles are one of the points of hot debate within Numerology. Many believe that first Cycle and Challenge are strongest from birth to age 28 and then each cycle following this is about 9 years in length. Some believe that the first cycle and challenges last until 36 years of age with each of the following cycles lasting up to 18 years in length. If the cycles are only 9 years in length one could live to see the end of the last cycles. When the fourth cycle and challenge ends, the cycles start over at the first with each one lasting nine years.

As you can see in the example, the month (5) minus the day (7) = 2. Therefore, 2 is the NAC of the First Cycle Challenge. The apex of its influence is felt from birth until age 28. The Major Challenge is the subtraction of all the components of the birth date. First the day and month are subtracted, which yields the First Cycle Challenge, then the day and year are subtracted, which yields the Second Cycle Challenge, then the First Cycle Challenge and the Second Cycle Challenge are subtracted from each other. This yields the Major Challenge.

If we assume the 18 years rule then the Major Challenge is actually a Life Challenge since its effects can be seen throughout the entire life. However, it seems to do more damage beginning 18 years after the First Cycle ends. Remember that the First Cycle lasts 28 years, and the Second Cycle lasts for 18 years. So from ages 28 to 45 the Second Cycle and Challenge is strongest. From ages 45 to 63 the Major Challenge is strongest. The last Challenge cycle is calculated from subtraction of the month and year. It is also in effect for 18 years.

After all of the cycles have passed, they rotate back to the First Cycle. That is, for 18 years, then the second for 18 years, and so on. There is a theory that all of the cycles last 18 years and do not rotate back around, but instead hold on the last cycle until death. However, 81 is the age of rebirth; therefore, this numerology program purports that at age 81 we recycle to the First Cycle again. A man is a man once, but a child twice.

The NAC represents the conditions that we lived through that changed us and taught us. The NAC Challenge are those things that damaged us and may cause us to stumble, often repeating the same errors in judgment throughout our lives. Please refer to the notes given at the end of 9 First Cycle. Look very closely at these numbers as they apply to you. Try to see through the habits that hold you in blindness to them. Identify, acknowledge, and change.

In both the First Cycle and the First Cycle Challenge charts there are notations that appear to be fractions. These numbers, such as 5/2, indicate a 5 First Cycle attainment with a 2 First Cycle Challenge. At times there will be a notation of other cycles. In all cases, the cycles and challenges will go together. This will mean that the Second Cycle may only go with the Second Cycle Challenge, the Third Cycle can only go with the Third Cycle

Challenge, and so forth. The cycle number is always on top, and the challenge is always the bottom number.

The strongest and most important challenge is the subtraction of the parts of the birth date. This is the Major Challenge. It can be seen all through life, but is at its strongest at 36 years minus Life Path + 9. Or, according to other theories, from age 28 until 45.

Assuming a birth date of March 10 1960, the components of the birth date would be:

March = 3   10 (1+0) = 1   1960 (1+9+6+0)= 16(1=6)=7
So the birth date reduces to   3 1 7

To get the Major Challenge, subtract the first and middle numbers. 3-1=2,   then subtract the middle and last numbers. 7-1=6. Lastly, subtract the two remainders. 2-6=4. The Major Challenge is 4.

EXPLANATION OF THE MAJOR CHALLENGE
The Major Challenge is calculated by first subtracting birth day and month, then subtracting birth day from year, and finally subtracting these two numbers.
Example: 5/25/1955 is reduced to 5 month / 7 day / 2 year.
Month – day is 5 – 7 = 2   Day – year is 7 – 2 = 5

Subtracting these two numbers is 5 - 2 = 3. The major challenge is 3. The major challenge can be seen throughout all of life, but is at its strongest between the ages of 36 and about 45. This challenge is an overview of the situations in childhood that caused the most damage to the psyche. It indicates weak points that are likely to arise from this. It is assumed that these are not dealt with completely until later in life, usually from ages 35 to 45, if then. This number, therefore, gives an idea of how the stresses of mid-life will overtake you.

The Major Challenge is in fact the challenge to the Life Path. Its influence is felt from start to finish. It is a general description of environment and the effect on the personality that can hold one back from one's true potential.

The second cycle and challenge start their influence at age 28 but do not fully come into play until age 36. They point toward a direction that life will take between the ages of 36 to 45. At age 45 their energies are spent.

The third cycle and challenge are seen mostly between 45 and 54. Although the Major Challenge it seems to be more focused in this time frame. This is probably why most mid-life changes occur at that time.

The 4th Cycle and Challenge begin at age 54 and continue until age 63. As with the other cycles and challenges, these show a general direction and challenge of life at this stage. Here we have two view points regarding what happens next. Some think that the life direction tends to stay here until death. Some think that we circle back to repeat the First Cycle again. This seems to make more sense to me since all things cycle. The timing seems to last 9 years and then move on to the Second Cycle, which will in turn last 9 years, and so on.

EFFECTS OF TIMES ON PERSONALITY

In this most recent 7 year a friend called to console me regarding some stressful events - the news of the deaths of two friends within six hours of one another had followed hard on the heels of the fact that someone had shot my dog. I was not having a good day. As I looked with confusion at my chart I saw that it was a 7 month and a 7 day. That's a duality. (A duality is when the day and month Vibrations are the same - the result is a 0 Challenge for the period).

In a 7 year many times people fall away. Part of this may be due to a need for the person to pull back and think, re-evaluate life, and try to solve life's problems. Sometimes it is because secrets don't stay hidden in a 7 year and the truth hurts. Now and then it is simply because in a 7 year there is already an inner tension and nervousness and we are not likely to put up with as much garbage and interference from others. Obviously, there can be a certain amount of loss due to death at this time; 7 and 9 years are known for that kind of thing.

My friend said, "There are many ties being cut now, aren't there? We are always faced with a choice in these times. We can either free-fall or we can float free." In times of change, that is a simple but profound rule. We can either get caught up in the nothingness of it all and be overtaken by the lack of direction, motivation, and connections, or we can see it as another stage in life. Death and change are painful things, stress-filled and depressing, but they are part of our lives. They bring about a kaleidoscope effect that is the constant dance of nature.

As we experience change it is essential that we float free from the old ways. We should do it with a graceful push toward new possibilities. Never allow yourself to free-fall - aimless, at the mercy of fate, without a goal or a passion in life. The trip is all downhill, the ride is swift, and the last stop is a huge problem .

First Cycle or Natal Attainment

The First Cycle is also called the First Attainment. It starts at the time of birth. It is also referred to as the natal attainment cycle, or simply NAC The NAC is the addition of the month and day. It is a strong indicator of the conditions under which a person grew up. This cycle gives insight into the childhood. It also is an indicator of how the child viewed his parents, environment, and the feelings of the years that molded the child.

We should keep in mind that this cycle has a lasting impact throughout the life of the person since it represents the formative years. However, the strongest influence is felt from birth to approximately 28 years of age. This number is an attainment number. Any number that is derived from the addition of any two numbers in a birth date or year will be an attainment. This does not mean that it will not have its negative influences, but it does mean that because of the conditions it represents, and the stresses thereof, the person will have grown, learned lessons from, and have been strongly impacted by the respective area that the attainment number represents.

For example:

05/25/1955 = (5)

2 + 5 = 7

1 + 9 + 5 + 5 = 20; 2 + 0 = 2

      5 + 7 + 2 = 5 Life Path

      7 = 12; 1 + 2 = 3 NAC

The First Cycle is derived from the addition of the month and the day. If the birth date is 5/25 then the First Cycle is calculated 5 + (2 + 5); 5 +7 = 12; 1 + 2 = 3 so the First Cycle is a 3. We should note the numbers that the 3 is reduced from - 12. Occasionally the double-digit numbers are mentioned as having a certain meaning.

Throughout the texts on NAC and NAC Challenge there will appear numbers that are expressed as if they are fractions. These numbers are the cycles and Challenges. The top number is the cycle. The bottom number is the challenge. It is a strange phenomenon in humans, that even though we see a situation in our youth as damaging, we tend to allow its recurrence in our adult years. It isn't because we think that it is right, but to the child inside of us, it is familiar. You see, when a trauma occurs to us as children, (and even as adults), if the trauma is intense enough, a part of us stops growing.

We stop moving forward in order to stay and work out a solution to the problem that caused the pain. Our downfall comes from not being whole people any longer. We have left too much of ourselves behind to be functional. If the drive is good it could lead to solid business ventures or foreign travel. With compassion, tolerance and understanding, this is a powerful cycle. It is one of powerful compassion, self-expression, deeply felt moral and spiritual beliefs. Completeness. We then try to go back, through our thought processes, our situations, and even our actions, to try to understand and fix the pain, abuse, abandonment, or dysfunctions of the past.

This is why, even though we know logically that we do not want a dysfunctional relationship, we keep ending up there. There is something in that relationship that has triggered a feeling or need from the past, and drawn us back to see if we can work it out "this time." If you find yourself in one of these recurring patterns, you must ask yourself what in this situation or the feelings that it commands reminds you of painful times in your youth. In some cases it will be obvious. Broken homes breed broken homes, alcoholic parents call forth addictive or emotionally abusive mates, etc.

But some insights are not so easy; they are hidden by our own choices. Like someone who is standing in his own light, the shadow he casts obscures his view. You must try to look from a different angle to see. Once you have identified it you can work on forgiving those responsible, healing the child within, and watching the adult in order to make yourself accountable for making the mistake again. You have the capacity to be compassionate, understanding and giving. You just need to understand your child within first.

1 NAC (1st Cycle)

1 --- Driven, self-sufficient, leader, creative. They are people who have had to stand on their own. This brought a sense of isolation at times. One can be a rather harsh Vibration for a small child struggling inordinately hard to discover and test its independence. To soften it, help and guide a child, don't give too much freedom, don't suppress its gifts. Help bring out the child's decision making ability. They will usually bond with one parent more than the other. This number indicates an off-balance of the mother or father influence. There are several conditions that can cause this. One parent could be critical, stern, or absent for times because of work. Another way an imbalance may occur is in a situation by which the child receives to much attention. This tends to bring about egocentricity. This is the key word for a 1 First Cycle. The child is put in a situation wherein they learn to look out for number one, either because they had to, or because they were taught to. The child gets "tough." It becomes a survivor.

To help this child, it's spirit must not be broken. Love and patience are needed, along with set boundaries and rules which are enforced with consistency and love in order to raise the strong-willed child. This is a warning not to be too headstrong and stubborn as an adult. Listen to advice, making sure your own ego isn't isolating you. You may have had feelings of being left on your own, at times even deserted. You may have been leaned on to take care of siblings, a sick parent, or to fend for yourself. You may have been forced to take on too much responsibility and grow up too fast or in some way had a portion of your childhood cut short. You may have said to yourself, "This will make me stronger in the long run," but chances are that you have not fully dealt with the pain of the situations that caused that feeling.

There is a 25% chance of a parent missing by death, divorce, working to the exclusion of the family, or alcoholism. With a 1 NAC and a 2 First Cycle Challenge, there is a slightly higher percentage of abuse or abandonment from the father image.

2 NAC (1st Cycle)

2 -- Tact, diplomacy, sensitivity to others and their feelings. Love of closeness, bonding, cooperation, harmony, and gentleness are the results of this cycle. There is a tendency to be nervous, sensitive, or high-strung. They were raised under the influence of an imbalanced mother image. (It is the mother's place in our young lives to teach us the proper place for sensitivity and emotions.) This number can be found when one parent tries to compensate for the deficit that they perceive in the other. They may be spoiled or pampered, even into late teen years. They may marry young or be dominated in early life by a mate.

With an 8 in the Soul or Expression the child will have a strong will and will revolt against the dominant influences in his life especially in the 30's. They will be more independent than most 2 NAC's. The balance to be learned is between bonding to someone and being dominated by someone. 2s must learn how to cooperate while maintaining their identity. Since this is an attainment position, it indicates that through the struggles the child will develop sensitivity because of the influences of this number.

2s need affection and closeness more than most, whether they admit it or not. They may be religious, musical and/or artistic. The ability to notice details, and a sense of how to cooperate is indicated. Just as in the case of the 1 NAC, the stress of the 2 can cause pain and resentment as the child struggles for a clear identity. It may mean divorce or death of a parent (25% of the time). The mother may be overbearing or overprotective; more times than not, it simply means one parent has a larger place in the raising of the child than the other.

Usually the mother has influenced child more than the father. I have seen the mother influence the child's development more by her absence than the father did by his presence.; especially if the 2 is reduced from an 11. There may have been a father missing because of work, death, alcoholism, or simply emotionally distant. (Interestingly, a higher percentage of homosexuals have this number which is reduced from an 11. (5+6=11 1+1=2). It should also be noted here that a high percentage of children with an 11 First Cycle or an 11 Life Path, die before the age of 2 years, frequently of sudden infant death syndrome.

2/0 may waver while deciding but once decided they tend to work in absolutes. They listen but seldom change their minds. Although they are generous with friends, they are rigid and not forgiving to enemies. Zeal, independent, ambition.

3 NAC (1st Cycle)

3 -- Social, the ability to communicate, ability to meet and mingle. May be praised too much as a child. This can make them self-confident or cocky. Friends are top priority. Child may have been told that they were beautiful, bright, or special so much that it felt "doted over" and a false pride developed. May have lead a protected childhood, followed by a search for independence in the teen years. Artistic, verbally expressive, social graces. You are more likely to be influenced by people other than parents during this period.

Romance and sex are important. Art and skill with words: speaking, writing, designing. (Love triangles may appear often.) Parents usually listened to child's point of view. This number may be attributed to the fact that grandparents, especially the grandmother, aunts, uncles, or others paid a lot of attention to the child. The child may have stayed frequently with grandparents (or aunts and uncles). Possibly out in the country so as to allow the child an escape to relax and have fun. Pleasant childhood memories often accompany this number.

4 NAC (1st Cycle)

4 - Hard working, high endurance, patient with others who try, logical, methodical, tenacious. You will have to work for what you get. There was a serious and demanding childhood in which there were restrictions. You may have started to work young. The childhood niceties could have been lacking because of money problems. This is number most often found in children raised in a "blue collar" environment. The father was usually a mill, factory, or construction worker, mechanic, military or farmer.

13, 22 are mechanical, technological, or have an above-average memory or logic (storing information). This number goes along with a lonely, restrictive, poor or harsh childhood. A situation where many fall into trouble with the law. One parent may drink or be strict and overbearing. With 2 NAC Challenge, father may restrict and mother may overprotect in order to counter-balance the negative influences. The father may have set standards too high for the child to live up to. This causes an inferiority complex. Watch for escapism through drugs or drink. Learn temperance and moderation. The family unit may not have been a warm or friendly family. Kisses and hugs were not freely exchanged. They may not have been the kind of family that showed or talked of their affections. Restricted emotional flow in family can render the adult incapable of finding words for their feelings.

5 NAC (1st. Cycle)

5 - This number represents travel, movement, freedom, and sensuality. The child should have freedom with guidance.   They will have an adventurous spirit. Watch for early sexual experimentation, wanderlust, or marriage for the sake of sex. They are restless, changeable, energetic, impulsive, and love to travel (especially if born in May).   They may have lived with grandparents or aunts and uncles, or away from home. It is an indication of a child that could have had parents that moved a lot. Military brats can have this number.

If this vibration is squelched by a parent who was too stern, or a religious upbringing that functioned through guilt, they will be forever frustrated. They will not be able to keep still for long, but they won't know how to express the need for travel and experience. A love of nature and the land is indicated. Sex will influences their lives, either by its expression, or by its repression. An indication of which way it will go is based on the influence of the challenges in the birth date. They must guard against unwanted consequences from sexual activity. If there is a problem in sexual expression, it may be because of an unbalanced view of the parents' ethics. This is an interesting number in this position because its effect is most dramatic. It swings either way sexually.

Many 5 NAC will have open lusty expressions, while others are somewhat repressed. Many people under this influence are raised under a mother influence that taught the Victorian concept that sex is dirty, or shouldn't be enjoyed. In this same vein, sex may not have been discussed at all. This sends a message to the child also. This seems to occur more with a 5/0 in the First Cycle.

The other extreme is a parent that was not faithful, and may have had an overly free sexual expression. In this side of the swing the parent may have drank too much and ignored the child. Since this position represents the childhood and youth, we must assume that the sexual influence of this number could mean sexual abuse, a parent who was to caught up in their own pleasures and desires to function as a parent. Or a parent who conveyed an out of balance sexual picture in either extreme. There could be anger and emotions that need to be dealt with in order to achieve a balanced view of sex.

6 NAC (1st Cycle)

6 - Most of the time this will indicate a stern parent, (usually the father), who was harsh enough on the child to set up a love/hate relationship with authority figures. These people can be responsible, devoted, protectors, parental, family, and group oriented. The 6 likes kids, family gatherings, and the security that a caring group can bring. Many 6s have a religious upbringing, heavy family ties and responsibility. However, if they rebel, they will have a chip on their shoulder and will resent authority figures. This is because it is tied back to their father image in their minds. Many 6s have a one parent image (usually the father), that was emotionally distant, a disciplinarian, or was missing due to divorce, death, or a job that consumed them.

The 6 is likely to put things and people that they care about on a pedestal. They are usually popular with their peer group. They tend to be good and fair supervisors. The overemphasis of this parent image in the child's mind sets up a love-hate relationship with authority figures. In not knowing its' relationship to authority, a child can not clearly see where it belongs. This can lead to an identity crisis which may cause them to rebel against parents' teachings, such as religious or moral standards. The fuel for the crisis usually comes from a situation where the child is

207

called on to be a parent image to siblings at a young age, or where parents put too much pressure on the child to conform and belong to the church or family groups. If taken too far, this represses the child's identity and will cause problems later in life. The child may marry young to get away from home. 33 is spontaneously artistic. Money and advance in business will come early if you're settled down. Marriage or love in a settled environment is important. Moral upbringing is probably strong.

7 NAC (1st. Cycle)

7 - Pensive, seeker of truth, quiet, questioner, life long student. The early years are a studious, lonely, introspective time. The child should be helped out of introversion. In the teen years a search for knowledge and purpose of being will ensue. 7 does not do well in early marriage. Many times the first marriage doesn't last.

With a 1 or 2 NAC Challenge, it usually indicates an emotionally abusive childhood. The father is either a stern, abusive or alcoholic man, or missing as an emotional anchor for the child. The child may not have connected deeply enough with the father, leading to insecurity and the inner pain of self doubt. Self confidence is painfully low. There is a feeling of being lost. Their identity or worth is unsure. This is doubly possible with a 4 Major Challenge or a 4 Life Path.

Problems in expressing their true feelings is due to a fear of rejection. They should be helped out of this, and the passive/aggressive expression that comes with trying to control and suppress emotions. (Remember, emotions will always come out one way or another). The child can be moody and very stubborn. An interest in science, psychology, religion, or metaphysics is indicated. Maturation is slow. Possible family troubles such as parents who fought often, or divorce caused the child to put

209

up a wall or pull in to itself. This can lead to insecurity and trouble in finding happiness in love or marriage because of problems in expressing feelings. Since the numbers 5 and 7 are related in an esoteric way, this can be a precursor to a lonely or sexually abusive childhood. The parents should watch for this and make sure that the child has friendships and time to play with other children. Make sure that the work load that the child bears is not too heavy, and lastly, make sure that they are taught about abuse and what to do about it.

8 NAC (1st Cycle)

8 -Value, justice, power, strong will, administration, stubborn, a leader. This number indicate an off balance of materialistic values brought about by a poor childhood or the child coming from a wealthy family, therefore it is an imbalance in the teaching of the proper value of money. Parent may have simply been too tight with money. Material gain possible early in life. They may decide life goals early. Lucky breaks with money and business are likely.

This cycle is too powerful for most. A balance of drive and selfishness versus justice and giving is needed. Pride, especially in doing things right, is high on the 8s list. Making a good showing of themselves is important. Many 8s own their own business or hold high position in business early in their careers. The 8 could mean an intense learning period and reading on their own in childhood. Money, home, real estate, or business is dealt with at an early age. The overemphasis on money and power can lead the 8 to be stingy, selfish, or very careful with funds. This picky or selfish Vibration is softened by a 9 Soul, Expression, or Life Path position.

There are indications that under this influence, and especially with an 8/4 First Cycle, the child had to grow up too quickly. This may be because of a parent behaved more

211

like a drill sergeant as far as discipline was concerned than a parent. The child may have been put in a situation in which it had to fend for itself or even worse, itself and its siblings at a young age. The child could continue to try and be stoic and strong later in life after stoicism is no longer needed. This may hamper communications of the heart. If a child can not trust and thereby fears the parent because of the misuse of parental authority or strength, the child will not be able to open up and trust later in its adult life.

9 NAC (1st. Cycle)

9 - Giver, caregiver, soft hearted, emotional, learning from life's school of hard knocks. 9s are emotionally open people. 75% of this vibration have come from, or will be in, broken marriages or broken homes due to divorce and/or the death of a parent or spouse. They have seen love unfulfilled, and they will experience hard luck in love. They may set themselves up to be misused in love. 9s are dramatic and tend to confuse emotions. If the child grows up with natural parents, they could be unusually oppressive. If their drive is good, this could lead to solid business ventures or foreign travel. With compassion, tolerance and understanding, this is a powerful cycle. It is one of compassion, self expression, and deeply felt moral and spiritual beliefs. They may have been deeply affected by the death of someone close to them. They could have had a difficult childhood due to poverty, loss, or abuse.

NAC CHALLENGE OR FIRST CHALLENGE

Like the First Cycle, this vibration is also calculated from the month and day of the birth date. It is the subtraction of them. Its meaning allows us to look at the problems, challenges, and deficits of the formative years. Like the First Cycle or NAC, this NAC Challenge lasts from birth until the age of 27. This is one of the most important numbers to understand since it represents the negative and possibly crippling influences exerted by parents, environment, and society in the most vulnerable times. The NAC Challenge should be read in conjunction with the Major Challenge. The Major Challenge represents those anomalies that are deep enough to follow us throughout our lives, and even seem to become worse at the midway point. Thus the Major Challenge can indicate how and in what direction the mid-life crisis will overtake us.

Example: 5/25/1955   (5)   (2 + 5 = 7)   (1 + 9 + 5 + 5 = 20; 2 + 0 = 2)

      5 + 7 + 2 = 14; 1 + 4 = 5

      First Cycle Challenge: 2

      Second Cycle Challenge: 5

      Major Challenge: 3

As you can see, the month (5) minus the day (7) = 2. Therefore 2 is the NAC of First Cycle Challenge. The apex of its influence is felt from birth until age 27. The Major Challenge is the subtraction of all the components of the birth date. First the day and month are subtracted, which yields the First Cycle Challenge, then the day and year are subtracted, which yields the Second Cycle Challenge, then the First Cycle Challenge and the Second Cycle Challenge are subtracted from each other. This yields the Major Challenge.

The Major Challenge is actually a Life Challenge since its effects can be seen throughout the entire life. However, it seems to do more damage beginning 18 years after the First Cycle ends. Remember that the First Cycle lasts 27 years, and the Second Cycle lasts for 18 years. So from ages 27 to 45 the Second Cycle and Challenge is strongest. From ages 45 to 63 the Major Challenge is strongest. The last challenge cycle is calculated from subtraction of the month and year. It is also in effect for 18 years.

After all of the cycles have passed, they rotate back to the First Cycle. That is, the first for 18 years, then the second for 18 years, and so on. There is a theory that all of the cycles last 18 years and do not rotate back around, but instead hold on the last cycle until death. However, 81 is the age of rebirth; therefore, this numerology program purports that at age 81 we recycle to the First Cycle again. A man is a man once, but a child twice.

The NAC represents the conditions that we lived through that changed us and taught us. The NAC Challenge are those things that damaged us and may cause us to stumble, often repeating the same errors in judgment throughout our lives. Please refer to the notes given in A-, and at the end of 9 First Cycle. Look very closely at these numbers as they apply to you. Try to see through the habits that hold you in blindness to them. Identify, acknowledge, and change.

In both the First Cycle and the First Cycle Challenge charts there are notations that appear to be fractions. These numbers, such as 5/2, indicate a 5 First Cycle with a 2 First Cycle Challenge. At times there will be a notation of other cycles. In all cases, the cycles and challenges will go together. This will mean that the Second

Cycle may only go with the Second Cycle Challenge, the Third Cycle can only go with the Third Cycle Challenge, and so forth. The cycle number is always on top, and the challenge is always the bottom number.

0 CHALLENGE

Zero pulls in all directions with no motivation in any one direction. There is a need to learn one point of concentration and direction. It is a warning of rashness, or excess. Lack of discipline is possible. At times we see them having trouble applying themselves.

Many people with all 0's in Challenges tend to drop out of high school. A 0 Challenge is, in a large percentage of cases, related to those who must be untangled from a material or social problem. Many people in jail have 0 Challenges in NAC; this may also be related to drug use. It is "misdirection" and/or "miss-motivation." The 0 suggests an unwillingness or inability to think of the long-term consequences. To beat this challenge you must act with long-term forethought and calculated deliberateness. You must see to cover all of the bases and act for the best interests of yourself, your children, and society. Act with determination.

There is a large percent of missing and/or abused children with 0 as a Challenge. This indicates emotional abuse (due to neglect, divorce, or actual abuse), but often emotional abuse is accompanied by physical or sexual abuse. This is why negative self-image and life expectation stand in the way of accomplishment and happiness. There is a lack of ability to discern the proper direction; there is instead immobility, fear, indiscretion. The 0 Challenge could indicate learning problems in the school years because of lack of motivation.

1/0 - Impulsive, headstrong, overly self-critical, a thinker, a busy mind. All things are important to them and are taken as a challenge.

2/0 - May waver while deciding but they seldom change their mind. Ambitious, zealous, independent. They are generous to friends, rigid and unforgiving to enemies.

3/0 - Feelings of inferiority hold them back from things that they want to do. Family is important and they may not feel comfortable with venturing out. They may seem detached.

4/0 - Sensitive and impulsive. There is a need for order and control. They are creatures of habit and good with details. They take things personally.

5/0 - A vague restlessness. A missionary type (especially to the young and elderly). May have been mistreated as a child. They may seek to impose their ethics and ideas on others. A need to control their environment.

6/0 - Are good with finances and entertaining. They are fiery and firm; determined and strong-minded.

7/0 - A crusader, stubborn, ruthless, with a keen business sense and a need to prove themselves. Family ties are important.

8/0 - Precise, stubborn, opinionated, domestic, just, but fair.

9/0 - Aloof, confident, a straight shooter. Tenacious, they can see the big picture and specifics. They have the ability to sense the right and wrong of things. They are meticulous when it comes to their looks.

1 CHALLENGE

This person has a poor self-image. They don't really think that they are valuable as a person. There was a message sent to the child from his environment with the effect of undermining the child's worth. Although there are many causes of this, it is certain that the child's worth and ego were not dealt with properly. Four out of five times this is due to an imbalance of the father influence. He could be a missing or out of balance in part of the child's life. This can be by death, alcohol, weak will, divorce or by being too involved with a job to the exclusion of the family.

If the mother is allowed to dominate and overshadow the father, the child's perception of him is damaged, and the child is taught that people can run over other people. Because of the lack of a father's influence, females may seek a father image in love. The mate could be selected to continue the feeling that the child had while growing up. The abusive cycle is much stronger in women since the 1 Challenge represents the husband.

The 1 Challenge tends to make people overly sensitive and unable to balance blame and criticism. They will either feel attacked, or they will take the blame for everything. The complex may be caused because they are unsure of the father's love for them as a child. This leads to a weak ego since it is primarily the father image that teaches us our self worth.

Procrastination, or a false bravado, are two results of this. Procrastination comes from not wanting to try something and falling short, so it seems safer to the psyche to do nothing at all. A person's area of procrastination indicates a general area of fear. The false bravado and pride are simple over-compensations to attempt to hide, even from themselves, what is lacking. They must learn to stand up for their rights, but not belligerently. They should please themselves and not everyone else. They must learn to make their own decisions and live their own lives, and learn to think and act for themselves.

Many feel oppressed or held down by people of stronger wills, and unduly influenced by people with a 2 Life Path or a 2 Soul. The mother could be so overbearing that the father becomes a silent partner. If you have a 4 Life Path or Soul, your father may have been alcoholic and abusive. He may have beaten the mother. His violence caused the child to distrust and reject his influence.

Overall, this is a subtle vibration that father and child are not close enough, are simply not getting along, or are not being together enough. The father may have been up in years at child's birth. The strong spiritual or moral teachings of a 7 NAC may overcome the 1 Challenge.

1/1 - May mean weak mother, strong father. Father under a

7/1 - May be almost too strong.

2/1 - Wants applause but aren't daring enough to seize the chance. They are behind-the-scenes people. They have a quiet strength. They are committed mates. They may have trouble with their family not accepting them. With a 4 Life Path this can indicate an abusive or alcoholic father. He may have beaten the mother.

3/1 - Person of vision; takes things and themselves too seriously. They tend to act quickly. There is a pride and ego problem. They tend to dodge blame. They do well as executives or adversaries. They tend to sulk or pout when angry.

4/1 - Finds it hard to balance work and play, order and escape, and may be workaholics. Job and income mean stability to them.

5/1 - Saint or sinner. They like action (enough that they may stir things up). They are the helpers of the needy. They act well under pressure.

6/1 - Have a quick intellect, and a different outlook than most. Often they don't fit in with their families. They may swing between rigid and moody, stoic and nostalgic. They are loyal friends. They need to pay less attention to work and more to spouse and family.

7/1 - Plays to win and doesn't like to stick around if they lose. They have strong egos yet they are sensitive. They have strong moral beliefs. High expectation of others may lead to disappointment. They prefer a domain that is under their control.

8/1 - Are planners, bargain hunters, and understated autocrats. They are seldom ruffled. They have a need to prove their point. They can appear to be aloof or cool in relationships.

9/1 - Swings between self and others. They are usually social and romantic. They can be blinded by love. They are humanitarian people; interest in law or public office is common.

2 CHALLENGE

Nerves may cause health problems.   2s are impatient, and hurt easily (especially by the opinions of others). They are overly sensitive, and thus have trouble in finding, keeping, or maintaining meaningful personal relationships. Mother is the cause of a wall surrounding the person. The wall deals with the unwillingness of the person to truly open up. This may lead to shallow conversations and interaction as a deterrent to intimate relationships. Bluntness may also occur to impede closeness. There is a tendency to overlook details and concentrate more on the "big picture" to the exclusion of needed details.

There is an off balance of the mother influence. She had a negative influence on the child either by her absence and neglect, or by her need to emotionally control the child. In some situations the mother may have known about incidence of abuse of the child, but she did nothing about it.

The child is unable to get his emotional balance and self-worth due to the mother making the child doubt his ability. The child tries harder and harder to please this parent image that uses guilt or shame to control the child. This shatters the child's self-image. The 1 and 2 Challenges are both shame driven. Guilt requires only a change of action or restitution to set things right. If you stop the action that causes the guilt, the guilt stops, but shame is not based in what you do but in what you are. Since the parent did not celebrate you as a child, or sent you a message that you were inadequate, you are driven by a need to be different. You are shame driven.

On the other hand, if a parent does too much for the child it can send a message to the child that he is incompetent. This can also go for offering too many opinions, as well as hovering and manipulating. The child may leave home or marry due to a need to prove that he can handle the challenges of life. Since this indicates an imbalance in the area of the mother, it must be pointed out that the influence of an absent mother may be greater on children than the influence of a father who is there. If the mother is in a position where she usually exerts a passive/aggressive influence, using guilt or shame as the tools of choice, then she undermines the child's self-confidence. There are problems in reading the 1 and 2 Challenges correctly since they seem to start with the interaction between the parents first. The child may be only the bystander, but may inadvertently be a recipient of the message sent between husband and wife.

If the father beat or degraded the mother, it would set a pattern in the child's mind not to value or trust one or the other of them; neither the father image for doing the deed, nor the mother image for allowing it to be done. So in certain cases the father can, by his actions, force a child into a lack of balance regarding the mother image by sending a message to the child the he does not trust, respect, or value her.

Many things hinge on the way that the child sees the issue. The child may view the mother as innocent, helpless, pitiful, or perhaps as worthless, devalued, at fault. Thus a 2 Challenge can mean a tyrant for a father, which causes an effect in the child likened to a broken home. If the mother uses guilt to control the child, he will not want to go against her for fear that he is at fault for not being good enough to want to do the things she asks. This annihilates self-confidence, which in turn causes sensitivity; a subjective sensitivity in the form of referring everything to themselves and their own feelings.

2s may go along with others to avoid arguments. At times they won't stand up for their rights or wishes. They pay too much attention to what others say or think. Men may resent women because of their mother's influence over them. They have trouble opening up and sharing their feelings with others. When sensitivity and self-confidence is balanced, this challenge is met. Most 2s have trouble in forgiving and forgetting because of a subjective viewpoint. In the First Challenge there is a possible problem with dealing with school or other social environments.

3/2 - On the move and looking ahead. They are outspoken and good in situations demanding quick, decisive action. They form ideas quickly. They tend to feel that the ends justify the means. They can form attachments quickly. They survive by wit and hustle. They have explosive tempers.

4/2 - Creative, sophisticated, romantic, and open. They are technical and methodical. They like to know the ins and outs of things and how they work. They need to feel needed. They crave the company of others. With a 0 Major Challenge there is a high percentage of alcoholism in the family. With a 5 Life Path there may be problems opening up emotionally or sexually; this can cause problems in orgasm.

5/2 - People of action, physically quick, independent, gamblers. They like helping others, but their help has strings attached. They need appreciation.

6/2 - Communicates, organizes, and has an air of authority. They enjoy directing others, usually with a parental air. They have a quick temper in their youth.

7/2 - Their identity comes from who they are with. They are not loners. They are very exacting and committed in what they do, and in relationships. There is a fear of rejection or abandonment in many of this cycle. They are sensitive and need approval. They may blame themselves if things don't work out. They are serious, committed mates.

8/2 - Unconventional, varied, changeable, they love travel. They have an executive ability. They enjoy the spotlight. They can drive a hard bargain.

3 CHALLENGE

Possible trouble in self-expression, introverted, (quiet with 3/5). This is a challenge of expression, pride, cockiness, and ego, in as far as it relates to self-image and what others think. With a 4 Major Challenge they may want to be center of attention. May lead to complaining or hypochondria, especially with 4s missing in the name. This number must balance a need for attention and being alone. They will try to manipulate through sympathy or by wrapping around their little finger. Self-pity or pride may hinder them. They can be "prissy" and very image-conscious. They often have trouble in admitting their mistakes. They need to balance their self-expression. Social interaction could help them get the attention they desire. The 3 Challenge is subject to depression and melancholia. It appears much the same as a 7 Soul in its influence.

2/3 - Perfectionists. They think that they know what is best for others. They feel more at ease if they are in control. They have a sense of mood and taste.

4/3 - Act on their principles and won't admit that they are wrong. They are candid, bright and methodical. They are determined, demanding and persuasive. They feel responsibility for others.

5/3 - Daring, intense, and adventurous. They can have a magnetic personality. They like variety but not confusion. They love a good mystery. They would make good doctors. They may over-extend themselves.

6/3 - Tend to change fields of work a lot. They are straightforward and solitary. They need to be careful of alcohol, drugs, and other addictions. This can be brought about by depression. They are drawn to people and politics. They can be professional students.

7/3 - Could indicate affairs. This challenge could have been formed when parents or grandparents fussed over the child too much, or paid too little attention to the child except when ill or hurt. Scattered energy leads to distractions. They are intolerant of criticism since it hurts their feelings. They may gossip. If they withdraw due to depression caused by not feeling accepted socially, it may make the 3 Challenge appear as a 7 influence. They should take care not to speak impulsively. Insecurity leads to a need for attention or approval. Parents or grandparents may have spoiled child leading to a false pride. Child may have spent a lot of time with aunts, uncles, or grandparents who probably spoiled the child. Hates idleness or inactivity. They desire results. They want their own way. They are curious. They love attention. They want to be socially accepted, and they want their mate to be socially in or be in the 'avant guard.' They relate best one to one. They can be a loyal friend. They are capable of keeping secrets.

9/3 - Sees the connection between commerce and society, or between self and humanity (the big picture). They may be hung up on appearance and image. They are astute with money but foolish in love. They can have an addictive personality.

4 CHALLENGE

You need to learn order and discipline. You may be prone to procrastinate. Don't be lazy, or intolerant. You dislike menial tasks. There is a tendency to be stubborn or rigid in your opinion. There seems to be at least two ways of experiencing a 4 Challenge - parents did not force child to do delegated duties and/or chores resulting in no discipline. This number is usually authority-resistant and may not respect authority. If hard knocks are shown in chart, the 4 Challenge may indicate a restricted childhood. This is found to be true in 4 as a Major Challenge also. They may find it hard to be on time.

Since this is a challenge of self-discipline, it also means that their authority and leadership capacity is down. Lack of self-control must always result in lack of control of others. In the overcoming of this Challenge, they will be drawn toward body and other disciplines and hobbies that need self-control. They need to stay away from alcohol, drugs, and over-eating. May need to change eating habits and keep body in shape.

With an 8 NAC, they may be very precise and nitpicking. This is an over-compensation for having an inner problem concerning discipline. Remember that a challenge can be in either extreme.

233

In certain instances, they may have trouble in expressing their feelings. Many times this is caused by an oppressive home environment. One parent could have been very strong-willed. They could have been raised under a father influence who was a military type; who drank, who was raising the child alone, or was a harsh disciplinarian. It simply indicates that the ability to emotionally yield and verbalize was not taught correctly. They may be sensitive with feelings of insecurity about the body (size, weight).

1/4 - Parents, especially father, could have been very strict. Many women may seek a man to take care of them so they won't have to work (especially with 3 Soul). Father, in some cases, may have been lazy or unstable. This did not teach the child application or discipline. They are earthy and witty with an outgoing style. They can survive with little sleep. They like to keep busy. Because of the extremes of this challenge, they can either be very close or very removed from family.

3/4 - Are outspoken. They have the answers or they know where to find them. There is a strong need to control. They may change their beliefs but they never doubt the one they hold at the time. They love animals and kids. Indication of physical defects or raised under too much discipline or an overbearing parent. Watch your escapism (drugs and drink). Learn temperance and moderation. Balance order, discipline, and fluidity.

5/4 - Have inquiring minds. They like analyzing and understanding things. They tend to be perfectionists. They can get irritated over details yet are hard to please.

6/4 - Youthful attitude. Happy go lucky. They like to be the center of attention.

8/4 - May view a situation as a conflict of good vs evil. Tend to change views between liberal and conservative during their life. They tend to express their views very strongly and they like to debate. (Especially with a 3 Major Challenge; this could mean that the mother was abusive or too stern.)

5 CHALLENGE

This represents extremes in indulgence. Change and adapting could be issues. It can go in either direction. They may find it difficult to express their freedom. May indicate trouble in reproductive organs and warnings of miscarriage. Females may be tense or taking long foreplay to climax, or may rely on sex as an escape. May be prudish. They show a need to experience and loosen up (Victorian ethics) or a need to curb indulgence.

It can indicate a promiscuous childhood. You need to learn when to let go but don't throw it away as soon as it is gained or hold on too long. Unorthodox, nonconformist, drugs. Possibility that early sex may lead to unwanted child. For men, premature climax; in some cases, sterility is a possibility. In this Vibration, nothing is certain but a problem or blockage in the body or emotions in sexual or reproductive expression, or unwanted child.

2/5 - Loves novelty and the unusual. Life can revolve around relationships. They are insecure, idealistic, and even obsessive in relationships.

4/5 - Are bundles of desire that tend to conflict. Sex, freedom, luxury vs. order, stability, and purpose. They need direction so as not to spin their wheels. They are loyal to friends and pull for the underdog. May seem cranky but they have a wry sense of humor.

7/5 - Can indicate incest or sexual molestation in a few cases. A dramatic swing from one emotion to another due to the inner anger resulting from mistreatment in youth. Good problem-solving ability. They are prone to extremes. These people are emotional users. They may use feelings to manipulate people.

9/5 - Seek self-discovery and to understand self and others. They are compassionate and sensitive. They are good at putting others first. They are social with small groups of people. They may tend toward escapism.

6 CHALLENGE

Insecurity may lead them to an unbending attitude. They can be victims of their own idealism. The search for perfection in relations can end in unhappiness or disappointment. They need to learn to accept responsibility. They must be more tolerant and less dogmatic of others' opinions. Don't think your way is the only way. This may indicate that the family did not function as a unit. It seems to indicate that they are closer to one parent than the other; this can indicate an overly strict parental influence, even to the point of being a tyrant. Many of the people with this number come from broken homes. They usually lose a parent before they are 15 years old. Marriage and close relations are threatened. Loyalty and desire to be the boss come into play. Guilt or restrictions from parent, usually the mother, is used to control the child. Trouble with infidelity in your life. Quarrels over children. In-law problems.

1/6 - Collector, pack rat, and somewhat introverted. They are easily distracted by new ideas. They are long-suffering, but selective of friends.

3/6 - Can be designers, stylish, clever and willful. They have a desire to be unique, but also to fit in.

8/6 - Want to lead and direct people. They have a good sense of timing when it comes to business. They are ambitious and seek power. They have high standards and find it difficult to admit their mistakes. They may seek to blame others for their failures.

7 CHALLENGE

Lack of spiritual awareness, lack of faith (in self), skeptical, lonely, materialistic. This can make for a nervous or high-strung person. They may lack common sense and try to live by misunderstood spiritual laws. They may be devious or aloof. They could stand back and watch the world go by. Because of the nervousness, they need to learn patience. They appear to be rebellious and somewhat melancholy. A "James Dean" type. Moody or brooding. There is a need to find a personal philosophy and purpose in life. Learn to express self and uncover feelings. There is a need to develop agape' (a spiritual love). Because of this there is much pride, much reserve of feeling and hidden emotions. Check for 7 missing in the name; this may be more introverted. With a 6 Soul or Expression it may tend to pull people down through criticism. Many have trouble with controlling passions, leading at times to being unethical.

2/7 - Resilient, tenacious, changeable, chameleon, wanderlust. Sensitive but they usually won't show it. Loves to be wined and dined.

9/7 - Competitive, ambitious, a daredevil. Opinionated, ruthless, successful, possessions are important, but there is an added softness. They have a hard time finding moderation in things. 50% possibility of abortion, loss or death of a child, stillborn child.

They could have been abused as a young child. This may lead to dwelling too much on sex, or other obsessive, compulsive behavior such as eating or nervous disorders. Another facet, and probably the strongest part of this Vibration, is one of religious or social rebellion. This includes drink, drugs, or sex. In later years (after maturity), the need for faith or personal philosophy will start to draw them back to the church and tradition.

8 CHALLENGE

A fear of lack of money, or loss, leads to a false sense of values. They tend to be materialistic. There is an off-balance of the spiritual and material. They can be ruthless. Many are self-made people. Fears and passions can run high. Watch heart and stomach. They may lack a solid personal philosophy.

This number may indicate a childhood in which a proper value of money and materialism was not taught. This may indicate a poor or rich childhood, a childhood where there was a drastic change in living standards, or a family that taught the child not to trust people because people were out to take from them.

1/8 - Leans toward the dramatic. They are innovators, leaders, and have a good sense of humor. They thrive on appreciation. They possess good concentration. They may be aloof or elitist.

9 CHALLENGE

Although this cannot exist unless the month and day is not reduced, it may be of value to look at it at this point. Rejecting wisdom. Stubbornness and won't learn from past mistakes. Lack of control of emotions and passions. A problem in emotional expression is indicated.

This is the Major Challenge. It can be seen all through life, but is at its strongest at 36 years minus Life Path + 9. Or, according to other theories, from ages 27 through 45.

WHAT IS A MAJOR CHALLENGE?

The First Cycle lasts for 27 years, while the Second Cycle always lasts for 18 years. So from ages 27 to 45 the Second Cycle and Challenge are strongest. From 45 to 63 the Major Challenge is strongest. The last Challenge Cycle is obtained from subtraction of the month and year. It is in effect for 18 years (ages 63-81). After all of the cycles have been seen, they rotate back to the First Cycle for 18 years, then the second for 18 years, and so on. There is a theory that all of the cycles last 18 years and do not rotate back around, but instead remain in the last cycle until death. However, 81 is the age of rebirth; therefore, it is my opinion that at age 81 we recycle to the First Cycle again. "A man is a man once, but a child twice..."

The Major Challenge indicates the environmental stresses that shape us - those anomalies that are deep enough to follow us throughout our lives, and even seem to become worse at the midway point. Thus the Major Challenge can indicate how and in what direction the mid-life crisis will overtake us.

The Major Challenge is the subtraction of all of the components of the birth date. First the day and month are subtracted, which yields the First Cycle Challenge, which is also called the NAC Challenge. Then the day and year are subtracted, which yields the Second Cycle Challenge. Then the First Cycle Challenge and the Second Cycle Challenge are subtracted. This yields the Major Challenge. The Major Challenge is actually a Life Challenge since its effects can be seen throughout the entire life; however, it seems to do more damage beginning nine years after the First Cycle ends.

Example: 5-25-1955

5 7 2 = 5 Life Path   2 5

3 Major Challenge

First subtract the day and month, then subtract the day and the year. Now subtract those two numbers to find the Major Challenge.

0 MAJOR CHALLENGE

This is an "all or nothing" Challenge in which lack of motivation or direction stands in the way. This represents a problem in truly applying one's self. This may be due to a broken home, dead or missing parent, parent who drank heavily, poor family, or, strangely enough, a child who came into money in their teens or twenties and lost the motivation to "get ahead in the world." These people may work but they seem to lack the extra drive for self-improvement and upward mobility. It has been noticed that most of those in jails have 4 Soul or Expression numbers and 0 Major Challenges.

On the positive side, this is a number that indicates that your Challenges are those you bring on yourself, so there is no real challenge to this number. There is nothing but your own excuses and motivation standing in your way. So decide what you want to do and go for it! With a 1 in a major position such as Life Path, Soul, or Expression the 0 Challenge is overcome. It represents most of the positive side of the challenge. There will be little to stand in the way of reaching your major goals. These may include your own business, inventions, or projects.

There are two types of 0 Challenges. The first tends toward being passive-indecisive. This type seems to just float along, letting life do with them what it will. They may have plans but they have trouble getting motivated enough to act on them.

The second type is much harder to spot. They seem to have few obstacles that aren't brought on by themselves. Although this is a truism for all, it is doubly true for them. Those individuals who claim the years don't match or make sense, tend to have this number. If you do not see any noticeable differences in some years, it may be that the 0 Challenge has blurred the picture. This is due to the fact that the play of the Life Challenges bring about part of the problems, issues and changes that show as a year Vibration. If you have no challenge, you have fewer things to shift during the balance of the years so they show up less.

1 MAJOR CHALLENGE

This person has trouble coming to grips with their worth and value as a person. There is a deeply felt inferiority or insecurity that is covered and is oft-times undetected by others. At times it may appear as a childlike uncertainty. They may allow themselves to be mistreated, or they could attempt to compensate with a false bravado. There are many reasons that this could evolve as a weak point. One is a parent who put the child down. They made the child feel like less of a person. It could have been that the father was missing, as a result of death, alcohol, weak will or divorce. At times it can indicate a personality clash between parent and child. This also sends a message that the child was incorrect as a person.

There are a few who will say that their father was a good man and a good father, but still, somehow, the same symptoms exist. These symptoms can include poor self-image, divorce, infidelity or abuse by a mate. A small percentage of the fathers are missing by being too involved with job, or following a pattern that didn't include spending much time with the family.

In the families with weak-willed fathers, the mother image is always dominant. They usually tend to control the child to the degree that it crushes the child's independence and personhood. The child is faced with a choice of succumbing to the parent or rebelling.

Because of the lack of father influence, females may seek a father image in love. This causes a complex because they are unsure of the father's love. It may lead to a weak ego and procrastination. They need to plan and look ahead. They should learn to stand up for themselves, but not to be pushy; to please themselves and not everyone else. They must learn to make their own decisions and live their own lives. To learn to think and act for themselves. This represents a distortion of self-image and ego brought about by a missing or imbalanced father image. (Especially strong with a 2 Vibration such as a 2 Soul or Expression. They may not have had enough attention as a child, which drives them to seek attention as adults.)

Think enough of yourself to be an individual. At times you may have a chip on your shoulder from lack of self-confidence. Since the proper orienting to a male image was never established, this number shows up in a high percentage of male homosexuals with a strong 2 influence. Those with a 1 Challenge must learn the balance between self-respect and being egocentric. They may feel oppressed or held down by people of stronger wills.

With a 2 Life Path or a 2 Soul, the mother could have been so overbearing that the father became a silent partner. With a 4 Life Path or Soul, the father may have been alcoholic and abusive. He may have beaten the mother or have been emotionally abusive. His violence caused the child to mistrust and reject his influence. Overall, this is a subtle vibration that father and child are not close, are simply not getting along, or are not being together enough. The father may have been up in years at the child's birth. Weak-willed, or, on the other end of the spectrum, abusive or alcoholic.

The father under a 7/1 may be almost too strong. 7/1 may mean weak mother, or strong father. Occasionally this could indicate learning problems in the teenage years. There is a small percentage who view their family as intact and healthy, but they exhibit all of the symptoms of the opposite. Women usually choose men who take advantage of them. An ego deficit makes them allow themselves to be taken advantage of.

With a 5 NAC Challenge, the person may feel like things are just out of reach, like things never seem to work out right. Jobs or promotions are given to others, and they don't know why.

2 MAJOR CHALLENGE

Nerves may cause health problems. 2s are impatient, and hurt easily (especially by the opinions of others). They are overly sensitive, and thus have trouble in finding, keeping, or maintaining meaningful personal relationships. Mother is the cause of a wall surrounding the person. The wall deals with the unwillingness of the person to truly open up. This may lead to shallow conversations and interaction as a deterrent to intimate relationships. Bluntness may also occur to impede closeness. There is a tendency to overlook details and concentrate more on the "big picture" to the exclusion of necessary details.

There is an off balance of the mother influence. She has a negative influence on the child either by her absence and neglect, or by her need to emotionally control the child. In some situations the mother may have known about incidences of abuse of the child, but she did nothing about it. The child is unable to get his emotional balance and self-worth due to the mother making the child doubt his ability. The child tries harder and harder to please this parent image who uses guilt or shame to control the child. This shatters the child's self-image.

The 1 and 2 Challenges are both shame driven. Guilt requires only a change of action or restitution to set things right. If you stop the action that causes the guilt, the guilt stops, but shame is not based in what you do but in what you are. Since the parent did not celebrate you as a child, or sent you a message that you were inadequate, you are driven by a need to be different. You are shame driven. On the other hand, if a parent does too much for the child it can send a message to the child that he is incompetent. This can also go for offering too many opinions, as well as hovering and manipulating.

The child may leave home or marry due to a need to prove that he can handle the challenges of life. Since this indicates an imbalance in the area of the mother, it must be pointed out that the influence of an absent mother may be greater on children than the influence of a father who is there. If the mother is in a position where she usually exerts a passive/aggressive influence, using guilt or shame as the tools of choice, then she undermines the child's self-confidence. There are problems in reading the 1 and 2 Challenges correctly since they seem to start with the interaction between the parents first. The child may be only the bystander, but may inadvertently be a recipient of the message sent between husband and wife. If the father beat or degraded the mother, it would set a pattern in the child's mind not to value or trust one or the other of them; neither the father image for doing the deed, nor the mother image for allowing it to be done. So in certain cases the father can, by his actions, force a child into a lack of balance regarding the mother image by sending a message to the child the he does not trust, respect, or value her.

Many things hinge on the way that the child sees the issue. The child may view the mother as innocent, helpless, pitiful, or perhaps as worthless, devalued, at fault. Thus a 2 Challenge can mean a tyrant for a father, which causes an effect in the child likened to a broken home. If the mother uses guilt to control the child, he will not want to go against her, for fear that he is at fault for not being good enough to want to do the things she asks. This annihilates self-confidence, which in turn causes sensitivity; a subjective sensitivity in the form of referring everything to themselves and their own feelings.

2s may go along with others to avoid arguments. At times they won't stand up for their rights or wishes. They pay too much attention to what others say or think. Men may resent women because of their mother's influence over them. They have trouble opening up and sharing their feelings with others. When sensitivity and self-confidence is balanced, this challenge is met. Most 2s have trouble in forgiving and forgetting because of a subjective viewpoint. In the first challenge there is a possible problem with dealing with school or other social environments.

3 MAJOR CHALLENGE

Possible trouble in self-expression. They tend to be introverted. This is a challenge of expression, pride, cockiness, and ego, in as far as it relates to self-image and what others think. They may want to be center of attention. May lead to complaining or hypochondria, especially with 4s missing in the name. This number must balance a need for attention and being alone.

They will try to manipulate through sympathy or by wrapping around their little finger. Self-pity or pride may hinder them. They can be "prissy" and very image-conscious. They often have trouble in admitting their mistakes. They need to balance their self-expression. Social interaction could help them get the attention they desire. The 3 Challenge is subject to depression and melancholia. It appears much the same as a 7 Soul in its influence.

4 MAJOR CHALLENGE

They need to learn order and discipline. They may be prone to procrastinate. They could be lazy, or intolerant. Dislike of menial tasks. There is a tendency to be stubborn or rigid in opinion. There seem to be at least two ways of experiencing a 4 Challenge - The parents did not force child to do delegated duties and/or chores resulting in no discipline. This number is usually authority-resistant and may not respect authority.

If hard knocks are shown in chart, the 4 Challenge may indicate a restricted childhood. They may find it hard to be on time. Since this is a challenge of self-discipline, it also means that their authority and leadership capacity needs work to develop. Lack of self-control must always result in lack of control of others. In the overcoming of this challenge, they will be drawn toward body and other disciplines and hobbies that need self-control. They need to stay away from alcohol, drugs, and over-eating. May need to change eating habits and keep body in shape.

With an 8 NAC, they may be very precise and nitpicking. This is an over-compensation for having an inner problem concerning discipline. (Remember that a challenge can be in either extreme.) In certain instances, they may have trouble in expressing their feelings. Many times this is caused by an oppressive home environment.

255

One parent could have been very strong-willed. They could have been raised under a father influence who was a military type, who drank, who was raising the child alone, or was a harsh disciplinarian. It simply indicates that the ability to emotionally yield and verbalize was not taught correctly. They may be sensitive with feelings of insecurity about the body (size, weight).

5 MAJOR CHALLENGE

This represents extremes in indulgence. Change and adapting could be an issue. It can go in either direction. They may find it difficult to express their freedom. May indicate trouble in reproductive organs and warnings of miscarriage. Females may be tense or take long foreplay to climax, or may rely on sex as an escape. May be prudish. They show a need to experience and loosen up or a need to curb indulgence. It can indicate a promiscuous childhood. You need to learn when to let go but don't throw it away as soon as it is gained, nor hold on too long. Unorthodox, nonconformist, drugs. Possibility that early sex may lead to unwanted child. For men, premature climax; in some cases, sterility is a possibility.

In this vibration, nothing is certain but a problem or blockage in the body or emotions, in sexual or reproductive expression, or an unwanted child.

6 MAJOR CHALLENGE

Insecurity may lead them to an unbending attitude. They can be a victim of their own idealism. They need to learn to accept responsibility. They must be more tolerant and less dogmatic of others' opinions. They think theirs is the only way.

This may indicate that the family did not function as a unit. It seems to indicate that they are closer to one parent than the other; this can indicate an overly strict parental influence, even to the point of being a tyrant. Many of the people with this number come from broken homes. Some lose a parent before they are 15 years old. Marriage and close relations are threatened. Loyalty and desire to be the boss come into play. Guilt or restrictions from parent, usually the mother, is used to control the child. Trouble with infidelity in your life. Quarrels over children. In-law problems.

7 MAJOR CHALLENGE

Lack of spiritual awareness, lack of faith in self, skeptical, lonely, materialistic. This can make for a nervous or high-strung person. They may lack common sense and try to live by misunderstood spiritual laws. They may be devious or aloof. They could stand back and watch the world go by. Because of the nervousness they need to learn patience. They appear to be rebellious and somewhat melancholy. A "James Dean" type. Moody or brooding. There is a need to find a personal philosophy and purpose in life. Learn to express self and uncover feelings. There is a need to develop agape' (a spiritual love). Because of this there is much pride, much reserve of feeling and hidden emotions.

Check for 7 missing in the name; this may be more introverted. With a 6 Soul or Expression it may tend to pull people down through criticism. Many have trouble with controlling passions, leading at times to being unethical.

2/7 - Resilient, tenacious, changeable, chameleon, wanderlust. Sensitive but they usually won't show it. Loves to be wined and dined.

9/7 - Competitive, ambitious, a daredevil. Opinionated, ruthless, successful, possessions are important, but there is an added softness. They have a hard time finding moderation in things. 50% possibility of abortion, loss or death of a child, stillborn child. They could have been abused as a young child. This may lead to dwelling too much on sex, or other obsessive, compulsive behavior such as eating or nervous disorders. Another facet, and probably the strongest part of this Vibration, is one of religious or social rebellion. This included drink, drugs, or sex. In later years (after maturity), the need for faith or personal philosophy will start to draw them back to the church and tradition.

8 MAJOR CHALLENGE

A fear of lack of money, or loss, leads to a false sense of values. They tend to be materialistic. There is an off-balance of the spiritual and material. They can be ruthless. Many are self-made people. Fears and passions can run high. Watch heart and stomach. They may lack a solid personal philosophy. This number may indicate a childhood in which a proper value of money and materialism was not taught. This may indicate a poor or rich childhood, a childhood where there was a drastic change in living standards, or a family that taught the child not to trust people because people were out to take from them.

OTHER CYCLES AND CHALLENGES

Beyond the first cycle and challenge, and the major challenge there are other cycles that represent minor influences. All of these cycles and challenges have the same basic meanings within their individual time frames. The application differs only in the range of age that their influence is felt. They represent shifts in environment and attitude that takes place after the basic growth process is over. Influences of the second cycle and challenge are first seen around the age of 28. The influence grows until the age of 36 and then begins to subside until it fades away by age 45. Vibrations of the 4th cycle, and 4th Challenge interplay until death. They are all weak in their influence.

Example: if the date of birth is 05/25/1955

Month 0+5=5, Day 2+5=7, Year 1+9+5+5=20 2+0=2

Therefore, the numbers used to calculate the Life Path and cycles are 5 7 2.

5+2=7 (M+Y=4TH CYCLE)

Month + day 5+7 = 2 and Day + year 7 + 2 = 9 3 + 9 = 12

1 + 2 = 3

5(M)   7(D)   2(Y)

CYCLES

(D+M= First Cycle) 7+5=2

(D+Y=second Cycle) 7+2=5

(First cycle + Second cycle = Third cycle which is also called

the Major Cycle) 5-2=3

(M+Y=4TH cycle) 5+2=3

CHALLENGES

(D-M= First Challenge) 7-5=2

(D-Y=second challenge) 7-2=5

(First challenge – Second challenge = Third challenge which

is also called the Major Challenge) 5-2=3

(M-Y=4TH Challenge) 5-2=3

OVERVIEW OF CYCLES AND CHALLENGES

1) New starts, new beginnings, independence. Going it alone.

2) Partnerships, co-operation, nervous, picky, dependent. Time details.

3) Social, children, pets, art, expression, writing, selling, pride.

4) Hard work, building, sickness, setting foundations, escapism.

5) Freedom, travel, trying new things, over indulging.

6) Family, caretaking, devotion, child and parent relationships, responsibility.

7) Learning, study, meditation, seeking answers within. Inner loneliness.

8) Money, job, land, boss, acquiring, demanding, stress.

9) Tendency to remain in a bad situation, loss, emotion, giving, altruism.

0) No Challenge but no drive either. Nothing stands in your way but you. Find a way to drive yourself harder and succeed.

YEAR CYCLES

The year is derived from the age and the Life Path. Add the digits of the age together and then add the Life Path. Next reduce this to a single digit by adding the digits together if necessary.

If a person is 34 years old and has a 9 Life Path the formula would be:

$3 + 4 + 9$; $3 + 4 = 7$; $7 + 9 = 16$; $1 + 6 = 7$ so the person is in a 7 year.

If the year and the Soul or Expression are the same, there is likely to be dramatic change in that year within those areas indicated by the year number. For example, if a person is a 1 Expression, and is in a 1 year, the areas of independence and a new lease on life will be dramatic.

YEAR VIBRATION 1

Master of ship, new ideas, lifestyle, job, interest and romance. Go it alone and be individualistic. Assert yourself. Self-sufficiency, cultivation of faith in self. New relations will or should last. New lease on life. Make it happen on your own and feeling alone, go together. Possible with 9 (4 month): separation or divorce because of the "alone" aspect (or a 4 or 6 month Challenge).

April brings a change or a chance to move ahead. June - home may be affected. August/September - things coming to a head.

Births from pregnancies late in the 9 year are a small possibility. Change of residence possible. Nurture and use faith in self. Travel possible. This is a good time to have important occasions. Taking opportunities that are offered, building, inventing, directing, organizing. A good time for moving, buying a home. A 9 four month cycle within this year brings emotional tension and upset. This is a period of restoration from that which was damaged in the 9 year. 19 = promise, success, honor, love.

YEAR VIBRATION 2

Give the reins to someone else. Partnership, teamwork, charm, tact. Waiting patiently, studying, learning. Refurbishing home and putting it in order. Possible problems in home. Try not to be overly sensitive or gullible. Focus of the year is on female or mother influences. Companionship is important. Friendships develop along with professional skills and talents.

Emotionally open dealings with mate (marriage, divorce). There seems to be a certain need for companionship and yet a need to be alone. If the mate realizes this, there will be closeness. Problems with someone close could arise in May. June, July, and August bring closing or finishing of things. Usually a companion is found in the winter months November, December, February. There is often stress in relationships that can lead to separation. Vulnerable. Steady but slow, financially. A time of the earth and of the female. The question of offspring may be raised. For the male, timing is critical for success. School or other training may be indicated.

Secrets are revealed by fate. Betrayal by a friend if you have trusted the wrong ones. This year seems to bring a time of stress due to the details of life. You may be stretched too thin and your energy will be depleted at times by many small and nagging demands.

If the 2 year is derived from an 11 it takes on other possible meanings.. For a7 Soul or an 8 Soul in an 1 year money is down.
If the year is derived from 20 there may be new interests .
Also be prepared for death of the aged.

YEAR VIBRATION 3

Socialize, relate and relax. Getting together. Unexpected romance. Acting, expressing self, extravagant, jealous. Moody if left alone. A year of children. A lucky year. Gain financially through social contacts. A year for movement (change of residence). Job is at a lighter pace. Romance but it may be short lived. Karma in relationships.

May and June bring things to a head; July brings new directions. Clubs, group activity, pets, romance, a good year financially. Changes in physical appearance (new clothes, diet, exercise). Style conscious. Sex is important. Affairs, physical relationships. Marriage shaken or even broken if intentions are selfish. If single, marriage could be indicated. If married, fidelity may be threatened. This could lead to unwanted pregnancy. Avoid jealousy and watch pride. Be careful to avoid affairs. This could create an illusion of love which will likely be short-lived and detrimental to other relationships. 3, 4, & 5 month cycles bring trouble from close friends and relatives.

Friendships may falter. In the 3 year the time to advance is not now, at least not alone; wait and get help, (friends, contacts, insiders). Openness brings a certain type of closeness and happiness.

21 - Success, good time to travel.

30 -Birth, pregnancy.

YEAR VIBRATION 4

This is not the best time to start things as it will take much energy to make it last, but if you can endure, do it. Growth because of limits and responsibility, or organizing, repair, hard work. Not social. Job may be affected (watch health), work year. Manifest ideas. Don't put things off. Buying or repairing home, gardening. A chance to purchase land or a home. Partnerships in business affairs will start roughly but with patience and endurance it will pay off. You may lack drive to improve yourself. Try not to get into routines or ruts too much. Trials, testing. Test of endurance, not to turn away if things get physically or financially tough.

In a rut. Routine, military discipline, application is down. Don't expect much manifestation until the last of the year - 5 phases in then. April to September and October show signs of 5. Heart, veins, bones, joints, teeth are under stress. Major appliances, cars and water fixtures may fail. Energy is low. Body is in a stressful state. In November, nerves may be affected. Job becomes affected in the middle of the year. (Financial slowdown.) Marriage is stressful (especially for 4s and 8s). Business, career and life's work becomes important. Not usually the best physical year.

There is a period of growth and the laying of foundations. For 4s and 8s, this year is slightly karmic in relationships and jobs. It can mean a change in security of any type of job, household structure, family. This is a stressful time for relationships in relation to 4s. With an 8 four month cycle there is a good possibility of promotion and/or raise. Warning to keep paper work and administration in order and caught up; otherwise, it will snowball. This year teaches endurance, order, discipline and the value of hard work. It is a must that you have adequate knowledge and information before making decisions. Don't be afraid to ask, but don't be obsessive. Authority, leadership, government.

13 - Change of plans, place or job.

22 - A pivotal point. Not a good time for judgment since much is unstable.

YEAR VIBRATION 5

There is an internal nervousness and activity this year. A feeling of being caged is common. This will propel you to "run with the wolves" or to become depressed with that feeling being turned inward. If you are in a situation where this need to change, escape, or experience life can't be expressed, you can expect to feel confined, "antsy," and depressed. The depression can only be relieved through freedom or distractions. If the depression drives the person to lethargy, counseling and help should be sought since this indicates anger and frustration, or feelings of helplessness in regard to breaking free of the situation that makes you feel trapped.

This year calls you to vacation; writing, promoting, speaking and sex are all good. Experience life this year. There will be restlessness, change, travel, change of job and/or residence, indulgence, infatuation. Sex is important. Watch for being too active (4, 5 month + year = accidents). April brings conclusions and changes or decisions. September brings freedom and change, a lighter and quicker pace. Watch for affairs. A lot of what is started won't last. A lot will be realized in a 7 year.

5 brings exposure to the world; travel and experience will let you see and do new things, but running

from your problems or being immoral is the negative part of this. Increased sexual magnetism brings sexual discovery and power, but because of this, adultery, fornication, (and even possibly rape) is indicated. Remember to manifest the good and hold back the negative. With 5 Life Path or 5 year, could marry to get out of the house, for sex or sexual compatibility. If you cannot express your freedom, you may find yourself in a state of low energy and depression. Do not deny yourself freedom. People who seemed to have been blocking you are just playing out a game; you may proceed now.

Watch for a non-conformist attitude getting you in trouble. There is a comfort in being socially approved that you may miss when it is gone. For a 7 Expression, a 5 year can mean change in the job and/or marriage arena. The activity is very taxing. It yields upset nerves and depression at times.

14 - Changes, risk, divorce, more money-oriented than normal for a 5 year.

23 - Changes, settle affairs, travel, tension, nervousness, legality.

YEAR VIBRATION 6

Stress and/or changes within the family. The makeup of the family is likely to change this year. Responsibility, obligations, putting home in order. Life should be more stable than in the previous 5 year. Interest narrows from the 5 year. Adjustments to and within home and family. Divorce, marriage, living together. This could be a good money and job year. Don't meddle or butt in to the affairs of others. It could cost you a friend. Redecorate your home. Take an interest in art. Watch out for family troubles.

March: things come to a head. September: home affairs. Buying a house is indicated. Re-establishing household, cohabitate. Don't be unjust or overbearing this year. Grandchildren. If you do not center your attention around the home, there will be trouble. Do not over-indulge or be flighty. You will be counted on for your responsibility and strength. Don't let people down. Buy a home or a piece of land possibly. Redecorate or refurbish. Since 6 means a change in the family, or home environment, it could point toward birth, death, separation, divorce or marriage.

This year could go either way financially. Some things may seem to be at a standstill. 6 people may find burdens of home heavy. Seek counsel and wait for sound advice. Be careful. Actions taken in the 5 year could bring negative repercussions; however, you may escape payment if you are careful. If you take advantage of the romantic possibility of this year, you will find a type of freedom, even though it may mean a change such as divorce. This year is split between the highest and lowest of man. It offers both extremes of selfless family love, and the selfish love of wanting things only your own way to the exclusion of others. This is why it can contain marriage, family, children, love; or divorce and lonely adjustment.

If derived from 15 - Love, joy, marriage, divorce, sorrow.
If derived from 24 - Love, family, sickness at home.

YEAR VIBRATION 7

Not a social year. Learning, self-analysis, seriousness, being alone with thoughts, gaining personal knowledge. Poor material year. Watch nerves and/or legal trouble. Relationship problems can bring depression. Keep occupied - read, travel, or take up a new hobby to avoid depression. Strive for inner peace and faith. Seek direction in life. This includes job, beliefs, and dealing with anger, hurt and depression caused in the past.

A time of asking the big questions about life, such as "Is this all there is?" and "Where do I go from here?". Many times a 7 year will see minor illnesses or hospitalization. This forces one to take time to reflect and meditate on life and values. For a 5 Soul and/or Life Path this year can bring the loss of loved ones through death or breakups. Nerves and finances are stressed.

Even as the year approaches and certainly during the 7 year, you will see relationships that are shallow and not rooted , or physically sustained start to fall away. There will be a thinning of the ranks due to misunderstandings on their parts, and feelings of being stressed, over-taxed, and needing more peace and quiet on your part.

Feelings of solitude and melancholia will draw you to deeper thoughts. They will mingle to form a time of an inner hermitage. Listen to your heart, learn about yourself. Don't be afraid of feeling alone. There may be a forced respite due to illness, hospitalization, accident, mood, job slowdown, marital problems, or anything that can impede. Emotional problems are possible. It is usually nothing drastic or permanent. It's mostly a feeling, and feelings aren't facts; they just seem that way. There will still be people around, and friendships can take on a deeper facet. Thoughtful, quiet conversations can give way to wonderful relationships.

Keep in mind that the numbers 7 and 9 are related in the way of the endings and emotional stress that are caused. 7 tends to be a karmic cycle, so unwanted pregnancies can occur, as well as having secrets exposed, and gossip that you may have started uncovered. 7 is not a good legal time so check contracts, etc. before signing. If you are too worldly or materialistic you may end up being lonely. Brooding about the repercussions won't help. You must face them and learn from them. This is not a year for new starts. There is a need to be alone and yet a strong desire to be with others. This could lead to sexual encounters which would best be avoided. (Karma runs high now.) This is a time to analyze self and beliefs. (A spiritual and mental readjustment.) Physical and worldly attractions only serve to distract one from self.

Not a good financial year. Job may suffer. Exercise caution when dealing with people. Communication is stressed. Do not gamble or speculate. Do not be unduly critical of others since this is a time to be judged by whatever measures you use for others.

December through March brings new direction and possible confusion due to indecisiveness. April brings things to a head. Work can be slow and in some cases lay-offs may be indicated. With 7 Life Path, emotional hardship or emotional harmony is indicated depending on how you relate to others. Do not deprive yourself of the solitude you need, and also do not resent others for their seemingly outgoing lifestyles. They are likely to be in other cycles and will not understand your bitterness. Be careful with your outlook on life.

Watch nerves. Hospitalization and surgery are common in this year Vibration. If analysis and strategy are used, this can be a good time for a leadership position. Victory is accomplished through work and will. Conquest and control of self, and a responsible nature bring control of a situation. Parenthetically, there could be sickness this year. Hold on and don't let it force you into anything that you might regret. If you quit your job, marry, or move based on your immediate needs, you will regret it later, so think ahead and be careful.

16 - Accident, affair, contracts, the unexpected. Not good for contracts.

25 - Small trials, health unstable, sickness or death of the aged.

YEAR VIBRATION 8

A time to establish authority or territory. A time of responsibility. When negotiating, deal with those in charge. Job and finance adjustments, loss, change, promotion, bills may catch up with you. Unexpected costs. Business and money year - must control yourself. Important as a money-making year (Karmic year). Sell yourself. Make advancements. First part of year - money and/or job change. Usually picks up at middle of year. If money increases, then 8 year can be one of showing off with clothes, cars, etc. Change in weight. Responsibility of the year could mean divorce or marriage (especially for those with a 4 or 8 Soul or Expression). For those with a 7 or 5 in the Soul or Expression, this year could mean unexpected large expenses and tight finances. A bank loan is possible.

September is high point. July may mean adjustments between family and job. Often, people marry for security this year, taking money and stability into account when choosing a mate. In this year a drive to acquire is higher than usual. Year seems to be more dynamic in job, finances and family changes for those with a 4 or 8 or Life Path or Expression. Learn to communicate and to share. You must use proper strategy to carry out your plans. The ability to negotiate and bring conflicting sides to agreement. Due to the pressure that the eight year brings a greater amount of stomach problems, head aches, and other related conditions. In severe cases strokes and heart attacks can be more likely.

17 - Money and luck is good now.

26 - Money is up if you are conservative and good sense is used.

YEAR VIBRATION 9

Completion and debts paid. Ending. Loss of friends or lovers. Emotional ending of things that tie you down. Watch for fights with friends and family. Untangle yourself from the past mistakes. Old friends may pop up at last of year. Getting what you deserve. Emotional testing. Manifesting of plans and things worked for. The coming about of things deserved in the light of past attitudes and work. Could be a spiritual journey. Things dropped now to make room for better to come.

Spiritual pruning in order to cut away the vine and thus, produce more fruit. Pregnancy or birth are possibilities this year. Because of the emotionalism of this year, it is best to hold your tongue and not act before you think, for fear of overreacting. There will be a tendency to want to abandon things, possibly before their time. Try not to let go too soon. If you marry in this year, make sure it isn't just to have someone that is sweet and compassionate to take care of you in this rather unsettled time. Conversely, be sure before giving up things since your emotions and nerves are tattered.

Job stress or loss possible. Try to stay focused. The death of someone close to you is possible this year. Watch your health. 9 is the number of the emotions and passion.

Compassion, love, hate, loss, death, completion. Divorce, shedding an old skin. Emotionalism. Abortion. Moods of anxiety, expectation, and an impending problem. Your emotions will run the gambit. They will be tested. You must learn the balance of giving and feeling. (6/2 4 month, family breakup.) Guidance, open-mindedness, council given and received.

18 - This is a pivotal point. It is not for beginning anything, nor for travel. Death, loss, quarrels or disappointments are possible.

FOUR MONTH CYCLES

The four month cycle and Challenges take place within the year Vibration. It is derived from the age + Life Path. If a person is 25 years old with a 7 Life Path then the three cycles would be laid out as follows:

$$1$$
$$7 \quad 3$$
$$2 \quad 5 \quad 7 = 5$$
$$3 \quad 2$$
$$1$$

The First Cycle and Challenge are the two digits of the age added and subtracted:

$2 + 5 = 7 \quad 5 - 2 = 3$

The Second Cycle and Challenge are the last digit of the age and the Life Path added and subtracted:

$5 + 7 = 3 \quad 7 - 5 = 2$

The last cycle and Challenge are the First and Second Cycle added, and the first and Second Challenge subtracted:

$3 - 2 = 1$

The cycles last for 4 months each. The first begins at the birthday. The second takes over 4 months after that, and the last goes from 8 months after the birthday until the next birthday. If a person has a birthday of June 5 then the first 4 month cycle would start at June 5 and last until October 5. At that time the second 4 month cycle begins and runs until February 5. The last cycle runs from then until the next birthday on June 5.

When the 4 month cycle is the same as the birth date pattern, there will be stress along those lines. This goes for any cycle in the date of birth (DOB) For example, if the DOB is 5/22/1956, the First Cycle will be 9 / 1 (9 cycle and 1 challenge). If the age is 34 and the Life Path is 5, the second 4 month cycle will be 9 / 1. This will indicate a loss of a job or lifestyle. A 7/1 will be a mid-life type of crisis.

1 FOUR MONTH CYCLE

1 Cycle - attainment, leadership, drive, new starts in job, home, or love. Stubbornness, individualism, independence, going it alone. Deciding new directions. Time of father, son, brother, husband, government. Opportunity, direction, organization, invention, writing, building.

19 - Love, promise, success, birth.

28 - Contradictions, betrayal.

1 FOUR MONTH CHALLENGE

Hard to stand on your own. Troubles in expressing your individuality. You may be taken advantage of. Information or the truth is being withheld. You may be misused. Not good for starting anything. This Vibration is strong enough to stop the job change or new starts of an 8 year, or a 1 month. Things may get postponed. Insecurity about choices. Men, government, and big business may take advantage of you. Family or friends can try to hold you back. Drive and get-up-and-go are at a low. Not planning or looking ahead.

9/1 is the loss of a job or lifestyle.

2 FOUR MONTH CYCLE

2 Cycle - fixing up and putting things straight. Taking care of details. A time for cooperation and partnerships. More of a need to bond and get close. Friendship and love. A time to let others take the lead. Don't let the little things get you down. Mother, sister, daughter. Adjustments relating to friends, lovers, and spouse. Secrets, or virtues. Carry out plans of others. A time of spirituality and inspiration.

20 - Death of elderly; otherwise this is a good number.

29 - Deception, treachery, uncertainty.

2 FOUR MONTH CHALLENGE

Sensitive, loss of details. Not taking others' feelings into consideration, or others not taking your feelings into consideration. Relationships are threatened. Nervous time. Nerves will affect your health. Little things and details seem more overwhelming. Deceit or betrayal by friend or someone close. Dealing with affairs and problems with a loved one. Don't be selfish, conceited, or shallow.

3 FOUR MONTH CYCLE

3 Cycle - Socializing and groups, friends, communications. A lighter time. A good time for romance. A time for

affairs.   A slight possibility of   pregnancy.   Children,
grandparents, and pets come into play.   Sex is important in
the last part of cycle.   Marriage, fertility, creativity,
openness; brings contentment. Good for finances.
21- Success, attainment.

3 FOUR MONTH CHALLENGE

The challenge of pride, jealousy and moodiness.
Scattered   energy,   trouble   in   expressing   yourself.
Communication problems. Your words will be used
against you. Breaking from clubs, groups, churches. Loss
of loved one. Relationships may end at this time as though
its season were simply over. Breakups, affairs, infidelity,
melancholia.

4 FOUR MONTH CYCLE

4 Cycle - Work, too busy to play. Money may be
tight due to unexpected bills from repairs, sickness, or
accidents. Limitations. Appliances and cars may break
down. Restrictions and health problems. Muscle, bone,
teeth, and circulatory problems. Watch for escapism by
hiding from the world in work, drugs, or alcohol. Job
change possible, and this might spur a change of residence.

A time to get work done outside. Authority, leadership, government.

13 - Changes, warning, death\rebirth.

22 - Time of bad judgment. Unstable time. Pivotal state.

31 - Wavering, unstable, lonely.

4 FOUR MONTH CHALLENGE

Teeth, bones, circulation, accidents. Breakdowns with cars and major appliances. Administration, paperwork, preventive maintenance can all fall behind. Low energy, laziness, carelessness. Money decreases. A need to be more fluid and relax. Weak self-control, immaturity, injury, theft.

5 FOUR MONTH CYCLE

5 Cycle - Change, new experiences; can be a religious or spiritual time. Pleasurable time, travel, movement, vacation. Research, talk, discuss. This is a time in which haste makes waste. Sex is important; there is an animal magnetism. Sales, writing, communicating, freedom of spirit, impulsiveness. A time to make new friends, and find a lover. Beware of overindulgence with sex, food, drugs, alcohol, or accidents caused by haste. In a 6 year can mean a change of residence. Watch for overindulgence in sex, activity, drugs, drink, and the things of the flesh.

32 - Good if you follow your own judgment.

23 - Nervous tension, travel, legalities possible.

14 - Good for money and speculation. Unwise divorce. Family obligations more monotonous than usual.

5 FOUR MONTH CHALLENGE

Dodging responsibility. This is a swing Vibration, between the inability to express freedom, being confined, even a rut, or prudishness; and over- indulgence, irresponsibility, carnality. Nervous or moody if tied down. Levels of sex drive or energy may be erratic. Much energy spent with few results. You may want to get away but will feel tied down. Immorality and the consequences. Breakups. Unorthodox, nonconformist, impulsive behavior that will catch up with you. Over-activity, speed, or excessiveness will lead to accidents.

6 FOUR MONTH CYCLE

6 Cycle - Dealing with home, marriage, and family issues. 6/2 may yield serious marriage/divorce considerations. Direction changed in home, romance, education, or marriage environment. Obligations, responsibility. Adjustments of financial security. A good time for education. Share and you will receive. Give advice

only when asked. This is a good money time. Adjustments made in household. A time of parents and children (usually good). Family visits. A romantic and inspirational time. This is a split between the two natures of mankind. It yields closeness and family, or divorce and quarrels.

15 - Love, joy, sorrow, birth, affairs, good for money. If followed by an 18, death or divorce.

24 - Family, love. Illness at home is possible.

6 FOUR MONTH CHALLENGE

Time of family. Divorce, marriage, change. Don't seek perfection since nothing is perfect. You will just be disappointed, or bitter. There is a tendency to be dogmatic or intolerant with ideas that are not your own. May indicate problems with children or parents (usually parents). Infidelity, in-law troubles, quarrels.

7 FOUR MONTH CYCLE

7 Cycle - Quiet pleasures, or feeling lonely. Sorting things out by yourself. A time of reflection and repose due to sickness, accident, hospitalization, layoff, legal trouble; this will take you out of commission. It is good to use this time for reading and learning. An introverted time that can lead to moodiness, nervousness, or depression. Secrets are exposed. Time to look at what you're doing wrong, or what

has been done to you, socially or morally. This is a time of reaping what has been sown in the areas of the sexual, moral, or spiritual. Success through control of mind and will. Inventing, composing, researching, learning, meditation, sadness, depression, enlightenment. 7 is a slow time so there may be delays. Try to be on time; it may upset someone if you are not.

16 - Sometimes indicates the unexpected, accidents, opportunity, law, incarceration, or sickness of someone close.

25 - Petty problems.

7 FOUR MONTH CHALLENGE

Lonely period, pessimism, depression. Not a good job or money time. Introversion. Sickness for you or someone close to you. In a 4, 6, or 9 year, the sickness could be severe; it seems to be more directed toward the father. Imbalance of passions, unethical.

8 FOUR MONTH CYCLE

8 Cycle - Putting finances in order. Executive and business time. Able to endure. Stamina. Directing, decisions. Job changes, promotions. Stocks, bonds. Buying major appliances, home, car. Large sums of money can

change hands. Unexpected expenses can cause money to be tight. Take control of life. This is a time to press toward the goal. Watch not to step on anyone on your way up; it will come back to you. Watch your bills. Ability to bring opposing sides into compromise. A time of increased pressure due to job and financial stress. This can cause head aches, stomach problems, and related conditions.

17 - Good for finances and luck.

26 - Good money time. Invest.

8 FOUR MONTH CHALLENGE

Problems with money, bills, health. Most problems arise from overspending or being taken advantage of. Stress may cause digestive problems

9 FOUR MONTH CYCLE

9 Cycle - Faltering love and relationships. Endings, completions, disagreements with friends or loved ones. Casting off excess baggage. Nervous, emotional. Loss, death, endings. Giving of gifts, spiritual attainment. End of training or journey. Old friends contact you. A time to choose a new direction in your life or ways. There may be a feeling of things being out of control. You will want to throw the baby out with the bath water. Think and have a clear mind before you end things.

18 and 27 - Troubles. Calamity, deception in business and relations. Not good for travel.

9 FOUR MONTH CHALLENGE

This is only possible if the unordered (unreduced) numbers are used. It indicates jealousy, emotional extremes, selfishness, sorrow, loss. Being trapped in a situation.

0 FOUR MONTH CYCLE

0 Challenge. This is a window to the Soul showing flaws. Nothing to hold you down. Motivation problems. Watch for accidents. A time of choices. You must make up your mind and then go for it. This Challenge is like the "color" black, which isn't a color. The very fact that 0 is a motivation, position, or direction challenge means that it will show the pinnacle and personality stresses clearly.

EXPLANATION OF THE MONTH
VIBRATION

The month vibration is the number of months that you have been alive. It is calculated by multiplying the age times 12, then adding the number of months since the birth day. If a person is born on May 15, 1963 and you want to calculate the month: For June 20, 1993 you would take the age which is 20 times 12 (for the number of months in a year). This is 240; 2 + 4 + 0 = 6, so on the birthday of May 15, 1993 the person would have lived through their 6 month. Then you would add 2 for the number of months since the birth day. May 15 - June 15 is one, and June 15 - July 15 is two. This person is within the second month. 2 + 6 = 8; the person is in their 8 month.

If you get confused about the addition of the months just remember that if a child lives to be one year and one day old they are living in their 13th month of life. This would be a 4 month. The same thought process applies to the day influence.

MONTH VIBRATION 1

New friends, aims, ideas, and lifestyles. A time of leadership, drive, and motivation. Men, government, big business. Decisions made. Directions set. Time to take the initiative, but not to be argumentative or overbearing. This is a good time to make the change or break that has been planned for. Time of son, father, government, or business. A time of separating and breaking away from parents, spouse, roommate, partner, or lover in order to stand on your own. The new start can take place from a new location. Change or start of job may also occur. Good for important events.

Take opportunity that is offered. Direct, organize, build. Energy is up. The likelihood is that anything started in this cycle will last.

MONTH VIBRATION 2

A time of females - mother, daughter, sister. Cooperation, friendship, and romance. A need is felt to be close to the one you love. Refurbishing and putting home in order. Learn new techniques. Study and soft time. A good time for retaining details. May lack drive or decisiveness (stand up for beliefs, but use tact). Watch for over-sensitivity and nerves. A need for quiet. Use this month, if possible, to catch up on bills. Projects may be slow in coming. Shipping, repairs, agreements will seem slow. Timing is essential, especially for anything dealing with men. Watch out for secrets being told.

MONTH VIBRATION 3

Romance, sex, temptation. A social time. Somewhat carefree. Money freer at the first of the month, but down at the last of the month. May squander money or party. Lovers and good times. Pride and jealousy are up. Restless for need of contact. Art and self-expression, but don't brag. Lonely if left alone. Karmic relationships blossom quickly and deeply. Good time for seminars and short classes. Music and home entertainment systems may be purchased. Affairs may be found out if karmic. Short break or vacation. A time to wait for help, especially social contacts and inside information. Marriage, fertility, creativity, openness. Birth is possible.

MONTH VIBRATION 4

Be logical and methodical. Work and toil. Manifestation of plans. Saving money and planning for future. Money tight, repairs made on car and home. Job, money and work are keys to month. Watch laziness, bills and health. Money increases the last week of the month. Interest in house, yard and garden work (expect little to manifest until last of the month (when the 5 starts phasing in). Watch for accidents caused by too much or the wrong kind of activity. Trouble with cars, freezers, washer, dryer, other major appliances. Theft, break-ins, loss of an object. With a 4 four-month, 11 year, 4 year: may indicate a job change or layoff. Dropping things, breaking things, accidents. Health may become affected. May feel restricted or tied down.

This is not the time to move, but the time to plan and prepare and, to some extent, negotiate using logic not emotion. Don't let inexperience make you overlook possible trouble. Seek advice, do your homework. A time of leadership, government, authority, reasoning, making war.

MONTH VIBRATION 5

Change at home. Movement, adjustment, travel, restlessness, vacations. Nervous, broken dates, personal magnetism (affairs, sex). Check year - could mean change of residence or lifestyle. Change of environment or business. Don't be flighty. Use your common sense. May feel a need or urge to move or break free, but don't run. The people hindering you in the past are now off balance - it is a good time to forge ahead. Unorthodox behavior brings about social pressures.

MONTH VIBRATION 6

Obligations, realistic attitudes, marriage, divorce, family changes. Sharing is imperative. Entertaining friends at home, settling down, procreation. Responsibility, listing of obligations. Not very good for traveling. Visits within family. Financially stable. Have a sense of reliability. An opportunity to spend time with your family.

This could be because you are taking on family responsibilities or because the family has taken you on as a responsibility. You could need their help due to an emotionally or physically stressful time. It's okay - family is supposed to help one another. Keep in touch with your obligations. Change in domestic matters. Enjoy hobbies or special interests. Seek advice from the wise if needed; don't think it makes you less strong to ask for counsel. Can be a time of experiencing the split of human nature between love, family, and selflessness, and divorce, selfishness, infidelity.

MONTH VIBRATION 7

A serious and studious time. Contracts, agreements, legal trouble. Delays and a slowing down period. Watch your health. Self-analysis and bill-paying is advised. Don't run from debt. Nervousness, learning, knowledge, and searching. Money may decrease. Money is tight at first, but picks up during the last week or two. Tension at work. You may find yourself being too heavy. Practice patience and silence. Do not gamble or speculate. You may feel withdrawn. Friends may fall away. Relationships may weaken.

This is a time to be easily misunderstood. Feelings can get hurt. You may feel as if your friends have turned on you or forsaken you. This can be a lonely time and a time to turn inward and get to know more about yourself. It is a good time to develop strategies and personal philosophy. Analysis of situations, and the control of will and mind will bring about control and success. This is a time of slow downs, forced or otherwise. It could be due to sickness, accident, layoff, or money problems. Do not be surprised by minor health problems this month.

MONTH VIBRATION 8

Power and energy, opportunity, especially in business. Time to direct your affairs. Set patterns and follow through. This is a time to establish authority, and territory. With this comes responsibility. However, if you try to dodge responsibilities, they will catch up with you. Money/raise is possible. Responsibility and obligations become important.

You may become irritated at the irresponsibility of others. Invest, sell, clean up legal problems. Buy or sell car, home, property, stock, etc. Money changing hands. Business and job change. Promotion and hiring. Having developed proper strategy, carry out plans now. A good time to bring opposing forces into compromise; this goes for the mind and for the world.

MONTH VIBRATION 9

Getting rid of old habits or things that weigh you down. Seek inside yourself for answers. Keep in touch with distant friends (could lead to opportunities). People whom you have lost contact with or haven't heard from in a while may contact you. Cycles may seem to begin again. The number 9 is karmic, so self-seeking and indulgence of the past may catch up with you. Likewise, the attainment of a goal and preparation for breaking away is based on past and present actions. An emotional time - loss of friend and/or lover, or partner. Letting go of things. First half of month is slow financially. Old friends pop up. Scattered energy until the last week. More action, less manifestation.

Your attitudes are manifest in your life. Break-up of partnership, lover, friends, family by divorce or death or move. Emotionally trying time. Best to wait before acting or speaking. Try not to abandon things before their time. Your dissatisfaction may pass. Think before giving up on

301

things. Death of someone close to you. If karma is good, there is contentment. Pregnancy or birth in the family, including animals and pets. Attainment and completion in a good way. Moods of expectation, anxiety, or something impending is common. Guidance given and received. Remain open-minded.

EXPLANATION OF THE DAY

Simply put, the day Vibration is the number of days that you have been alive. In the calculation of this number there are some things that will make it easier. First reduce the years that you have lived to a single digit. If you are 25 years old that would be $2 + 5 = 7$. Next reduce the number of days in the year to a single digit: $3 + 6 + 5 = 14$; $1 + 4 = 5$. Then multiply the age digit and the year digit: $7 \times 5 = 35$; $3 + 5 = 8$. Next add the number of leap years that have passed since birth. Here is a list of leap years to help you. (Remember that if February 29 did not pass between a birthday and the day for which you are calculating, you should not count it.)

1900	1904	1908	1912	1916
1920	1924	1928	1932	1936
1940	1944	1948	1952	1956
1960	1964	1968	1972	1976
1980	1984	1988	1992	1996

and every four years after that.

Adding the number of leap years, the last step is to add the number of days since your birth day of this year. So if your birthday was 2/1/1966 and you want the day Vibration for 2/16/1993, you would add 7 leap year days and 15 for the number of days that have passed.

8 + 7 + 15 = 30; 3 + 0 = 3. So it is a 3 day.

Lastly, there are also Pinnacle and Challenge Vibrations for the day. It is the addition and the subtraction of the day and the month cycles. If you have calculated for a 3 day and you are in a 4 month, then the Pinnacle is 3 + 4 = 7 and the Challenge is 4 - 3 = 1. The Challenge is what will stand in your way of fulfilling the pinnacle. The Pinnacle is the best that can be attained from the situations of the day. One word of warning - if the Pinnacle and Challenge of the day/month matches any of the Pinnacles and Challenges of the birth date, stress and unexpected events will be likely. This is especially true for the First Cycle of the birth date.

If the day and month are the same there are unique factors put in play. These are noted. For example, if the day and month are 8 the line will read "8 DAY 8 MONTH."

DAY VIBRATIONS

1-DAY

Beginning anew. Catch up on things that you have put off. Your mental energy is up, and so is your will power. This is a great day to start something new. Take a situation by the horns and conquer it. New directions are indicated. Original concepts and a fresh new approach to situations will bring results. Business, appointments (apartment or house rental or purchase). Day of man, government, father, or business. Possible advancement. Good for sales. Birth is possible.

1 DAY 1MONTH

Accidents, relationships, injury, operations.

2 DAY

A slowdown. Peaceful day. Attend to details, retrospection, but watch your nerves and pettiness. Putting home in order. A sensitive, psychic flow. Depression, especially if alone. Crying spell when coupled with a 9. Friendships, cooperation, togetherness. Friends call to share their accomplishments and worries. Caught between warring factions. Good time to negotiate and work things out. Fair for gambling. Good for bonding and dating someone who is emotionally open and soft.

2 DAY 2 MONTH

Nervousness, accidents, breakdowns, cars malfunction. Stress could lead to fights or breakups.

3 DAY

A time of Love and affection. An Artistic and creative time. Short trips. Good day for relationships. Not a good work day. Social time and visits. Grandparents' and children's day. Money may be squandered on clothes, jewelry and partying. Talking with friends. Groups and gatherings work well. Birth in the family. Good public relations day. Charm, socializing, sex, giving, joy.

3 DAY 3 MONTH

Accidents, births, karma in relationships.

4 DAY

Bills due, order or priorities tested, money is tight. Systems may not work. Laying cornerstones, work, order and organization, planning, repairing. Cars and appliances may break down. If you are traveling, the trip may be hard or with no manifestation of interest. Watch for breaking law (speeding). Body may break down, accidents, sickness, may not feel well, may feel held down, may get lost.

4 DAY 4 MONTH

Accidents, breakdown, health, work.

5 DAY

Don't bother planning today, it won't help. Promote yourself. Change, travel, converse, take short trips, visit. Shopping, sex, food, buying, selling. Restless energy, sharing ideas. Personal magnetism. Ideas conveyed, communication, meeting new people, activity (fast thinking, good at sparring, verbally or otherwise). Watch not to overeat, or overindulge. A day for expanding frontiers and experiences.

5 DAY 5 MONTH

Communication, movement, travel, accidents, sex.

6 DAY

Assuming responsibility. Number of home and family. Closeness and fights. Job and money day, but could go either way. Quiet pleasures. Lasting accomplishments. Home-hunting. Car shopping. Watch for pushing your point too hard. Don't crusade or hard-sell. Not a great day for finances. Good for entertaining at home. Affections are strong.

6 DAY 6MONTH

Family, birth, accidents, breakup, affair.

7 DAY

Don't be depressed, get out. Books, learning, meditation, analysis, solitude. Personal decisions, philosophy, religion, legality. Inner tension and wanting to be alone. Follow hunches. Legality may include loss of money. Meeting of people for readings, church, spiritual purpose, or ceremony. Closeness is quick in coming under these conditions. Vibration is somewhat soft with nerves and a critical attitude inside. A need for quiet. Sensitivity to outside stimuli. High tension. Low energy, moodiness. A day to be a respite, forced by sickness, hospitalization, accident, or attitude. Usually it is nothing lasting or serious.

7 DAY 7MONTH

Accidents, movement, nervous energy, learning, spiritual quests, sadness.

8 DAY

Money, job, finances, administrative, executive, business. Lawsuits, court dates, hospitals. Use tact, but go for it. Good for gambling. Sell yourself, but not self-righteously. Put money matters in order. Do paperwork. 8 is also a number of the executive, boss. Watch not to oppress, or be oppressed. Organize, pay bills or receive payment. Authority day. A day for promotions and job changes. Be straightforward but use tact.

8 DAY 8MONTH

Job stress, accident, tickets.

9 DAY

Endings (trips end). Emotional. A giving time. Soft day. Not a good business day. Don't be selfish. Friends visit. 9 is a spiritual day. There is tension and emotion. Emotions very high and open. A need for reassurance. Outbursts, losses. The ending or pause of patterns, lifestyles. May want to leave work early. Friends may call or come by for a visit. The giving of gifts or receiving of gifts that are from the heart. Hearing from distant friends. You may receive news of sickness or death of someone you know.

9 DAY 9MONTH

Accident, loss, breakup, emotional time.

EXPLANATION OF THE DAY CHALLENGE.

This a what is likely to go wrong during the day. This is the area of weakness to watch, take precautions and overcome. The number is derived from the subtraction of month and day.

1-CHALLENGE OF THE DAY

You may feel oppressed or taken advantage of. Don't react with aggression. Orders and requests given by you may be carried out incorrectly. People may "be on your back." You may feel mentally tired. You may be in a situation in which information or the truth is being kept from you. False starts, postponements. Things may get put off, rescheduled or begin late.

2-CHALLENGE OF THE DAY

Nerves and pettiness get you down. A relationship is threatened by untruthfulness or over-sensitivity. There will be a need for peace and quiet. Best to keep your mouth shut today. Today is not good for gambling. Sensitivity leads to nervous depression.

3-CHALLENGE OF THE DAY

Self-expression is stifled. Watch your pride and ego. Don't try to impress people. Anti-social, depression, moodiness, scattered energy. Not good for social contact. You may come across as being cocky. Not a good day for gambling. People could want to communicate with you at inappropriate times or places making the contact strained and ineffective. You may pick inappropriate ways to make your point.

4-CHALLENGE OF THE DAY

Your patience will be tested. Order and priority have gone astray. Systems, body, car, or appliances could break down. Low energy or a feeling of lethargy may come over you for part of today. May be late for appointments. Watch for drinking or other forms of escapism; it could get you in trouble. Law and traffic tickets, court, or lawyers can come into play today. Be careful of clumsiness and accidents. Your energy and timing are off.

5-CHALLENGE OF THE DAY

Trouble in body and hand/eye coordination. You may feel slow or sluggish. Give yourself some slack because you will have trouble being on time. Running, wasted energy with few results. Problems related to traveling - breakdowns with transportation. Sex drive may swing dramatically. May overindulge with food, drink or sex. You could be moody today.

6-CHALLENGE OF THE DAY

Feeling oppressed by responsibility or obligations. Family tensions can bring emotions to the forefront. May want to run from responsibility. Doctor visits or minor illness in family. Traffic tickets, possible family squabbles, or conflicts with an authority figure, so it is best to keep a low profile. Trouble with people not living up to their words or responsibilities. People that you have put on a pedestal may fall off.

7-CHALLENGE OF THE DAY

Moodiness and high tension plague today. Low energy is caused by depression. Sex drive may be up because of an inner aloneness or disquieting (if depression hasn't weakened it). You may want to be left alone, but you may not want to be by yourself. The world overrides the spiritual realm. Possible stress, tension and depression in a 3 month. You may be sullen and quiet. Broken dates or missed-timing may be cause you to be alone for a while. Don't chastise people for what you have also done. Be careful of deception and backstabbing by others. This can indicate a setup in the worst case. Be careful of the dark side today.

8-CHALLENGE OF THE DAY

Watch for mishandling money, and problems with getting along with the boss. You may feel powerless to change a situation. Power is down. This is not a good day for gambling.

0-CHALLENGE OF THE DAY

Motivation is low. Check the duality chart. Accidents, breakdowns. Warning!! This is a day of the unexpected. Be careful. With proper motivation there is nothing to hold you down. Your choices will decide your direction.

DAY PINNACLE VIBRATION EXPLANATION.

The day pinnacle vibration is the sum of the month plus day numbers. It represents how the day will peak. It is a picture of the important points in the day. It is the thing that can be used for the good. It is the springboard to happenings, growth, and better self understanding.

1-DAY PINNACLE

Beginning anew. Catching up with things put off. Mental energy is up. New directions. Self-directing. Original concepts. New and fresh approach to situations.

Business appointments (apartment or house rental or purchase). Day of man, government, father, brother, husband, business. Possible advancement. Good for big occasions and sales. Birth is possible.

2-DAY PINNACLE

A slowdown. Peaceful day. Attend to details. A day of retrospection and introspection. Watch your nerves. There may be pettiness if the details get to you. Putting home in order. A sensitive, psychic flow is felt. Depression, especially if you are left alone. Dates. Crying spell when coupled with a 9 month. Friendships, cooperation, togetherness. Friends, mates, bonding. Mother, sister, wife, daughter. Sharing, cooperation, sensitivity, feelings, nervousness, are all key words for a 2 day. Friends call to share their accomplishments and worries. You could find yourself caught between warring factions. It is a good time to negotiate and work things out to a peaceful end. Fair for gambling. Timing is everything.

.

3-DAY PINNACLE

Personality. Love and affection; artistic and creative time. Short trips. Good day for relationships. Not a good work day, labor. Social time and a time of visits with friends. A day involving grandparents and children.

Money may be squandered on clothes, jewelry, and partying. Talking, groups, and gathering. Birth in the family. Good for public relations, charm, sex, communicating. Doing things with the help of others. Social contacts can bring opportunity.

4-DAY PINNACLE

Bills due, order or priority tested. Money is tight. Systems may not work. This is a period of breakdowns and accidents. Laying cornerstones, work, order, and organization. Planning a project, repairing things. Mechanical appliances may break down. If you are traveling, the trip may be hard, or with no manifestation of interest. Watch for breaking law (speeding). Body may break down, accidents, sickness, may not feel well. You may feel held down, limited, or restricted; may get lost. You must get all of the facts before acting.

5-DAY PINNACLE

Don't bother planning today; it won't help. Promote yourself. Change, travel, conversations, take short trips, short visits, shopping, sex, food, buying, selling. Restless energy, sharing ideas. Personal magnetism. Ideas conveyed, communication, meeting new people, activity, fast thinking, good at sparring (verbally or otherwise).

Overeating, overindulgence. A day of excesses. Expanding frontiers. Act now.

6-DAY PINNACLE

Assuming and taking care of responsibilities, especially with family and job. A day of home and family. Closeness and fights. Job and money day, but could go either way. Quiet pleasures. Lasting accomplishments. Home hunting. Watch for pushing your point too hard; don't crusade or hard-sell. Not a great day for finances. Good for entertaining at home. Affections are strong. Seek counsel if needed. Not a good day for new projects.

7-DAY PINNACLE

Reading, learning, meditation, analysis. You may feel a need to be alone. Personal decisions regarding philosophy, religion, or bills and legality. Inner tension requires you to watch your nerves. Follow hunches. Legality may include loss of money, a day in court, or answering for past violations. Meeting of people for readings, church, spiritual purposes or ceremonies. Closeness is quick in coming under these conditions. Vibration is somewhat soft with a critical attitude inside. A need for quiet. Sensitivity to outside stimuli. High tension. Low energy, moodiness. It is important to develop a strategy for life. This is a time to judge yourself first so that others won't have to.

8-DAY PINNACLE

Lawsuits, court dates, business decisions. Use tact, but go for it. Good for gambling. Sell yourself, but not self-righteously. Put money matters in order. Money will change hands. Paperwork should be done. This may be a spiritual day. This is a day to be the executive, or boss, but don't be too demanding. A day of working with authority figure such as government, law enforcement, judicial, business, boss. Establish your rights. A day of justice. Organize, pay bills, or receive payment. Authority. Use tact. It is very important to have a solid strategy before acting.

9-DAY PINNACLE

Endings (trips end), emotional, giving, occult, readings. This is a soft day (not a business day). Don't be selfish. A day for visiting with friends. Spiritual day especially with a 9 month. You won't want to work today. Emotions will be very high and open. There is a need for reassurance. Emotional outbursts, and losses. The ending or pause of patterns or lifestyles. May want to leave work early. Friends may call long distance. The giving of gifts or receiving of gifts that are from the heart. Visit distant friends. Feeling of anxiety is common.

INTERPRETING A CHART

The simplest rule of interpreting a chart divides the numbers into three families. These families will be referred to as the primary, secondary, and tertiary families. They are so named because of the degree of influence each of the families has on the individual. The primary family will always have the most influence on the person. Next will come the secondary family. Lastly, the tertiary family will have the least influence in the chart.

Here is the flow of influence in a person's chart:

1. Soul, Expression, Life Path.

2. Quiescent Self, First Cycle and Challenge, Major Challenge.

3. All other numbers in the chart.

Important notes:

A. The Soul, Expression, and Life Path make up the primary family. More information may be obtained by referring to the Enmass section and looking under the numbers that match the number of the Soul and Expression. Example: Enmass1 or Enmass5 .

B.   The Quiescent Self, First Cycle (Attainment and Challenge), and the Major Challenge of the birth date make up the secondary family.

C.   The Subconscious Self makes up the tertiary family.

D.   Any influence within any family will soften or cancel the influence of the opposing numbers.

E.   Any similar influences between numbers will increase those influences.

F.   A primary family vibration will always overcome any opposing influences of a secondary or tertiary family.

G.   Any vibration in a secondary family will overcome an opposing number in a tertiary family.

H.   The Plane Of Expression is the only tertiary vibration that can be clearly seen to influence the other families of numbers by causing stress or bending of the Expression even when the numbers are in opposition. It is like adding pigments to the established color of the Expression.

I.   When in doubt do not read the tertiary numbers. It all sounds reasonable, logical and simple, but there is a catch. When two opposing influences appear within the primary numbers they will set up a struggle within the psyche. It is how this stress is resolved that determines the personality of the individual. The opposing numbers can meet head on, and like two trains meeting on the same track, cancel out one another into rubble, at a combined speed of zero.

Or they could be like those same two trains pulling against each other; there would be a dynamic tension in the person as they seek for ways to satisfy two opposing wants, hope, paths, or desires. But the best is a harmony. This is where the numbers find a common meeting ground of attributes, and coexist, having merged their vectors in order to find a compromise natural to both as they react one with the other. If a person is a 5 Soul, 2 Quiescent Self, 7 Expression, and 5 Life Path, these numbers would make up the primary family. With a 2 First Cycle Attainment, 3 First Cycle Challenge, and a 5 Major Challenge; these numbers would make up the secondary family. All numbers remaining are considered tertiary numbers.

J. No one is just one number. All of the information listed under a number is the information for only that number. Any discrepancy between the personality and the information indicated by the number is due to the influences of other numbers in the person's chart. All numbers in the chart must be taken into account before a reading is done. Cancel out conflicting points, soften points that are in opposition, and stress points that are related and interdependent.

Anne Burton

NUMEROLOGY, PSYCHOLOGY, AND COUNSELING

PSYCHOLOGICAL PRINCIPLES

Before we counsel clients or examine ourselves there are certain psychological principles to observe. The first rule is that no matter what the number is it will have a yin (feminine), or yang (masculine) influence in part according to the sex of the person. There is more Eros, feminine, "relating" in the female matrix; and more logos, thinker, "provider" in the male matrix. This will slant the manifestation of the numbers in our society. In our culture today there may be stress for one to abandon part of their nature in order to build the inferior part. This can happen to a woman who gives up feeling in order to just think. This will produce an unhappy and stressed persona. And the more superior the suppressed type is, the more stress is produced. This stress will come out in the weakest point of the personality, (the challenge of the birth date or missing numbers in the name). Thank goodness our society is slowly changing to allow people to be individuals.

The id is made of basic urges and instincts. It is driven by the pleasure principles, Eros and survival instincts. Most of its energy is directed toward the discharge of tensions associated with sex and aggression. This energy is called libido. Although there is not an exact match in meaning, the system used herein refers to this area

323

of influence as the " child." The idea of the "child" will be explained in detail later. In Numerology this is the **Soul.**

The ego is the executive, taking the primary mental images from the id and balancing it with external reality. It is the thinking, planning, and deciding part of us. It is the consciousness that puts things off until it is appropriate, or squelches unwise actions. We shall label this part of the psyche as the adult. Since the adult is the only logical, reasonable part of our inner voices, it is the only one which should make our decisions for us. It roughly equates to the "adult" in our makeup, and the **Expression** in Numerology.

The superego is the judge or censor of the thoughts and actions of the ego. It is the conscience, the part that draws conclusions as to what is right or wrong based on past punishments and reactions. The superego contains the ego-ideal, which is all of the things that we perceived our parent image approved of. It is referred to as the parent herein. It is the internalized parent. To match the ego-ideal is to feel pride, accomplishment and success.

In Numerology this the **Quiescent Self.** It is this judge (superego), when under-developed that allows for criminal, delinquent, or sociopathic trends. If overly strict, the superego yields rigidity, inhibitions, and guilt. The superego and the id are unconscious, but the ego is partly conscious and partly not. It is, however, the personality that we see. It seems sociopaths are people with weak links between ego and superego. It could be that the ego is not functioning as a referee, or that the proper "parent" is not being supplied by the superego.

According to several texts, when we speak of sociopaths, we are talking about those who are not good at it, since many of the world leaders, entertainers, and people of power are sociopaths. It often takes manipulation, deceit, and cold use of others to rise to power. Strangely enough, that they don't learn from experience; thus they do not draw conclusions as to right and wrong behavior. The id is the child, the superego is the parent, and the ego is the adult.

The ego, however, is divided into three parts. First is that which is seen; this is our persona. Second is the subconscious. This is how we deal with our feelings. The third is the interface between the id and the superego. This interface is called the **Planes of Expression.**

It is the arbitrator between the "parent and child" which is responsible for finding a way to please both "child and parent." The ego decides if the time, place, and request is possible under the "parent's" restraints. It then uses this to subdue the id (child). When the interface is weak then the child seems to run wild, not hearing the parent as it should. Part of the Planes of Expression represents the views or positions of the parent with regard to the different aspects of life - emotional, mental, physical, intuitive. A more complete picture can be had by combining this with the insights from the Quiescent Self.

ACTING IT OUT OR WORKING IT OUT

All of us are either "acting out" or "working out" our problems. As we go through the day and receive different triggers that relate back to our youth, or bring up past emotions, we must, in some way, dissipate them. This is either done by working them out in such a way as to release us from their affects, or acting them out in a way as to relieve pressures while not addressing the true issue causing the pain.

In working out a problem there must be a conscious understanding and evaluation that not only takes care of the immediate feelings of anger or hurt, but also works toward a healthy emotional equilibrium concerning the basic problem.

In acting out, a person feels a stress brought about by the same mechanism, but there is no conscious understanding or healing. Instead, the person's emotions are repressed, anger and hurt are "swallowed down" and are harbored on some level until such time that the psyche is full. The unconscious overflow of this anger and hurt comes out in attitude and actions aimed at making a statement that their fear and repression has kept them from making consciously.

These statements are almost always designed to go in two directions. The first is regarding the self, and is self-worthlessness, self-destructiveness, or self-protection. The second is fear, anger, and hurt caused by the people or situations that brought about the first feelings.

We must ask ourselves, are we working things out, or are we acting things out? If we are working things out we will not keep repeating past mistakes. We will come to understand, and take responsibility for our lives and all of the things in it. Like a pendulum that seeks its center, we will find ourselves off balance less and less, and mistakes will occur less frequently.

If we are acting things out we will find it hard to take responsibility for our lives. It will always be the other person's fault. We will find ourselves consumed with an anger, fear, or pain, and striking out or acting without thought. Sometimes even before we realize it, we will say, "Look what you made me do." We will repeat patterns and mistakes over and over without getting any closer to having it right. Worst of all, we won't think about it, or, if we do, it will seem hopeless because we will not admit that we have control, and therefore responsibility, over our own actions.

There are always choices. Either change yourself, or change your situation. It is never an option to try and change another person. That's not your place. It can only cause them to have negative emotions toward you. And those, too, will either have to be worked out, or acted out. It is a logical but bizarre twist that can compel us to act out in a manner that seems opposite to what is our normal personality.

This same reflex will make the personality types associated with the numbers swing from extreme to extreme. They will be mirror images contained within the same person. As an example of this phenomenon, please consider the many priests and clergy that are being uncovered today as con-men, homosexuals, and abusers.

When we sense a problem in our personality, we are faced with the question of what to do about it. We could face the problem head on, start into therapy, and work through the pain until we are healed. This is the most difficult, but most rewarding choice. We could deny the existence of problems and continue to act without control.

Then there is the worst choice of all. We can decide to put ourselves in a situation that we believe will defuse the bomb within us. We believe that if we make it very difficult to act on any of our imbalanced impulses, we have fixed the problem. So we lock ourselves away in an environment that is the antithesis of the nature of the problem, as a shield between us and it.

Truth is like cream, it will always rise to the top. And as the stratification occurs, we start to act out again. We do so this time in an environment chosen for its purity and piety. In this environment we preach to ourselves, pray for ourselves, even do penance for what we are fighting within ourselves. We cloister ourselves away, and symbolically we cloister the sickness away inside of us. Day after day we beat them back, but like the dragon in the basement, they are always there; waiting and promising to one day break through. In spite of our walls, denials, or whips that we use to control it, we never dealt with the problem. Problems that are not solved forever will forever recur.

The difference between saint and sinner, then, is the wholeness of the person, and this wholeness is the integration of those levels in ourselves that we consider anathema. These hidden pockets must be faced, conquered, and integrated back into the personality. We can expect that while the "disintegration" is in progress, it will cause the affected numbers and types to appear as opposites. It must be remembered that they will usually swing within the extremes of the same type. A 5 could be either a communicator or a con artist. A 6 could be priest or pervert. An 8 could be a fair judge or ruthless.

When typing a person or examining ourselves, we have to remember this in order not to be deceived, or to deceive ourselves. If these blind and deaf areas of ours could be opened to us, and we could learn to hear and recognize the voices and feelings of our three parts; the child, the parent, and the adult. We could allow the adult to make our choices in its logical way. We would not have to be driven and blind sided by voices and feelings from our past that we barely recognize. Our life would be ours. While we would not get rid of the feelings and voices, we would learn to identify them in order to quantify, compensate, and mute their effects in our lives.

VOICES

Inside each of us there resides a trio of voices. The voices in the trio are hardly ever in harmony. The voice of the child that we were can be heard during the times of escapism and other more emotional behavior. The voice of the parent is usually associated with restrictive, more sterile, behavior. The voice of the adult that we have become represents a reasonable, moderate point of balance. It is the only part of us that has the ability to act with forethought and logic.

Child	Parent
Sex addiction	Prudishness
Alcoholism	Abstinence

Drug abuse	Self-condemnation
Being late	Anxiety about being punctual
Not keeping appointments	Stickler for details
Doesn't accept responsibility	Blames self for everything
Passive/aggressive	Disciplinarian
Passive / indecisive	Sternness
Being silly	Always serious
Abused	Abuser
Sloppy	Obsessively clean
Chaotic	An order addict
Emotional	Repressed
Food addiction	Eating disorders
Hypochondria	Stoicism

The above is a list of common actions and attitudes. It gives a general idea of the voice that we are listening to and by what we are being driven, based on the outward manifestation of our problem. The adult is the side of us that is reasonable, logical, understanding, moderate, and balanced. Here are two quick checks to see how in touch with the adult you are:

1. Ask yourself how immature and selfish you really are. The honesty of this answer will reveal volumes.

2. Remember the last time that you made a serious mistake in a relationship. Weren't you aware that it was a foolish choice when you made it?

These answers will add insight into yourself. If you have arrived at the point that you in touch with your own behavior, it is only a short step to being in control of it.

IF YOU ARE CONFUSED BETWEEN WHAT IS RIGHT AND WRONG SIMPLY EXAMINE THE INTENT.

MOTIVES

One of the most frequent causes of friction in relationships is the misinterpretation of another person's intentions, based on their words or actions. More often than not, we attribute our motives to their actions. We fail to realize that each number functions from a different base of motives. The worst thing that we could do is to apply our basic motives and drives to the responses of others.

As an example, let us assume a situation of conflict or disagreement between an 8 type and a 2 type. As the issue heats up the 2, operating from a base that seeks to help and empathize and is afraid of rejection, is likely to take a more passive, even manipulative stance. Women are more likely to be passive-aggressive than men. This is probably because in the societies of the world, generally women used to be less educated and usually physically weaker. Those who are weaker, or see themselves as being weaker, physically and/or educationally, find other ways to persuade and to preserve their individuality. This is done with emotional manipulation.

2s hate confrontation; it frightens them on a deeper level, so they turn more toward manipulative means first in order to get their way. After all, everyone wants to get their wishes met. Everyone has an agenda. The 8, on the other hand, is likely to become aggressive and will seek to control the situation from a base that is power and control-oriented and a fear of being taken advantage of. The 8 will view the pattern of the 2 as being unsure, weak, even cowardly. It is not.

The 2 is probably quite sure of how he/she feels, and knows what he/she wants. They are simply going to try to keep harmony and try to help the 8. This does not mean that they won't try to manipulate the 8, but it will be a passive/aggressive stance that the 8 is not likely to see. The 8 may interpret the actions of the 2 as a retreat. 8s will attempt to advance to fill the space in the argument that they think has been vacated by the 2. The result can only be that the 2 is going to view the 8 as a bully who can not be reasoned with. Actually the 8 loves to reach a compromise by "banging heads" at times. They believe in a peace through testing and trying one another. This is a type of territorial behavior.

The 8 will be confused by the 2s lack of steadfastness. They will assume that they don't care about the issue as much as the 8, or that they aren't willing to fight for what they believe in. The 2 may lose respect in the eyes of the 8, simply because they interpreted the actions of the other in the light of their own motives. The de-evolution of the relationship into the bully verses the victim is one possible outcome of this scenario.

Yet, if at any time either of them stopped and truly understood the basic motives of the other, they could have saved themselves from this. By understanding the other person we can try to speak and understand their language. We can know their fears and work around them. We can gently try to reassure them that we are not trying to do to them what they fear most. By knowing where the other person is coming from, we can help and not hinder the aim of harmony and peace in our families, work places, and lives.

Here is a quick reference list of the types, and their likely base of operations and how it will manifest in a fight.

Type 1 - Intolerant of others' ideas, fears being wrong and the condemnation that it may bring. Egocentric, arrogant, judgmental, critical, cold. The base is one of uncertainty and the fear of coming up short. Fear of falling short of their ideals and being judged harshly. They fight against the parents' critical attitude of them which they hear in the voices of others.

Type 2 - Histrionic, prying, emotionally intrusive. Insincere, uses false flattery, manipulative. They beat around the bush, and express aggression in an indirect way. They try to put themselves on the moral high ground. From there they will fight the side issues that they can win without directly attacking the main argument which they may lose. The base of the 2 is a fear of abandonment and rejection. They want to keep the peace and be a helper. They need to know that they have a place in the hearts of others, but this is only to insure that they will not be disregarded.

Type 3 - Haughty, holier-than-thou, arrogant, sarcastic. The 3 assumes that they should be admired all of the time, even when they are wrong. The basic drive of the 3 is fear of losing face. They refuse to be just one of the crowd. Their egos are very strong, and they demand attention.

Type 4 - Escapes through drugs, alcohol, sex, religion. Stubborn. Hides feelings. Trouble in expressing emotions.

Type 5 - Quick-witted, sarcastic, tries to jump quickly between subjects to confuse the opponent. The motive of the 5 seems to be a fear of losing their freedom.

Type 6 - Tries to take control as a parent/authority figure. Self-righteous, possessive, passive/aggressive.

Type 7 - Can be devious and sneaky. They tend to hide and/or distort the truth. Their favorite game is to tell part of the truth in order to back up their claims. They are brooding and withdrawn when angry. The drive that the seven feels is a type of paranoia.

Type 8 - Will not admit that they are wrong. No compromise. A tyrant, the boss.

Type 9 - Scattered energy. Wants things to remain the same. Fearful of change. Temper and theatrics when threatened.

THE PARENT TRAP

As with any idea or system that attempts to pigeonhole or categorize, there are obvious drawbacks. The main problem is that people are not simple so they do not fit neatly into one category. If the system being used is functional, and the categories are defined properly, you will be able to see yourself, or those who you are applying the system to, in one main category. There will be secondary applications in other categories, but they will be weaker and their effects will be weaker. This rule applies to this list as well as any other system of pigeonholing.

One night while a lady and I sat and talked over our latest revelation, she mentioned that after forty years of feeling put down by her mother she realized that her mother was jealous of her. This started my mind wandering. In the following days I thought of all the parents that I knew and how they related to their children. Some were very good and supportive. Others pushed their children relentlessly.

Last night I fell asleep trying to find some similarities between this plethora of parents. In the morning I had the answer. It seemed to have bubbled up from my subconscious in a way that only Carl Jung could appreciate. All parents interact with their children in the following ways: supportive, manipulative, dismissive, vicarious, jealous, abusive. Each of these postures will produce several responses in the child.

The supportive parent is one with no agenda or personal expectations laid on the child. The parent allows the child his own goals and then supports the child in his endeavors. It takes a healthy, balanced parent to love and support their child with no strings attached. This is the kind of parent that is most likely to produce an emotionally healthy child. Before you go grabbing this label for yourself let me point out that only ten to twenty out of a hundred parents can even come close to this type...so dig deeper.

The manipulative parent is the parent who tries to interfere, run, orchestrate, detour, plan, or otherwise manipulate the child's life. It can be as apparently kind as showing up uninvited to clean the house, (which says to the child that he can't even clean correctly), or as intrusive as always offering an opinion when not asked. The manipulative parent wants to navigate the child through life in various degrees.

The strange thing is that the parent is usually unhappy with their own life. The parent could be wanting another chance to get it right through the child's life. This is a form of the vicarious type. They could simply be a dominating, controlling type which is forever seeking to increase their base of control and power. Whatever the reason, they are attempting to take the child's life from it and run it to one degree or another. We all have a right to our own opinions, to learn, to live our own lives, and to be wrong while doing it. If the ploy of manipulation, which is normally covert, becomes stronger or more overt, the manipulation becomes control. This parent controls through threats, blustering, force of will, or force of intellect. They simply shout the child down or reason the child out of their feelings.

Like the jealous parent, the manipulative type will also steal the child's joy. They are convinced that their child should live, believe and act as they do. It hasn't dawned on them that they are not happy in life, and anyone who follows their path may not be happy either. This parent tends to raise children who are somewhat rebellious. They had to get strong to save their individualism. Sadly, if the

338

parent's personality overtakes the child's and the child's will is broken, the child can turn inward and become incapable of making clear or strong choices or commitments.

The manipulative parent is one of the most common. They slowly eat away at the child's self-esteem and confidence. This is done by trying to tell the child what to do or trying to manipulate the child, which sends a clear message to the child that they don't know enough, aren't capable enough, or aren't adult enough to run their own lives. This is very damaging to the ego and can only end in resentment for both. The parent will raise the kind of child which he is fighting so hard against, and the child will be resentful for not being able to simply be a person without having to wage a war to get that right.

The dismissive parent is one who is detached from the ups and downs of their child. They are usually too caught up in their own life to give much thought or care about the problems that may be faced by a child. The parents that fit this category are either very self-absorbed or are very stressed out due to the demands of life. This doesn't matter to the child, however. All they know is that they are not important. No matter how good the child is, the parent doesn't seem to notice.

They send the message to the child that they are not important nor loved enough. This causes some children to seek more negative or destructive means of gaining attention. As a general rule, a child will try first to gain approval, when he cannot obtain the parents' approval, he will then try simply to get attention. This is a situation that can escalate quickly into acts that are designed for their shock value in order to simply get a reaction from the parent.

A subcategory of the dismissive parent is that parent who lets the child get away with anything. A child that runs rough-shod over Mom or Dad is a child who does not feel cared for. The message is that the child can do whatever he wants because the parent doesn't care. A wholesome discipline is a way to show love. It says that you care enough to watch out for the child. It forms a feeling of love and security. It also will serve as a blueprint for their life choices in later years. It is sad to think that there are children whose very existence is acknowledged so seldom that they aren't comfortable with their own worth or personhood.

The vicarious parent has many hidden agendas that they heap on the child. All of their wishes and dreams, even those things that they always wished that they could have done, are written into the child's life plan. Fathers drive their sons in sports. Others coax them to follow in their footsteps. Mothers drive their daughters to be beauty pageant contestants, cheerleaders, or other favorite dreams. Parents demand that the children exceed all normal expectations in academia.

The parent has two reasons for doing these things. First is ego. They demand the privilege of being proud, even to brag about their child. It is as if the child were their property to be displayed. The child feels driven. If the child can live up to the parent's demands they will be constantly displayed and touted as something special. This can quickly build an over-inflated ego and an expectation that they should be admired by all.

The jealous parent is the most dangerous of all. They are difficult to spot and covert in their attacks. These parents are usually unhappy with their lives. They are reminded of this fact whenever someone, even their child, seems to do well or be happy. They will demean, cut, and sabotage the child or their feelings. The parent may not attend significant events in the child's life, and in the more unguarded moments the parent will let their resentment slip.

There is a saying that within flashes of anger true feelings are revealed. The child will feel as if they do not deserve to succeed, much less exceed. They may feel that it is wrong because it makes Mom or Dad feel bad when they do well.

The last and easiest to identify is the abusive parent. They can either be emotionally abusive, physically abusive, or sexually abusive. Emotional abuse most often takes the form of verbal abuse, but not always. Sometimes it can be a mean spirited emotional tyranny. The abuse type has anger, rage, or a need to ultimately control others.

There isn't enough time to tell of all that this can do to the child. The abused can grow up to abuse. Abused wives can choose abusive husbands to continue the pattern. The abused child grows up to have a distorted self-image, and most of all, they are filled with pain and anger. It is these two feelings that will be the stumbling blocks until they are dealt with. Look at your parents from an objective point of view and categorize them by placing them into one of the basic categories. All parents will fit into one primary place and possibly a secondary place. For example, abusive parents are often dismissive also. A jealous parent will probably be dismissive in order to vent jealousy in a passive/aggressive way.

You must turn this mirror on yourself in order to learn and grow. Keep in mind that only 20 percent or less of children actually receive healthy parenting, so don't be too easy on yourself. Are you supportive, manipulative, dismissive, jealous, vicarious, or abusive? Any type number can be any type of parent, but there are noticeably higher percentages of correlations between certain numbers and Enneagram types to parent types. This makes sense when we consider that there are types of people more prone to nurture, and others more prone to abuse.

The nurturing types are usually manipulators, by the way, so they don't get off that easily either. Any healthy type can be a supportive parent, but the other types, which represent specific anomalies, are more prone to be found in certain Enneagram and numerological types. The manipulative type is prone to be a 2, 3, or 8. The 8 and the 1 will step over the line into the area of controlling, However, I have placed these two types together since I view them as greater and lesser degrees of one another.

The dismissive parent is usually the 1, 4, or 5 type. They are too involved with their own life or escapism to be bothered by others. The jealous parent can be a 3, 6, or 8. Any unhappy person tends to be jealous or envious, but these numbers show a greater bent in that direction.

The 1, 3 and 9 can get more from vicarious living than others. They do it for their own pride in the child as if it makes them look better as parents. 4, 6, and 8 are the tyrannical and abusive types. They do so because of anger, rage, or a need to control. Remember, any number can be any type. Within the context of relationships there are many ways of classifying reaction.

More 1s, 6s, and 8s tend to express anger, aggression, tyranny, and confrontation in their relationships. 5s, 7s, and 9s tend to express appetite, sensuality, and a peculiar drive to consume things, including the relationship. 2s, 3s, and 4s are prone toward control, ownership, and control of the relationship. This can be overt or by passive/aggressive means.

Since any number can express any type, these are only a higher percentage of occurrences. Don't assume that just because you are not a number mentioned for that type of parent that you can't be in that category. You can be anything you choose to be, good or bad.

WHAT TO DO NEXT

So you have read the personality profiles and the psychological overview, and you are thinking that you may have a problem... don't we all!

The first thing to do is to allow the shock of having identified and admitted your strengths and weaknesses sink in. This is the first in a three-step procedure. Most people will not admit to having a problem, therefore most people never start getting better. You must hold on to the realization. Write it down in detail. Keep it, and read it over again later when your zeal for improving yourself starts to wane. Be specific in your insights, and don't let yourself off the hook.

If your problem relates to choosing a particular mate, don't excuse yourself by saying that you didn't know how he was when you married him/her. I want you to understand that you did indeed know. There is no way that a person can hide all that they are from anyone who is around them for more than a few days. Our subconscious is more observant than that. It picks up on every nuance, slip of the tongue, and faux pas.

The axiom that should always be remembered is that you are as damaged as the people that you choose. It is difficult to take responsibility for the actions that get us into bad situations, and even more difficult to take responsibility for actions that keep us in abusive situations. Weak and trite excuses are those such as, "I stay with this person for the children." This is a "hot button" of mine since what you are saying is that you are staying in an abusive relationship so that the kids can experience a bad childhood, and by being exposed to abuse within the home, grow up to be abused, or to abuse.

The next most stated excuse for staying is that there is no place to go. There are many homes for battered women and children. The services are free and confidential. Your whereabouts are kept secret. Many will even train you for a job and allow you to start life anew.

Given, there are not as many places for the abused man to go, which is a shame, since the dysfunctional woman is capable of inflicting as much harm as a man. Usually women inflict their harm in more passive/aggressive and covert means so as not to openly attack and suffer open physical conflict. It is nonetheless just as damaging. The man in this type of relationship should be just as concerned with the long-term emotional scars.

The last of the three big excuses is that of, "I just love them too much to leave them." If they are abusive, then you are saying that you literally love them more than life itself, since you are willing to allow your possible death. These are worst case problems but they are numerous and growing. I am not saying that anyone in a dysfunctional relationship should leave. I speak only to those whose very minds and bodies are under attack.

I strongly believe that the fastest way to start healing is to stop the injury first, and then begin the treatment. The highest percentage of success comes from couples who begin the sojourn together. Just as the abused is suffering from lack of wholeness in order to allow the actions, so is the abuser suffering from a lack of wholeness in having the rage and anger built up in them to do these things.

If you are the abuser and you are reading this right now, you may even be feeling resentment and anger at having to examine this issue. If you throw this book down you may keep repeating the actions that you yourself find embarrassing and not acceptable. You must get in touch with the fact that you are willfully hurting another human being. By your actions you are saying that their battered psyche and broken heart is not as important as the release you get by beating them, yelling at them or hurting them emotionally. The same rules apply for emotional or physical abuse. If you are one of these people, admit it. We must recognize our problems, admit and take responsibility for our problems, and then put forth the effort to fix our problem.

Strangely enough, this is where the majority of people stop. Almost everyone runs into the truth about themselves at one time or another, but most shrug it off and go on as if nothing has happened. They are the ones that say, "It is my life and I can live it the way I want." Some will say, "Well, at least I'm not as bad as some." Well, you're bad enough, and you might as well admit it now before things get any worse.

Of those people who enter into therapy or a self-help program, most get stuck in a stage of recognition. That is to say, that they recognize and understand the problem, but they are not putting forth the effort to change. The last and most painful step is the effort to fix the problem.

Thus far we have looked with objectivity at our numbers, specifically our Soul, Expression, First Cycle, First Challenge, and Major Challenge. We have discerned from the numbers, along with our ability to look at ourselves, that we have areas of imbalance. We have noted parallels between our, childhood problems and the problems described in this manual. We can then assume that the effects of these problems are also, at least in part, ours. The Soul and Expression numbers should be studied along with those numbers in the "Enmass" section.

Some of the common causes and effects are discussed in these pages. If you do not believe that there is any problem or area of dysfunction in your life, there is no point in reading further except for the gaining of general knowledge. We can't fix other people, and it usually causes confusion and resentment when we try, so I urge you once again to attend to the log in your own eye before attempting a speck-ecthyma on anyone else.

Now we must talk about what to do. First ask yourself how much pain, insecurity, or misunderstanding your blind spot caused you and those you love. Next ask yourself if you truly wish to change. Would you go through the pain of brutal self-examination? Do you want it enough to be totally honest about your motives, actions, and intentions? Do you want to change enough to police yourself and be consistent just about your insights? If so, then we will begin.

Let us take an action, almost any action. Examine that action and its purpose. The purpose that is on the surface which you relate to at first, is not the true purpose. The true purpose can only be seen when you have answered the question "why" for the final time. Let us suppose that a person had an affair. If I asked them why they did it they would probably say that their mate didn't love them or make them happy. This would peg the question of whose voice they were hearing, and whether this feeling was due to a blind spot in them, the mate, or both.

No one can force you to do anything. Anyone can do, or not do, whatever they want, if they are willing to pay the price. The price may be high. It may mean your life. But if an action is worth the giving of your life, then there is nothing to stop you from trying. So let us quickly bypass the trap of, "They made me do it." "Now why did you have the affair?", I asked. "To be happy." "Why did you think that would make you happy?" "Because it makes me feel like somebody loves and wants me."

"Why does the fact that you are wanted make you feel happy?" "Because it makes me feel as if I am worth something." "Why do you feel that the worth that others ascribe to you makes you more worthy?" "Because I am unsure of my own worth."

At this point of the scenario, a long silence ensued and then a story emerged of a child who had been alone and lonely for years. From the time that he was in the first grade he had few friends. His parents had drunk socially, and his father began to drink excessively. They were always surrounded by their friends, but the child had few friends of his own. Since the lifestyle of the parents was so different from the child's in this area, it sent a message to the child that his way was wrong.

At that time the child had no way of correcting it, but slowly he sharpened his social skills and developed a somewhat magnetic personality. As time went on he amassed a group of friends, mostly women. He became a womanizer. As the image matched more and more closely that of the parents, the man felt like he was on target. The only problem was that the adoration of others was necessary in order to fulfill the image, and to quiet the voice of the parent.

Inconsistency of attention and lack of insight to the child's needs, had produced this blind spot. It could have gone in many different ways, but with this individual this was the result. By asking why? why? why? we get down to a point where there is no longer an easy answer. At this point the digging begins, and the needed insights come. It may be painful to admit to your own selfishness.

This man had to admit that it was more important for him to feel good than for him to be faithful to his wife. That is selfish, but we all have areas like that.

Why do you do those things that hurt you and your loved ones? Chances are you are being driven by voices that you don't understand. The numbers and types will give you some insight into whose voices you are listening to, and what they are saying. After this head start you must clarify and focus on the area. No two people are alike, so the information contained in the numbers is designed to be a general starting place. As anti-climactic as it seems, the only cure for a blind spot is awareness and discipline. Once you are aware of the existence of an inner voice that makes you feel a certain way, you must come to understand that feelings are not facts.

Feelings do not have to be acted upon. They do not impel you, they compel you. The difference is that in the final analysis, you are in control. It may help to repeat that when certain feelings come up. Feelings are not facts. I do not have to act on feelings. If there isn't anything that caused the feeling, it is only an inner voice anyway. You cannot trust your inner voices of the parent or child. Would you let a five year old plan and control your life? Would

351

you let someone who didn't care for you try to make you happy? The voices of the child and parent are like that. That is not to say that your real parents didn't love you; that is a separate issue; but because the voices usually come out of times of pain or trauma where a piece of you has been left behind, they are not balanced voices.

After you have found the problem you must start to recognize and identify whose voice you are hearing. It is only the adult that can be allowed to plan your actions, not the voice that says "Nobody loves me," or "You are never good enough," or "You will feel like your worth more if that person wants you." Only the adult is to be listened to and acted upon. That voice is the one asking, "What will be the final outcome?" or "Is this the best course of action for the most lasting good?"

The adult can suggest that we go through suffering in order to improve ourselves, the child cannot. The parent can suggest that we serve and suffer in a situation indefinitely, but the adult would not. In order not to repress feelings, the child and parent voices should be allowed to "feel and say" what ever they wish. It is normal to feel afraid at times as long as you admit that it is the child's voice and fear. It is normal to feel guilty for not going to work even though you are on your death bed - you know that it is the parent. They do not have to be acted on.

352

When you understand which voice is which, you can allow expression, but not action. In this way you will learn to live your life as an adult. It takes recognition, understanding, and the commitment to examine your thoughts and feelings before they become actions. As time goes by this will become second nature. This is what balanced adults do. They are people who may have some unpleasant feelings at times, but they are not driven by them. They are in control of their lives, their voices are not.

NOTES ON TIME AND PERSONALITY

In the calculations and predictions that emerge from the year, four month, month and day cycles, there is a simple but nebulous influence to take into account, the personality. Whether you are reading yourself or someone else, we must be forever aware that different personalities function and react quite differently to outside stimuli. Like a jewel that is turned so that the appropriate facets are in line, you must contemplate, feel, and sense the strengths and weaknesses of the personality, and line that up with the time and situations being encountered.

The numbers and Enmass sections of this book will give you insights into the various points to watch. If, for example, the year is a 9 and the person is primarily a 5 type, we can assume that they are accustomed to changes in their life, and that while ends are always stressful, they will handle it well. On the other hand, if the person is mostly a 4 type, we can expect there to be emotions that tend to be repressed and not handled well. There may even be a journey into escapism.

Instead of there being a never-ending list of comparisons between types and times at this point, it is best if you get firmly in your mind what the year and other cycles have to offer as an environment and then place the personality type in that environment.

No person is only one number, so we can suggest what attributes would be best accentuated, and what pitfalls to watch for, in order to make things better for them in this period. The same rules apply for the mixing of personalities. If two 5s married there would be lots of activity and sensuality, but not a great amount of responsibility.

If a 5 and a 6 married there would be a balance; however, there would be friction as the 6 wanted to nest and be at home with the responsibilities that they are comfortable with, while the 5 wanted to run away and have fun. You see, time and personalities are carved from the same stuff, just as energy and matter are the same substance wearing different disguises.

GOING UP, GOING DOWN, OR GOING TO SLEEP?

In an earthquake there is no place to run, nowhere to hide, and nothing to hold on to. The very thing that you have put your trust in is shaken. Solid as a rock has no meaning here. In each type there is a fault line and just as with mother earth, when enough pressure builds up at the fault it will give way and slip. The result is change in the psychic terrain.

According to the health and integration of the individual, this can mean growth or the descent of the psyche. The metamorphosis takes place when the personality is stressed in such a way that the positive or negative traits line up similar traits in another type. What happens next is nothing short of quantum physics. Though a person's type will not change; if an ascent occurs, the main personality type begins to spread out into the next type adding more possibilities of expression, balance, and understanding. If a descent occurs, the main type is crowded into the space that the two types have in common. This area is accented and the result is an imbalance.

As in quantum physics, the personality either gains enormous potential as it seeks the next level, or it loses most of itself and descends into the negativity that the types have in common.

355

Anne Burton

The path of ascent: 1-5 5-7 7-8 8-2 2-4 4-1 3-6 6-9 9-3

The path of descent: 1-4 4-2 2-8 8-7 7-5 5-1 3-9 9-6 6-3

TYPE ONE

Positive ones are self-assured natural leaders, reliable, productive, motivated, self starters, and they are idealists.

Negative ones are judgmental, inflexible, self-righteous, critical, controlling, perfectionist. They can't stand to be wrong.

Fault line - reactive, angry, over reaction to a critical internal voice leads to a defensive anger. In their fight not to be wrong they turn to a false self righteousness.

Ascent- from 1 to 5. The release from anger and the need to be right will lead to a freedom and spontaneity that will open up new experiences and energies. You will be lighter and more carefree.

Descent- from 1 to 4. By getting locked into self criticism, the one can spiral down into depression and moodiness. The result is a self absorbed guilt.

TYPE TWO

Positive twos are loving, helping, caring, empathic, supportive. They have good attention to detail. They are the diplomats.

Negative twos are passive/aggressive, manipulative, emotionally weak, given to feelings of martyrdom. They have the egotism that comes from thinking that they are secretly behind the scenes making things happen. They have the idea that people could not get along without them.

Fault line - emotion repression. Unsure of their own feelings. Taking on the feelings of others. Trying to control though passive/aggressive manipulation. They can become hostile if they don't think that they are properly appreciated, even though they have manipulated to get things done.

Ascent - from 2 to 4. By attending to their own feelings and learning how to be assertive the two will uncover a genuine warmth and earthiness. When the repressed emotions are swept away, a discerning logic will show though.

Descent- from 2 to 8. As the two's emotional repression and manipulation continues, it declines into an insensitivity, aggression, and crassness. If they can't get their way through compromise or manipulation, they try a demanding, aggressive approach.

TYPE THREE

Positive threes are optimistic, confident, energetic, outgoing, social, good networkers and communicators.

Negative threes are vain, deceptive, shallow, vindictive, jealous, competitive, perfectionists. They play the part that they have chosen to the hilt.

Fault line - deceit of self and others. An identity crisis occurs when their likes, dislikes, and feelings are suspended in order to portray what they decide is appropriate...the need to fit into the character that they have chosen means that at times they loose themselves in their part.

Ascent- from 3 to 6. By dropping all pretense and facades, along with the need to be accepted, the three will be loyal and caring. They will climb from the childlike approach of the three to the parental caring and solidness of the healthy six. Being true to their feelings, brings the three to a place of likable solidness.

Descent - as the three identity crisis reaches its breaking point the three starts to shut down. They start to vacillate between apathetic, and obsessive. As they loose themselves they sink in to an unassertive despair.

TYPE FOUR

Positive fours are warm, physical, creative, logical, down to earth, with a realistic approach to life.

Negative fours are depressed, guilt driven, stubborn, moody, self-absorbed, obsessed with what they think they could have been.

Fault line - a feeling of being wronged or held down. Self pity.   A dramatic or uncentered way of expressing feelings such as addictions.

Ascent- from 4 to 1.   By taking responsibility for their own actions and consequences, the four takes control over his own life. They become leaders and reliable, self disciplined people.

Descent - from 4 to 2. From depressed to repressed, the four devolves from self-absorbed to emotionally weak. From feelings of being wronged and held down to martyrdom.

TYPE FIVE

Positive fives are fun loving, spontaneous, imaginative, productive, quick, confident, curious, charming.

Negative fives are narcissistic, impulsive, undisciplined, restless, rebellious, unfocussed, critical, curt. They are masters at rationalization.

Fault line - a pervading feeling of emptiness is the force which drives the five to try and find an experience, or something in the physical world to fill the void. Greed and gluttony is the fault line.

Ascent - from 5 to 7. By realizing that the void within can't be filled from the outside, the five becomes stable. They turn experience into wisdom and impulsiveness into objectivity.

Descent- from 5 to 1. As more and more experiences are taken in, the five begins to fear that nothing can fill their emptiness, which then creates anger. This is acted out in the form of a critical, anxious, inflexible attitude.

TYPE SIX

Positive sixes are loyal, caring, practical, parental, responsible, care-givers.

Negative sixes are judgmental, ridged, defensive, unpredictable, paranoid. They distrust authority but need approval. This sets up a love\hate relationship.

Fault line - the fear of not being approved, together with the fear of authority figures, can get strong enough to tint the entire outlook. This is paranoia.

Ascent - from 6 to 9. Freeing themselves from the need of approval and the fears associated with this, the six becomes less limited and more universal in its outlook. The result is more open-mindedness, generosity, and inner peace.

Descent- from 6 to 3. As the fear of being approved of by their authority figures increases the paranoia starts to show itself. The six becomes more jealous and competitive, not wanting others to have more friends or approval than they. Judgment attitudes becomes vindictiveness as they slip into a shallow, vain posture.

TYPE SEVEN

Positive sevens are objective, wise, self-contained observers.

Negative sevens are snobbish, arrogant, stingy, critical, aloof, and emotionally removed.

Fault line - an attempt to fill the emptiness within is done with knowledge. As long as they are evolved with the mind, it takes their attention off of what they are feeling, (and what they are not feeling). They believe completely in the old adage that knowledge is power, especially when it is a secret to control someone with.

Ascent - from 7 to 8. As the seven gets more involved in the world, they start to put to use all that knowledge. They stop living in theory and start applying themselves. The result is a person to be looked up to and reckoned with. Capable, confident, direct, and in charge.

Descent - from 7 to 5. As the seven is wearied of more and more information and its lack of application to improve the human heart, they become restless. Nothing seems to satisfy them. They descend into a critical curtness. They become unfocused and sense the primary reason for gaining their knowledge is abandoned.

TYPE EIGHT

Positive eights are direct, authoritative, driven, self-confident, capable, assertive people with a strong sense of self.

Negative eights are controlling, insensitive, self-centered, domineering, aggressive, intimidating, bullies.

Fault line - a lust for power and control of their environment spreads out to include the people in it. There is an anger at not having everything in control and operating correctly or according to their wishes.

Ascent - from 8 to 2. When eights become truly secure with themselves, they drop the bravado and bossiness. They then let others make their own choices. They become supportive. They use their abilities to help and support others.

Descent - there are two problems with needing an ever increasing power base. First, there is no end to the desire. Second, as the area of control increases so does the energy requirements it takes to keep and run the territory. This will spread the eight so thin it will eventually collapse or stop and be dissatisfied. When this happens the eight becomes even more critical, negative, and arrogant. In an attempt to keep what they have, they become stingy and emotionally removed.

TYPE NINE

The positive nine is pleasant, peaceful, generous, receptive, and open minded.

The negative nine is apathetic, and forgetful. They vacillate between unassertive and stubborn; obsessive and apathetic.

Fault line - nines have the tendency to "zone-out or space-out". They think that if they do nothing then what is bothering them may go away. They can become passive/aggressive as they try to ignore their anger and disappointment. They fear change and want to keep things as they are. A known condition is preferable even if it is bad.

Ascent - from 9 to 3 When the nine takes things in hand, they free up all the energy that it took to keep their feelings suppressed. This energy shows itself as an outgoing, social confidence.

Descent - from 9 to 6. No feelings can be kept hidden without causing damage. In this case the strain takes its toll starting with unpredictability and emotional swings. The control of emotions turns to rigidity. The weakness it causes needs security to bolster and soothe the nine. If they do not get the security, the nine crystallizes into judgmental defensiveness.

I'VE ALWAYS HEARD VOICES INSIDE MY HEAD

Mimic, oppose, compensate. These are the only ways to deal with the voices in our heads, or almost anything for that matter. To mimic implies approval or agreement. To oppose implies disagreement to such a degree that a middle ground cannot be found. To compensate implies partial agreement, with some modifications in those areas of dispute to make them acceptable. Therefore, as in politics, be it the politics of nations, or of the psyche, we either agree, disagree, or reach a compromise with the voices from within or without.

Generally speaking, in childhood we mimic the parental voice since children always assume that the parental voice is correct. In adolescence we attempt to establish our own identity, so we oppose our parental voice. And in adulthood we attempt to find ways to compensate and find a balance in order to live in peace, somewhere between the parental voice and the voice of our own established self-identity.

Appendix

Table of Inclusion

1	2	3	4	5	6	7
AJS	BKT	CLU	DMV	ENW	FOX	GPY

8	9
HQZ	IR

The Table of Inclusion represents all of the numbers in the full name as it represented when converting al letter to their number equivalent. If the name is missing a number it represents a challenge to the personality. We are drawn to overcome our challenges and will seek out opportunities to do so .

The Planes of Expression

Physical	Mental	Emotional	Intuition
D M V	A J S	B K T	G P Y
E N W	H Q Z	C L U	I R

Physical Numbers reflect how we experience life, and what our strengths and weaknesses are on the physical plane, which is the material world.

Mental Numbers reveals our mental strengths and weaknesses, as well as how we think and resolve problems.

Emotional Numbers reveal our inner or emotional experiences, how we react to emotions and how they affect us.

Intuitive Numbers represent intuitive abilities. It reveals how the person deals with that gut feeling that is unsubstantiated by facts.

Anne Burton

Look for other fine books published by Fifth Estate

The Lost Book Of Enoch:
A Comprehensive Transliteration,
ISBN: 0974633666

The Gospel of Thomas: A Contemporary Translation
ISBN: 0976823349

Fallen Angels, The Watchers, and the Origins of Evil:
A Problem of Choice
ISBN: 1933580100

Dark Night of the Soul - A Journey to the Heart of God
ISBN: 0974633631

The Tao Te Ching: A Contemporary Translation
ISBN: 0976823314

Christian Counseling – Healing the Tribes of Man
ISBN: 1933589970

Anne Burton

The Gnostic Gospels of Philip, Mary Magdalene, and
Thomas: Inside The Da Vinci Code and Holy Blood, Holy
Grail
ISBN: 1933580135

The Book of Jubilees; The Little Genesis, The Apocalypse
of Moses
ISBN: 1933580097

The Book of Jasher
The J. H. Parry Text in Modern English
ISBN: 1933580143

The Lost Books of the Old Testament
ISBN: 1933580119

Anne Burton

www.ingramcontent.com/pod-product-compliance
Lightning Source LLC
Chambersburg PA
CBHW060928030726
47503CB00003B/514